HOME
RUN
HEART

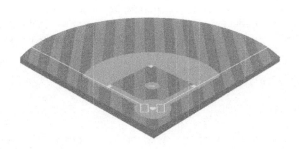

HAILEY GARDINER

Cover design by Yummy Book Covers

Editing by Heather Austin and Ascension Edits

www.haileygardiner.com

To my sweet Grandpa Bagby.
You taught me that the celestial sport of baseball is mentioned in
the Bible...in the "big inning".

ONE

Nora

August

Two hours into my Saturday morning shift at Delia's Diner, I accidentally slam into a busboy. Our collision causes the plates of hot waffles I'm carrying to flip onto my chest, after which the waffles slide ceremoniously down the front of my body before plopping onto the diner floor. Servers rush to my aid and clean up the plates and spilled food in a flurry of efficient teamwork that makes my manager's heart sing. I'm frantically trying to scrub the sticky syrup off of my black polo shirt when I glance towards the front door, only to realize that Tommy Collins just entered the diner.

I curse under my breath and inspect my shirt. Thankfully, the syrup stain is hardly noticeable anymore.

Tommy's gangly frame and eager gaze is visible from the waiting area near the hostess stand. Molly, our hostess, glances back at the dining area helplessly, no doubt feeling pressured to seat the ever-growing crowd of locals also waiting for a table. I wouldn't put it past Tommy to buck protocol and weasel his way past Molly to get to me, so I hastily duck my head and

1

make a beeline for the kitchen. I don't have the energy to fight off another invitation to dinner or a movie today. Ever since my divorce two years ago, Tommy has felt like it's his duty and his alone to swoop in and bind me up in matrimony before someone else does.

I desperately hope Tommy hasn't already spotted me as I weave past crowded tables, servers balancing plates of hot breakfasts, and busboys filling plastic bins with dirty dishes at record speed.

Just as I'm about to enter the beverage prep station, I overhear a half-whispered conversation coming from within. I pause, angling my ear towards the doorway to listen.

"It's him!" I hear Kate say in her signature, enthusiastic tone.

"Are you sure? He looks shorter in person," Audrey replies, ever rational.

"I swear, Kate, if you don't get back out there, you're going to be on lemon-cutting duty tomorrow morning. Get moving!" That's Roman, my right-hand man. I don't think I could successfully manage Delia's without him.

The conversation between the three servers is cut short as I make my presence known by joining them inside.

"Hey, boss." Audrey resumes filling her table's drink orders without missing a beat. Kate, on the other hand, looks like she's about to combust.

"It's him!" she squeaks again, her cheeks and neck patchy with pink splotches. "It's him, Nora! In the flesh!"

Roman gives her a withering, albeit amused look.

"I know, I'm sorry," I say. "Can you guys make sure Tommy stays seated once he gets a table? I can't handle him today."

"Tommy?" Roman says, looking confused. "Good gracious. That's not who Kate is talking about, Nora. She's freaking out over..." he clears his throat, "someone else."

"How can you stand there and act like you don't care one bit that a famous person just set foot in our restaurant?" Kate asks Roman in disbelief.

"Because," Roman drags out. "I was born and bred with a class that you, miss ma'am, do not possess. You're a disgrace to your namesake."

Kate frowns. "My namesake?"

Roman looks at me in miserable commiseration. "I swear this child was born under a rock."

"Catherine, Princess of Wales," I clarify. "Who are you talking about?"

"It's him, Nora," Audrey says calmly. "Your ex."

"Nate?" I breathe. I don't believe it. There's no way my ex-husband would have the guts to show up at my place of work. He'd end up dipped in batter, fried, and dusted with powdered sugar.

"No, your other ex," Roman clarifies. "The hot one."

"He requested an outside table," Kate squeaks.

"I tried to cut in at the host stand, but it was too late. Molly sat him outside," Roman adds.

Understanding settles over me. *That* ex. The one who usually requests to be seated at Booth Six, which results in me hiding out until he's gone. I must have missed his grand entrance while cleaning up the waffle debacle.

Seeing him always sets me on edge, and not just because he's by far the most attractive player on the Seattle Stormbreakers' roster.

"I can't serve him," Kate says in a rush, clinging to my hands. "I can't do it. Nora, I forgot my name the moment I looked into his eyes."

Roman snorts.

"Here," Audrey says, shoving two glasses filled to the brim with Diet Coke into Kate's hands. "Your high-top is waiting."

"Nora, please," Kate pleads, resisting as Roman and Audrey start shoving her from behind. "I already got their drink orders in, but I'm going to screw everything up if you send me back out there. I'll single-handedly put this place out of business."

It would take a lot more than a flustered server to put Delia's Diner under. It's been around for nearly thirty years and is still as packed as ever.

"There's nothing to be afraid of," I say in an attempt to reassure Kate and tamp down my own skittering nerves. "Treat him just like you would any other customer."

"There's no way I can pretend like he's a normal person. He's not. He's got this presence, Nora. I'm begging you. Send Roman out there. Send anyone else. Molly talked to him just fine, maybe she can cover my table."

"Molly is *not* a server," Roman cuts in. "Besides, she reached her flirting quota for the day two minutes after he walked in the door. You should have seen the eyes she was making at him, Nor. Inappropriate."

"Please!" Kate is unraveling before my very eyes. She's young and relatively new to the team, but she's a hard worker and desperate to please. I know she wouldn't ask for me to cover for her unless she really felt she couldn't handle it.

"I'll do it," Audrey offers. "Let me take care of that six-top in the back that Molly just sat first, and then I can–"

"No," I hear myself say before I can reel the words back in. "No, it's okay. I've got it. I'll take his table. That way I can avoid Tommy."

Kate sags with relief. Audrey shrugs and goes on her way, unaffected by the drama, as usual. I feel like I just swallowed an entire bottle of maple syrup at the thought of seeing my ex-boyfriend again. Sure, he comes into the diner every once in a while with his family, but I haven't allowed myself to look directly at him since we broke up in high school. I think part of me has been afraid that it would still hurt to do so. But what else am I supposed to do? Try to work with Tommy breathing down my neck and gazing at me longingly from across the diner?

"Thank you!" Kate breathes, lifting her Diet Coke cups into the air and nearly sloshing the liquid all over the floor.

"Le-mons," Roman says slowly. "Tomorrow. The next day. Every day for a week."

Kate sticks her tongue out at Roman like a toddler before happily bouncing away, relieved of the burden of waiting on the local celebrity who decided to dine at Delia's with his family this busy Saturday morning.

"Need this?" Roman flicks his unused notepad in my direction. Like me, he's been here long enough that he can mentally record all his orders.

"I don't think so," I say initially, then my confidence falters. "Actually, maybe I'll take it just in case." My brain might flatline once I actually have to speak to him.

"You sure you want to take that table? I've got your back if you want to stay cloistered away in here like an old maid."

"I've got it," I laugh, trying to look confident. "I'm not sure why Kate is losing her mind."

The corner of Roman's mouth lifts knowingly.

"Right. Why would anyone lose their mind over a professional baseball player who looks as deliciously expensive as he smells?" He leans in closer. "Think about it, though, honey. I have it on good authority that you're the only one in this place he's kissed." He gives me a saucy wink before sauntering off to take care of the tables in his section.

My stomach lurches at Roman's bold declaration. We've worked together long enough that the line between boss and employee pretty much doesn't exist anymore. He's one of my best friends, and I love him to death.

You're the only one in this place he's kissed.

I curb the train of thoughts that involve my ex-boyfriend and kissing and Booth Six by focusing on the familiarity of my surroundings. I listen to the clatter of silverware reverberating through the dining area and clanging of cookware coming from the kitchen, the murmured conversations and bursts of laughter. I inhale the smell of sizzling bacon and pancake batter being ladled onto the griddle. I place a hand on the countertop that divides the beverage prep area from the rest of the diner, feeling the tacky pull of syrup and spilled soda under my fingertips.

I'm at home here at Delia's, as comfortable here as I am in my own kitchen. I know our menu inside and out, can rattle off the orders our regular customers request when they come in, and can tell you which part Maisy Montgomery got in her seventh-grade class play and how sweet Mr. Herbert's recovering from his fall last month.

I handled my son's meltdown of epic proportions over me asking him to put his shoes on before daycare this morning without batting an eye. I can handle this.

I steel myself for the task of seeing *him* again. Looking into those grey-blue eyes that always reminded me of calm, clear skies after a thunderstorm's blown over. Dodging his smiles while I parrot back my stilted answers to the polite questions his mother asks whenever she comes by. Trying not to think about the fact that *I know what he tastes like.*

Or rather, what he tasted like back when we were in high school. Before he dumped me to play college baseball at Oregon State while I stayed here and ended up marrying someone else. Before my marriage fell apart and I became a single mother to a beautiful little boy.

Before, before, before.

I slap the notepad down on the countertop, resolving to put to good use the sliver of my brain reserved for cataloguing orders and not rely on writing things down. I've worked here for eleven years, for goodness' sake. *How would you like your eggs? Bacon or sausage? Wheat or white toast? Can I get you anything else to drink?*

"Do you want to put on some lipstick first?" Roman mutters to me as I pass him, reaching for the side door that leads to our outdoor seating area. "You're looking a little pale, honey."

"Get back to work, or I'll dock your pay."

"Do it. See how well this restaurant fares without me."

"You know I love you," I call out as I push open the door. I step out onto the dock that extends over the little stretch of harbor Delia had her restaurant built on. The morning sun prickles my forehead, and I blink in the bright light glittering off the surface of the water. Gulls are singing their morning song, most circling overhead, but a brave few land on the dock and scuttle under tables to snatch up fallen scraps of food. The briny tang of the salty air mixes with the scent of pancakes drenched in buttermilk syrup. I'm almost lulled into a false sense of security by the ease of it all when my eyes fall to the table in the far corner of the dock.

He's laughing at something his sister is saying, the drink Kate brought him half-raised to his mouth. He's got his other arm casually resting over the back of the empty chair beside him. The sound of his laughter carries on the late-summer breeze, tugging somewhere deep in my belly and stirring up memories. Memories I haven't dared to revisit in a long, long time.

Roman was right. He looks expensive in his head-to-toe black athleisure with his blue baseball hat pulled down over his dark hair. He probably wore the hat to avoid being recognized, but it does nothing but draw the eye to the masculine set of his handsome features. Those bright eyes that used to hold mine are probably only going to pass over me with polite regard. I won't blame him. I've avoided him pretty much every time he's come to the diner, and up until two years ago, I was a married woman. But now? I can't help but wonder what it would feel like to see the sparkle of affection in his eyes again. For him to look at me the way he did in high school.

Pushing my shoulders back and my feelings down, I approach his table with a bright smile. My heart takes a little tumble as Brooks Alden's piercing eyes dart up to meet mine.

Bubblicious bubble gum.

That's what he tasted like.

TWO

Brooks

THERE HAVE ONLY BEEN two things I can say I have truly loved in my life: baseball and Nora Foster.

Every time I visit Delia's Diner, it feels like stepping into a time capsule. I'm sixteen again, grabbing a bite to eat with a few of my teammates after practice or stopping by to catch a glimpse of the pretty, dark-haired waitress who's also in my English class. The girl who stole my heart by causing a spectacularly clumsy dessert disaster, which led to me helping her scrub chocolate syrup and foamy, melted ice cream off the diner floor. Before I'd left the diner that night, I'd asked for her number.

For some reason, those faded memories came to the forefront of my mind today, and I couldn't do it. Booth Six is the last booth at the back of the restaurant, which usually offers my family privacy when we visit Delia's. But today when we'd entered, I'd seen Nora near the kitchen and my gut had bottomed out at the sight of her. Usually, she's nowhere to be seen when I come around, and something about catching a glimpse of her today left me feeling surprisingly vulnerable. Memories started clambering to the surface of my mind, and I needed to snuff them out.

I'd asked to be seated outside in the hopes of shoving down all of the frozen bits of my past this place holds, but as she approaches our table, my pulse starts to pound. All chances of forgetting have just gone out the window.

"Nora!" Mom says cheerily. "How lucky are we to get the manager herself waiting on us today?"

"How are you, Mrs. Alden?" Nora says warmly, the glint of her bright smile making something twinge in my chest. It's a gorgeous smile. One I'd love for her to turn on me.

But she won't. She can't.

"It's great to see you all," she says, giving a courteous sweep of her gaze over everyone except for me. "I'm sorry to keep you waiting. We're a little busy this morning."

"That's okay," my sister Caroline chimes in. "We're in no hurry."

"Brooks has the weekend off," Mom says, reaching over to pat my hand. Nora has no choice but to acknowledge me then. She tips her head in my direction, her soft brown eyes widening slightly as they meet mine. She gives me a hesitant, polite smile.

"How nice. Glad you decided to stop by."

She doesn't ask me any follow-up questions or attempt to hold my attention like most women would do, given the chance. But she's not like most women in my social circle. She's more...real. Soft in all the right ways and naturally beautiful. She's always been beautiful.

I cut my eyes back down to my menu, pretending to contemplate my order even though I eat the same thing every time I come in. A veggie omelet with a side of bacon and breakfast potatoes. Nora probably knows this.

"How's the season going?" It takes a kick from my other sister, Claire, under the table for me to realize that Nora is talking to me. Acknowledging my existence.

"It's going great," I say, looking her full-on in the face for the first time in a long while. It feels forbidden. I shouldn't feel an automatic, visceral pull towards her still. But it's hard not to. She's lovely. Her skin is tan and smooth, freckled from the sun, her full, dark hair lifting in the sea breeze.

My mom and sisters are staring at me. Claire lets out a little sniff of amusement, and I'm tempted to kick her right back under the table.

"Gearing up for play-offs," I tack on. "It's a busy time."

"We're all cheering you on," Nora says. "Especially my dad. He's got his heart set on the Stormbreakers winning the Wild Card this year."

Her dad isn't the only one. I've felt the pressure to perform well this postseason after a killer rookie season last year.

"I'll keep that in mind," I say.

"Are you all ready to order?" Nora says, bringing her hands together. My pulse skitters under my neck as I register something else that's new about Nora.

I notice the chipped pink polish on her fingernails. The glint of two silver rings on her right hand. The bare stretch of tan skin on a certain finger of her left hand.

There's no diamond blinding me in the sunlight. No gemstone-inlaid piece of jewelry circling her ring finger. There's not even a tan line where it used to be.

Nora Foster isn't wearing a wedding ring anymore.

"She seems to be doing well, all things considered," Mom says once Nora's gone.

I'm not big into gossip, but in this case my curiosity gets the better of me. "All things considered?"

"We all swore to never speak of Nora around you after you broke up, remember?" Claire points out.

"What happened to her?" I say.

"You sure you want to know?" Caroline asks. "Because I specifically remember the last time I brought her up you threatened to burn all my books."

"No, I didn't," I scoff.

"You did," Claire says.

"Okay, well, I'm sorry. Your books are safe now. You can tell me what happened."

My sisters and mom exchange glances, hesitant to speak. Whatever it is I'm about to learn about the girl who I let get away is making me nervous. She's still my biggest regret.

"Nora and Nate got divorced two years ago," my mom finally says. "They were pretty quiet about things." She has firsthand experience with divorce, having finally separated from our dad several years ago while I was playing in the minors. "I've talked with her mother a few times, and it's really quite sad."

"He was unfaithful," Caroline adds. "Nate."

"What?" I stare at my mom and sisters in turn, my grip tightening around my fork. I'm struck with the sudden desire to go back and shake my eighteen-year-old self who asked his family to never speak of Nora again. How did I not know about this? Nate had been my friend in high school. When I eventually found out that he and Nora were together, yeah, I was insanely jealous. But I also knew that even if I couldn't be the man she deserved, she'd at least chosen a decent guy as her husband. He'd always been respectful and kind to her.

But evidently, Nate was no longer the guy I'd been friends with all those years ago.

"He cheated on her?" I ask in disbelief. "With who?"

"Someone he worked with. They're married now," Claire says softly. "Nora found out she was pregnant shortly after she found out about the affair."

Pregnant? Affair? I have no right to feel anything towards Nora, but my head is buzzing, and a wave of protectiveness rises within me. I want to track Nate down and deck him in his jaw.

"I'm sorry I didn't tell you," Claire says, looking apologetic. "But I thought you didn't want me to. I honestly thought maybe you'd come across something about their divorce on social media or hear about it from someone else."

"I don't follow either of them," I say. I used to. But once I was out of the picture and they were happily married, I couldn't stomach their posts. Call me immature, but I'd had to do it in order to move on.

"So, they're no longer together? But they've got a kid?"

"A little boy," Caroline says. "Ollie. He's adorable."

"I'm sure he is," I say. "No thanks to Nate." I'm hoping nobody picked up on the bitterness that slithered into my tone. I'd better keep my mouth shut while out here in public where gossip spreads faster than one of Cortez's hundred-mile-an-hour pitches.

"Like I said," Mom says. "She seems to be doing much better lately. She's a brave girl, that Nora."

I register that Claire and Caroline are staring at each other with wide eyes, doing their twin telepathy thing that always makes me feel like an even bigger third wheel.

"Stop that," I mumble, pointing my fork at Caroline accusingly.

"I could find out if she's seeing anyone for you. Scope out the competition."

"You know I don't have time to date right now," I say, but secretly I'm wondering how I could obtain that information myself without involving my nosy sisters. Could Nora really be available again? I never dared to let myself think of the possibility.

"I hate to tell you this," Claire says with a heavy sigh. "But you're getting old, Brooks."

"Tell that to *Sports Weekly*."

"Past your prime."

"At twenty-seven?"

"Any day now, you're going to look around at all of the wealth you've amassed and think, 'Shoot. I don't even have an heir I can bequeath all of this to,'" Caroline says.

"You realize that if you don't find a wife soon, every penny you've made will go to us, right?" Claire says around a bite of food. "Your poor, lowly sisters who can barely make ends meet."

"On second thought," Caroline says. "Maybe we won't help you find a wife so we can inherit your fortune."

"You both know you'll get nothing from me either way. You're nothing but two big pains in my—"

"Did you hear that, Mother?" Claire cuts me off. "Brooks intends to leave us with nothing!"

"You're both capable of taking care of yourselves. I don't see either of you trying very hard to find husbands," I say.

"That's because we're not ancient like you."

"I've got plenty of child-bearing years left in me." It's just as Claire finishes this sentence that Nora reappears, balancing plates loaded with breakfast food.

"Oh, hi, Nora," Claire says, tossing me a wicked grin. "We were just discussing childbearing."

Nora sets a plate of French toast down in front of my loud-mouthed sister, looking like she's trying not to smile.

"How's Ollie doing?" Caroline asks, always adept at steering the conversation away from Claire's attempts to embarrass me in public.

"He's great," Nora says, setting my omelet down in front of me. "He keeps me busy."

The truth about Nora's situation is making me see her in a completely new light. Her eyes flick to mine for the briefest second, and I can't help but wonder what her little boy looks like. Does he have her beautiful, dark brown eyes? Is he the spitting image of Nate?

"How old is he?" I ask.

"He'll be two next month."

Two. That means she's been single for at least two years now? I guess I shouldn't assume. Maybe she's got a boyfriend. The thought makes me grip my fork even tighter.

"Who tends to Ollie while you work?" Claire asks.

"My mom helps me a few times a week, and my neighbor runs a daycare out of her house, so she takes him on the other days."

"If you ever need a babysitter, call me up," Claire says. "I've got lots of experience working with kids."

She's a fourth-grade teacher at Kitt's Harbor Elementary. One of the most requested, she likes to brag.

"That's very sweet of you."

"Her experience doesn't count for much. The kids she teaches are probably potty-trained and can speak in full sentences," Caroline teases, turning to Claire. "You wouldn't know the first thing about caring for a toddler."

"Of course I would. I've got Brooks here as my brother." She leans toward Nora and drops her voice to a hoarse whisper. "You should see the tantrums this man throws when the Stormbreakers lose a game."

Leave it to my sister to keep me humble. "Tantrums?" I repeat.

"Okay, maybe he's grown out of the tantrums," Claire says. "Now he just sulks and mopes about."

"You and Ollie have that in common," Nora says, giving me an understanding smile. "It's hard when you don't get something you want and have worked hard for. I get it." She somehow spun Claire's incessant teasing into a way to validate my dedication to my sport. "Is there anything else I can get for you at the moment?" she asks.

"We're all set," Mom says warmly.

"Just let me know if there's anything else you need," Nora says, smiling directly at me. That smile on her lips hits me in the dead center of my chest, and I decide, right then and there, that if the opportunity presents itself for me to see Nora again, I'm going to take it. No questions asked. Forget my *no dating during baseball season* rule.

"Everybody still doing okay over here?" A tall, redhead server asks as he approaches our table. "Nora's tied up at the moment, but I'd be happy to box up any leftovers you'd like to take home."

"That would be great. Thank you," I say, handing him my plate. Then I quickly slip him my credit card.

"There you go, girls," I say once he's left. "Your good-for-nothing brother just treated you to breakfast."

"Thank you, Brooks," they say in annoying unison.

The server returns a few minutes later, styrofoam box and receipt in hand. "These are for you," the server says, handing me the styrofoam box. I glance down and am surprised to see a name and a number scrawled across the top of the lid in black ink.

"From Nora," he says softly in an attempt to avoid drawing attention to the box. Unfortunately, I'm related to three bats who are staring beadily in our direction.

"Thanks, man. And thanks for the meal. Always good."

"I'm glad you enjoyed it. Come back and see us soon, okay?" he calls out cheerily, walking away. "Go Breakers!"

"What's on the box, Brooks?" Caroline asks.

"Yeah, what does it say?" Claire strains to get a look.

I try to keep it away from my nosy sisters by pushing my chair back from the table and standing up. "Don't worry about it."

Caroline quickly swipes the box out of my grasp and darts towards Claire's side of the table. Both girls gasp.

"It's her number!" Claire says gleefully. "She gave you her number!"

"Who?" Mom asks.

"Nora Foster!" Caroline whispers hoarsely. "I hereby give my approval." She stamps my box with her fist. "Hear, hear."

"I second the motion!" Claire stamps the box with her own fist.

"Quit manhandling my box. You're going to smash my leftovers."

"Who cares about the food!" Claire cries, slinging her arm around me as we descend the stairs that lead down from the pier at Delia's to the boardwalk that lines the harbor. "The only girlfriend of yours we've ever liked just gave you her number. This is a cause for celebration. Your bachelor days may finally be over!"

Claire then breaks out into a rousing chorus of "For He's A Jolly Good Fellow" at full volume, dancing a ridiculous jig with her arm still clenched around my neck. I wince, hoping Nora didn't hear a word of Claire's less-than-subtle outburst.

I'm no stranger to the desperate attempts of women who spontaneously seize the opportunity to throw their name in my proverbial dating hat. It makes all the difference in the world having history with the beautiful girl who scrawled her number on my to-go box.

I can't believe my luck. Who knew the opportunity to reconnect with Nora would come so soon after finding out that she's no longer married? But there's no way I'm about to let my meddling sisters see that Nora's gesture has affected me. They will never let it go if they feel there's any hope of the two of us reconnecting.

"I'm sorry to disappoint you both," I say. "But baseball season isn't over yet. You know my policy."

My sisters share a look that makes me feel like I just gave them the wrong answer.

"You're an idiot if you don't call her, Brooks," Claire says. "Even more of an idiot than we all thought."

"Thank you, Claire."

I had made a huge mistake in allowing my dad to persuade me that staying with Nora would somehow prevent me from playing professional baseball. That mistake still haunts me in moments like this. I hate that I'd let him manipulate and control me the way he had.

Don't worry, Claire, I think to myself. *I don't plan on being an idiot again.*

THREE

Nora

"OLLIE?" I CALL OUT, elbow deep in dish soap suds in the kitchen sink. "It's almost bath time! Are you ready?"

When he doesn't respond, my mom instincts begin tingling. Usually if things are quiet, it means something is afoot. Occasionally, I'll find my busy two-year-old playing quietly by himself, engaged in some sort of imaginative storyline that I try my best not to interrupt. But most often, he's either eating something that's not actually meant to be eaten, painting with something that's not meant to be used as paint, or emptying the contents of a drawer with incredible efficiency.

I set the ceramic bowl I'd washed aside, ears prickling for any sound that would give me a hint as to what sort of mischief Ollie's getting himself into. The craziest thing about moments like this is how much damage one little boy can do in such a short amount of time. It's impossible for a mother to keep an eye on her child every second of every day, and boy, does he make the most of those few minutes when he runs off alone.

"Ollie?" I call again, quickly drying my hands on a towel hanging from the oven rack. "Where are you, buddy?"

No answer. I first check my spare bedroom-turned-ceramics studio downstairs, where I spend most evenings throwing clay at the wheel. I open the door and glance around quickly, relieved to find that my shelves of ceramics remain untouched.

I peer into the downstairs bathroom. No sign of the sprite. I ascend the stairs, checking first in the upstairs bathroom, then checking Ollie's bedroom before wandering into my bedroom.

"Ollie bear," I say in a sing-song voice. "What are you up to?"

I hear a muffled giggle coming from my closet.

"Hmm," I say, reassured now that he's given his location away that the damage can't be too bad. There's not much to destroy in my closet. Maybe he was busy trying on my hats and shoes.

"Could he be..." I fling back my shower curtain, "...in the shower?"

Another giggle.

"Maybe..." I draw in a raspy gasp. "Oh, no. What if he..." I flick the toilet lid open, "...got *flushed down the toilet?*"

Laughter bubbles from my closet, and I hear hangers clacking together. Ollie emerges, eager to assuage my fears that he hasn't been forever lost to the plumbing.

"Mama!" he says in a gruff voice, running into the room like he's on a mission. "I'm right *here!*"

"Sweet relief!" I cry, flinging my arms around him and squeezing him tightly. "What were you doing in the closet?"

"Hiding."

"Hiding?" I cry, gripping him by the shoulders. "From *me?* Uh oh. You know what happens when you hide from me."

His brown eyes grow wide with gleeful anticipation. "Tickle bear?"

"*The tickle bear!* You'd better run!"

I roar, and he screams out another laugh, breaking away from my grasp and darting out of my room.

"I'm gonna get you!" The chase ensues. I stomp around, roaring and threatening to steal his honey stash and eat all his berries. Once he's caught and thoroughly tickled until he's breathless and my own ribs hurt from laughing, too, I lower him to my lap and kiss each of his soft cheeks.

"Let's get you in the bath."

He doesn't put up much of a fight; bath time is his favorite part of the entire day. Within a few minutes, I'm once again elbow-deep in bubbles, fishing out trucks and rubber bath toys for my water-loving boy.

Ollie's engaged in some kind of epic water battle with his toys when my phone buzzes in my back pocket. I slip it out and quickly read the text that's come through.

> **Unknown number:** Hey, Nora. This is Brooks. It was great to see you today. Thought I'd text you so you have my number.

I let out an audible gasp, fumbling my phone and nearly dropping it into the bath water.

"What, Mama?" Ollie asks.

My heart is flapping around my ribs like a caged bird.

This is Brooks.

Brooks Alden?

No way.

How in the world had he gotten my phone number?

My initial shock morphs into suspicion. There's no way *the* Brooks Alden could really be texting me right now.

But the unknown number's area code is the same as mine. And who else would have known that we'd seen each other at Delia's today? As far as I know, he doesn't publicize his outings in his hometown.

A splash erupts from the bath, drenching me in bubbles. I stand up and remove myself from the line of fire, too stunned to once again remind Ollie that the bath water belongs *inside* the bathtub.

I read over the text three more times, my heart ricocheting through every corner of my body.

Is this a joke? It's got to be a joke. One I wish I could find funny.

I'd survived an encounter with Brooks today without dropping a plate or making a social blunder. I'd maintained a cool indifference as Kate had pressed me for every detail of our conversation every time I'd re-entered the restaurant. Sure, I'd allowed myself a few brief moments to really look at him, to admire his athletic physique and handsome features. We'd even had a friendly, if brief, interaction. Nothing to write home about, but still. It was more than the few words we've exchanged over the years.

He was nice. I was nice. End of story.

After I'd clocked out, I'd returned to reality. I'd picked up Ollie from my neighbors' daycare that she runs out of her home. Then we'd gone to the park for a bit so we could both get some fresh air, enjoyed a gourmet dinner of mac n' cheese, and now I'm getting him ready for bed. I can't allow myself to dissect everything about my encounter with Brooks until I finish taking care of the little fish flopping around in the bath behind me. They both deserve my full attention.

A fresh wave of suds washes over the lip of the bathtub, and I decide I'd better intervene before we reach full-on flood status. Twenty minutes later, I'm sweating like I just finished a workout after wrangling Ollie into his pajamas and trapping him in his crib. Yes, he is still in a crib. I will use that method of containment as long as humanly possible. He's figured out how to climb out of the thing, but at least it buys me a few more minutes before the escape artist makes his first out-of-bed appearance than a toddler bed would.

"Goodnight, Mama," he says after we finish a bedtime story, lulling me into a false sense of security with a clinging hug and sweet, slobbery kiss he plants on my cheek.

"Goodnight, my boy. Sleep tight!"

I may be a first-time mom, but I can call a kid's bluff when I see one. Ollie squints at me through half-closed lids as I shut his door. I know I've got maybe two minutes before he's clambered out of his crib and is racing around, flinging random requests at me as an attempt to stall bedtime.

After nearly meeting my death by slipping in the puddle pooling on the bathroom floor, I mop up the spilled water on my hands and knees with Ollie's wet bath towel. I've barely tossed it into the laundry room when I hear his door creak open.

"Yes?" I say as he peers into the hallway, his hair still damp and eyes glittering.

"I thirsty."

"You already drank a bottle of milk."

"I need water. Please." He widens his big blue eyes. He's so dang cute, it makes it hard to say no.

"Go lay back down, and I'll bring you some."

I fetch the master his drink and lay him back down into his crib. "It's time to sleep now, Ollie. I'll see you tomorrow, okay?" He's surrounded by his favorite stuffed animals and fully hydrated. Fingers crossed he'll get cozy and actually fall asleep.

I close his door behind me, feeling the weariness of the day start to fully settle in. It's only once Ollie is safe in bed that I give myself permission to feel tired. If I sink into the fatigue at any other point during the day, I know I won't be able to get back up and do everything I need to do.

Sore feet? Keep standing.

Tired eyes? Don't close them.

Fuzzy brain? Stay awake.

Don't stop moving.

That's been my motto ever since Ollie was born.

Don't stop moving.

It was in the depths of the long nights shortly after my divorce that the darkness would take hold of my heart and squeeze all hope from my lungs. I never want to feel that way again, so I stay busy to keep my mind from being shrouded in shadows.

I shuffle downstairs, letting out a long, slow breath as I assess the work that still needs to be done. I'd gotten our house in the divorce settlement, and even though it's relatively small, it's still a lot for one person to take care of. I'm it, over here. The housekeeper, the cook, the parent, the primary provider. I'm doing it all. Sometimes the weight of my role weighs heavy on my shoulders. I try not to dwell on it these days, or the overwhelm gets lodged in my throat like it often used to in those early months of motherhood.

I have my coping methods, like throwing pottery at the wheel and working extra shifts at the diner, but sometimes I'm terrified that the depression is going to slip through the cracks and undo all of the hard work I've put in to take care of my mental and emotional health since having Ollie. Sometimes I feel so fragile, like there's a thin thread inside me just waiting to snap should something else go wrong in my life. It's why I haven't really dated since the divorce. The fear of getting my heart steamrolled by another selfish man keeps me from even trying.

Miraculously, Ollie doesn't emerge from his room again. The house is quiet as I finish up the dishes and tidy the house, and for once, despite my fears, I allow my mind to grab hold of a very enticing, pleasantly distracting thought. Brooks Alden.

How had he gotten my number? I'd seen the way his sisters perked up every time I returned to their table. Did they have something to do with it?

I contemplate asking my own sisters, Sydney and Bridget, what they make of this unexpected turn of events but decide against it. No point in getting their hopes up before I even reply.

I draft about fifteen responses, including one that reads:

Hey Brooks! I didn't give you my number. I'm not sure who did.

Luckily, I stop myself before sending that one. I can't tell him the truth until I find out who gave him my number. The only reason he'd texted me is because he thought I'd wanted him to, right?

There's only one thing left for me to do.

I've got to own up to this. Fake it until I make it. Respond in a neutral, friendly way that doesn't make me sound like I'm trying to pursue him because I most definitely am not. I type out another text.

Hey Brooks! It was great seeing you, too. Good luck on your games next week!

I'm about to send it when I hesitate...again. What if it isn't actually Brooks texting me right now? What if this is some kind of personal and painful joke someone decided to play on me?

I slowly backspace over my text, deciding it's probably best to at least sleep on it before I decide whether or not to respond. I put my phone on its charger and bury myself into my blankets, growing dizzy as memories of Brooks as I once knew him collide with who he is now. Who *I* am now.

It's been over two years since Nate and I divorced. Two years of doing life on my own. I can keep my mind occupied during the day. Ollie and work at the diner keep me plenty busy.

But at night?

Nights are long when you're alone. The bed feels too big, the house too quiet. Fears of raising my son and providing for the two of us on my own forever sometimes sneak into the space between wakefulness and sleep, preventing my mind from resting.

Tonight, Brooks is a welcome distraction. I'll happily stew on this mystery instead of discouraging thoughts, allowing my mind to dissect every word of his message, analyze every imaginable storyline that led to me getting a text from a now-famous baseball player I once fell for. Back when he was just Brooks, the boy I used to cheer for from the bleachers.

I decide to launch a full-scale inquiry of my staff when I arrive at work the following morning.

The kitchen staff, servers, and our hostess, Molly, are all gathered in the dining area for my usual morning briefing, unaware that they're about to get good-cop-bad-copped by their manager until someone fesses up.

"Audrey, do you mind updating the specials board to include Max's macadamia nut pancakes?" I ask, addressing the last item on my list before we split off to do our various opening tasks.

"On it," she says, moving to stand.

"But before you go," I say quickly. "I have something I'd like to ask you all."

My employees look at me expectantly.

"Yesterday, we were visited by a certain professional athlete," I say, staring each of them down in turn. Kate flushes at the mere mention of him, and Roman doesn't even attempt to hide his audible gasp. "This is super awkward for me to even ask this, but I need to know. Did one of you give him my phone number?"

Audrey chokes, fisting her hand over her mouth. Roman bites his lip. Molly stares at me in a mix of confusion and shock.

"Why would someone do that?" Molly says, smacking a piece of gum between her teeth annoyingly. I know for a fact that she's a huge Stormbreakers fan and has a photo of Brooks as her wallpaper on her phone.

"I'm asking myself the same question."

"Why not?" Kate pipes up. "You're a babe."

"A babe who hasn't been on a date, at least to my knowledge, in a very long time," Roman says.

"It was you, wasn't it?" I say. "You gave him my number."

"I don't know what you're talking about," Roman says innocently.

"Was it you, Kate?"

"I swear, I didn't do it!"

"Then who did? Or are all of you conspiring against me?"

"It was a golden opportunity, Nora," Audrey says matter-of-factly. "But if you're going to fire one of us, I'm pinning the blame on Roman. I need a steady paycheck."

"Way to throw me under the bus!"

I level Roman with what I hope is a censuring look. "Roman. Did you, or did you not give Brooks my number?"

"You know what, Nora? I did. And I'm not going to apologize for it. You would never have done it yourself, so I simply took matters into my own hands." He leans forward, his smile broadening. "He called you, didn't he? He called you last night."

A hot flush climbs my neck, and I clear my throat, trying to regain some control. "Okay, we'll be opening in a few minutes, so I'm going to need all of you to get your tasks done before we open those doors. The breakfast rush is coming and won't stop until–"

"Nora Foster," Roman claps his hands together to punctuate each word. "Did he or did he not call you last night?"

When I don't answer, he laughs. Excessively.

I can see Molly hovering in the corner of my eye, waiting in disbelief for me to confirm the seemingly impossible. No doubt she can't wrap her head around the fact that the gorgeous Brooks Alden would pay any attention to someone like me. But then again, she doesn't know our history.

"He did *not* call me last night," I say loudly for everyone to hear. "And I will not be taking any more questions on the subject, thank you. Move along."

What Roman doesn't know is that I *had* responded to Brooks this morning. I'd felt a sudden burst of courage that prompted me to throw caution to the wind and type out a reply. Ollie had come bursting in as I was agonizing over whether or not to send it, and my thumb moved of its own accord, tapping that send button before I could overthink things any further.

> **Nora**: It was great seeing you, too. Good luck with your games next week. We'll be cheering you on!

Am I deeply regretting this impulsive, un-Nora-like momentary absence of judgment? Absolutely. Brooks hasn't responded to me, and now I'm wondering if he texted me purely out of pity. Some little corner of my heart really hopes Brooks genuinely wants to reconnect with me, but the rational part of my mind is warning me not to be naive. If there's anything the past few years have taught me, it's that men can't be trusted. Even the one I thought was in it for the long haul.

I recognize that I'm spinning into an anxious spiral before the restaurant has even opened, but guess what? I know a super effective (probably unhealthy) way to deal with these pesky sorts of emotions. If I want to stay afloat today, I've got to forget all about this business with Brooks, put my head down and get to work. I refuse to look back at the text thread between us unless he actually replies.

Just keep moving.

FOUR

Nora

September

"You're not wearing that to the game, are you?"

My younger free-spirited sister, Sydney, grimaces as she takes in my old, faded Stormbreakers t-shirt and leggings. I'd even put on my favorite yellow Converse sneakers and had gone through the trouble of re-tying my laces into neat little knots. She's clearly unappreciative of this immense effort.

"What's wrong with my outfit?"

"Well…" she says, stepping inside my house and closing the door behind her. "There's nothing wrong with it, necessarily. It just feels a little…" she does a little swooshing motion with her hands, "…casual."

"Nobody told me there was a dress code."

"Leggings, Nor?"

"They're comfortable, okay?"

"Right, and comfort is key. Just not tonight."

"Why is that, Sydney?" I ask, my suspicions raised. A family trip to the ballpark in Seattle to celebrate my dad's birthday didn't strike me as an opportunity to strut my stuff. Not that

35

there's much stuff to strut, anyways. Every part of me has been stretched out and softened after having a baby.

She places her hands on my shoulders and steers me toward my bedroom. "Now, I know you've got to have something sexy hidden in the depths of that closet of yours."

"Sexy? We're going to a baseball game. Not the club." I stiffen when we reach the doorway of my bedroom. "You didn't lie to me, did you? Is this some ploy to get me out on the town?"

Sydney laughs. "We ain't clubbin' girl. Now get those leggings off so I don't have to peel them off you myself."

I sigh and comply, knowing that if I put up a fight, I'm going to make us late for the game. We've got a two-hour drive ahead of us to Seattle, and the last thing I want to do is be an inconvenience to the rest of my family. I'm already feeling super uneasy about watching the Stormbreakers play, harboring the knowledge that even after I'd bravely decided to text Brooks back, he never replied. It's been a month since we saw each other at the diner, and even that amount of time hasn't lessened my embarrassment around the fact that I really believed that he wanted to reconnect with me, his high school girlfriend from a past life.

But the joke was on me because he'd never responded. That's what I get for taking a leap of faith. And now I'm going to have to watch him play while knowing that he probably hasn't given me a second thought since our run-in. I'd sit tonight's game out if I could, but my dad bought my ticket, and I didn't have an excuse to give him that wouldn't require me spelling out all of the embarrassing details. So here I am. Allowing Sydney to dress me and keeping the truth to myself.

Within a miraculous few minutes, Sydney's scrounged up a fitted white tee and some cut-off shorts I haven't dared to wear since before I was pregnant.

"Nope. There's no way I can zip those shorts up!"

"What do you think I'm here for? Have a little faith in me, sister!"

She's true to her word. The shorts pinch my waist a little, but even I've got to admit that they're flattering. I'm not really sure why I haven't even attempted to wear them until now. I guess when your body changes so much after carrying and birthing a real-life human being, it can be a little like Russian roulette trying on your old clothes from your pre-mom life. You never know what's going to fit and what's going to suddenly feel like it was made for Polly Pocket.

Sydney scrutinizes me from head to toe. "Do you have any other shoes?"

"Sydney!"

"Okay, fine. You can wear the Chucks. But can we do something about your mouth?"

"You know I'm working on the swearing thing, especially now that Ollie understands–"

"Where's your makeup?" Sydney cuts me off, darting into my bathroom.

When she emerges with a tube of poppy-red lipstick and a bottle of perfume, I back away from her with both my hands raised defensively in the air.

"Sydney," I say slowly. "Put the weapons down."

"Come on!" Sydney pleads. "This lipstick will brighten up your face so much. You used to wear this all the time!"

She pops the lid off the perfume, yanks my wrist towards her, and then sprays it on my pulse points. I realize she's about to try to apply the lipstick to my face herself and snatch the tube from her hand.

"I can do that," I say testily. She follows me at a very Ollie-like distance into the bathroom and hovers over my shoulder as I carefully swipe the tube over my lips.

"There," I say impatiently. "Do I look acceptable now?"

A slow smile lifts her face as she meets my eyes in the mirror. "You look gorgeous, Nora."

My eyes dart to my own reflection, and I'm shocked to see a bright-eyed, red-lipped, dark-haired beauty looking back. I blink a few times. Where's the exhausted mom with purple smudges under her eyes, unidentifiable stains on her clothes, and a rat's nest for hair that I'm used to greeting in the mirror? Even though I'm still pretty casually dressed, I have to admit that I look more put-together thanks to my sister.

"What's this all about?" I say, pulling the bottom of my shirt down over the waistband of my shorts again as I face my sister. It's way tighter than anything I'd normally reach for.

She gives me a very suspicious, wide-eyed shrug. "Come on. Trent's waiting for us in the truck."

Sydney's husband Trent nods at me in the rearview mirror as I slide into the back seat of his truck.

"Sorry to keep you waiting," I say, buckling my seatbelt and feeling very much like I'm forgetting something. Ollie is at his dad's this weekend, but I feel a constant pull towards him even when he's gone. His absence is definitely contributing to my heightened anxiety. I'm missing my other half.

"You look nice," Trent says with a rare half-grin. "What's the occasion?"

"You tell me. Would you like to explain why your wife decided to play fairy godmother this evening?"

"Because," Sydney says. "Cinderella's going to the ball!"

"Tell me, once and for all, are we going clubbing? Because if so, I'm going to actually throw up."

"With this guy as our third wheel?" Sydney juts a thumb toward Trent. "I think not."

Trent's left eye twitches ever so slightly, and I know he's close to confessing.

"Trent," I say slowly. "What's going on? You know something, don't you?"

Trent shifts his grip on the steering wheel, his eyes glued to the road like his life depends on it. His silence speaks volumes.

"If the two of you don't tell me what sort of shenanigans you're up to, I'm going to–"

"So many threats, Princess," Sydney says, flicking a hand lazily in my direction. "There is nothing to worry about. We're all going to enjoy a Stormbreakers game on Dad's dime." I almost miss her next words because she drops her voice so low. "While sitting with the Alden family."

"I'm sorry...which family did you say?"

"The Alden family," Sydney repeats, refusing to meet my eyes.

"Alden," I lean forward, jutting my head between the front seats. "As in...*Brooks* Alden's family?"

"That would be the one," Sydney says, letting out a very fake cough.

Dread gathers in my belly. No, no, no. Things were not supposed to play out like this.

"Dare I ask who you murdered to pull this off?" I say, trying to hide the panic in my voice.

"It was actually much easier than I thought it would be." I can see a familiar mischievous gleam in my sister's eyes. "Remember Brooks' sister Claire? She and I have stayed in touch."

"You have? Why didn't I know that?"

"We're the admins of the Facebook page for our high school graduating class. We served on the student council together, remember? Wait, aren't you coming up on your ten-year reunion? I'm sure Fiona Hastings will be in charge of that. Always did like to be the center of attention."

"Stop trying to change the subject. So, you and Claire randomly got back in touch–"

"No, we've been in touch for a while now," Sydney clarifies. "We follow each other on Instagram. Anyways, I told her it was my dad's birthday, and we were planning on coming to the game. I asked her if there was a way we could upgrade our seats. You know, to get closer to the field. And instead, she offered to let us sit with them in the friends-and-family section!" She's turned around at this point, looking as pleased as punch. "Isn't that fun?"

"Does Brooks know about this?" I can barely get the words out.

"I'm assuming he does."

"You know what they say about assuming," I mutter. Trent snorts, earning him a sharp glare from his wife.

"I'm sure Claire had to ask Brooks first before she extended the invite," Sydney says, suddenly looking uncertain. "Right?"

My gaze flicks to Trent, who has stayed silent this whole time. "What do you have to say for yourself, Trent? You're partially at fault here, too."

"I am?"

"Why didn't you try to intervene?"

"I tried to," Trent insists. "But you know how she is."

Sydney scoffs. "You should be thanking me! I got you an in with the relatives of a gorgeous, single man, who I know would love a chance to see you again."

"How could you possibly know that he wants to see me?"

"Claire told me that you waited on their table last month when they came to the diner."

Rats.

"So you really are in touch," I say dryly. "Good to know the residents of Kitt's Harbor have nothing better to do than to discuss the comings and goings of Delia's Diner."

"Fess up, Nora. Why did you take their table? I thought you always hide when he comes in."

It's a simple explanation, really. Straightforward.

"For some reason, the Aldens requested a table outside rather than their usual booth. The server over that section didn't feel comfortable waiting on them, so I stepped in."

And because I was avoiding Tommy Collins at all costs. But I'm not about to tell Sydney that. No doubt if she knew that Tommy is still pathetically pursuing me, she'd track him down and tell him to back off.

Now that I'm thinking about it, maybe I *should* tell her.

"That's the whole story?" She narrows her eyes at me. "You might as well get the truth out. We've got a long drive ahead of us. I want all the details."

When I don't immediately start speaking, she begins a dramatized narration of the events for me.

"One beautiful Saturday morning, Brooks Alden walks into Delia's Diner, removing his baseball cap and running his hands through his luscious, dark locks. He scans the restaurant, eyes hopeful. Filled with longing."

I can't help but laugh at her theatrics. "You want the story? I'll give you the story. Once upon a time, Nora had a server who panicked at the sight of Brooks Alden, becoming too starstruck to wait on him and his family. So, Nora was then forced to take over their table. She was nothing but professional as she took their orders and made small talk."

"What kind of small talk?"

"I don't remember! I asked him about baseball, he asked me about Ollie, then Claire said something about childbearing..."

"See!" Sydney smacks my knee. "I knew he was filled with longing!"

"Then!" I interrupt before she takes things too far. "I got tied up with another table. A baby shower. Roman offered to take care of them after that and then he..."

"What?" Sydney asks eagerly.

"Well," I falter. "He did something he shouldn't have."

"What did he do?"

"Roman wrote my phone number," I sigh. "On Brooks' box of leftovers."

Sydney whips around again, and I swear her seatbelt is being tested to its limits.

"He did *what*?"

"I know."

"So then what happened? Did he call you?"

"Well...no." It's the truth. Brooks hadn't called me.

"Oh, no," Sydney says, her eyes softening. She thinks I got rejected by Brooks. A repeat of our high school breakup. We ate an insane amount of ice cream and cried over cheesy romcoms together after he dumped me. "I'm sorry. I wish you would have told me. I wouldn't have orchestrated all this for you and Dad had I known."

"Here's the worst part about it." I slide my phone out of the pocket of my shorts and scroll back through my texts. "Brooks didn't call me, but later that night, I got this text."

Sydney's eyes flick over my phone screen. "Nora!" she screams. "He texted you! He texted *you*! But wait...you never responded?"

"Wait, what? Yes, I did!"

"No, you didn't," Sydney said, turning my phone around to show me the screen. My heart sinks into my toes.

"I swear I replied..." I say, in shock. I take my phone back and stare down at Brooks' text. The screen is riddled with spidery cracks from all the times Ollie and I have dropped the poor thing. Maybe I thought I'd hit send, but really I hadn't. There's a sizable crack over the send button that sometimes requires a really firm thumb tap. I'd been so determined not to look back at the text that I hadn't even realized that it had never actually sent.

My whirling thoughts suddenly distill into frostbitten clarity.

For the last four weeks, I thought Brooks had ghosted me. But in reality, I had unknowingly ghosted *him*.

"If it makes you feel any better, I wouldn't have responded either," Trent says, trying to cheer me up.

"That's because you barely know how to use a cell phone." Sydney turns back to face me.

"I thought I had pressed send. Oh my gosh," I groan. "I can't believe this. I'm just going to pretend it wasn't him to make myself feel better."

"Who else would it have been?" Sydney scoffs.

"I don't know, one of my employees trying to play a prank on me?"

"Don't tell me you're serious." My silence must be answer enough because she takes my phone right out of my hands again. "Well, there's only one way to confirm that it really was Brooks who texted you." Sydney deposits my phone under her thigh, keeping it out of my reach.

"Sydney Stewart," I warn. "Don't you dare text him back now!"

"Yeah, Syd," Trent chimes in. "Don't text him. Need I remind you that you're already married? To *me*?"

"I'm not going to text Brooks! This isn't my first matchmaking rodeo," Sydney says defensively. She considers herself responsible for our sister Bridget's marriage to Trent's friend Javier. Sydney pulls out her own phone. "I'm texting Claire!"

"What on earth are you going to say?" I ask.

"I'm going to tell her you somehow lost his number. I guarantee she'll give it to me if she knows you're the one asking for it."

I'm about to unbuckle my own seatbelt to intervene, but her fingers are already flying across her phone keyboard. Too late.

I huff out a breath and fold my arms like Ollie does when I deny him a treat before dinner. If I'm entirely honest with myself, the blame in reality lies with me. I'd been so determined to not get my hopes up that I hadn't bothered to double check that my text had gone through. This is my fault. And Roman's, too. He had the gumption to give Brooks my number in the first place.

"It's done!" Sydney cries.

Trent grumbles something under his breath that sounds a lot like "crazy woman".

"And now," Sydney says ceremoniously, flourishing her phone through the air. "We wait. Enjoy the Seventh Inning Stretch, everyone."

I groan and bury the heels of my hands into my eyes.

FIVE

Brooks

162.

That's how many games we've already played in the regular season. That doesn't include the spring training games we play from late February through the end of March, and the playoff games we could potentially play in the postseason if we perform well.

We're two games deep into our postseason Wild Card series with the Utah Archers and have to take home the win tonight to advance to the American League Division Series. This is what the team has been working for all year. So much is riding on tonight, and I'm feeling the electric current of my nerves buzzing through my body.

I couldn't even tell you how many games I've played since getting drafted by the Stormbreakers out of college, playing three years in the minors before moving up to the majors last year to play shortstop. But what I can tell you is how many games I've played in recent years when I knew Nora Foster was somewhere in the crowd.

Zero.

Until tonight.

"It's Mr. Foster's birthday. You don't mind, do you?" Claire said coyly over the phone when she'd asked if the Foster family could join her in the friends-and-family section.

"Of course I mind," I mutter, still confused about the fact that Nora had blown me off when I'd reached out. But Claire doesn't need to know about that. Plus, I had never allowed myself to look at Nora during my high school games. It was too distracting. The last thing I need tonight is a distraction.

"You're lying to yourself," Claire said. "You'd like nothing better than to have a beautiful girl there, cheering you on. A beautiful, *nice* girl for once."

"What are you trying to say? I don't date nice girls?"

"Yep," Claire said brightly. "That's exactly what I'm trying to say. You always go for the ones with eyelash extensions."

"And that correlates to their personality...how?"

"It just does, okay? But I plan to help you attract the right kind of women. The kind who don't look like they've got spider legs for lashes. Starting now."

Sisters.

Ultimately, I'd agreed, not wanting to disclose the real reason I didn't want to see Nora again. I'm sure there's a reason she wasn't interested in reconnecting with me, but it still stung when I thought she'd given me the green light by writing her number on my to-go box. It's been a month, and my ego is still bruised.

The pressure is on tonight, and I'm feeling it. The fact that Nora and her family will be here watching me play isn't helping my stress levels, but I've played too many games in my career to let a woman get in my head before I step onto the field. I don't plan on starting tonight.

We still have a few hours before game time, and I'm twitching with excess energy that's got nothing to do with the Red Bull I downed before running some infield drills. I'm on my knees, catching fast ground balls from my trainer. I focus on the *thwack* of the ball as it lands in my well-worn glove, letting muscle memory take over.

I've always been known for my dynamics on the field, my speed and versatility as a player. So much of my performance during games depends on my preparation. The guys on the team call me superstitious for time-blocking my pregame routine down to the minute, but it's what works for me. I do not deviate from my schedule. Strictness is the name of the game.

And that's why, as much as I'd like to, I can't afford to think about Nora tonight. If I do, I'll lose focus, and my game will suffer. I'd had a bad streak of games after Nora had gotten married, and I can't allow myself to slip again like I had then. Texting her last month had been a mistake. It had given me ideas. Ideas that she clearly doesn't share.

I'm determined to forget about Nora all over again. Throwing myself into baseball has always seemed to do the trick in the past, so I let my game brain take over, trying to shove all thoughts of Nora out.

Nora

"It's a boy!" Sydney says, flipping her phone and mine around so I can see both screens. "Would you look at that."

I take my phone back with shaking hands, then blink at my sister fearfully.

"Oh, no," I say in an almost whisper. "It really was him?" I slump back into my seat, stunned. The number Claire had sent over is identical to the one from the mystery text on my phone. Brooks had texted me *for real*.

And I had unintentionally ignored him.

"He hates me," I say. "He hates me, and when he sees me tonight, he's going to throw me out of the stadium."

"Nobody's getting thrown out of the stadium. Well, except maybe Trent if he decides to toss his popcorn into the crowd again."

"I didn't toss my popcorn," Trent growls. "You knocked it out of my hand in a fit of rage when the umpire made a lousy call."

"There's an easy fix to this," Sydney says, ignoring her husband's point as she passes my phone back to me. "Send Brooks a text. Right now."

"Saying what?"

"Just tell him the truth. I'm sure he'll understand."

"Will he though? It's been a month since he texted me!"

"It'll be alright," Sydney pats my leg and then turns to her husband. "Tell her, Trent. He won't care that it looks like she purposefully ignored his advances and potentially bruised his ego."

Trent says nothing.

"Tell her!"

"If he really is interested," Trent finally says, "then he won't mind that he had to wait for you."

"There!" Sydney beams. "See? Everything will be fine."

The last thing I want is to cause more drama, especially when the Alden family is accommodating us tonight in honor of my dad's birthday. I think Sydney's right. I have to reach out to Brooks. Hopefully, I can temper the awkwardness that is bound to rise between us, should we end up speaking face-to-face tonight.

Not that I'm hoping for another encounter with Brooks. I'd like the complete opposite, actually. Someone grant me the power to become invisible tonight because I'm too mortified to be seen by Brooks or anyone in his family. Besides, baseball players are way too busy to say hi to anyone at any point before, during, or after a game, right? Especially in a qualifying game for the play-offs.

I bite the bullet and decide to take Sydney's advice. I type out a text, revealing the truth about what happened, which Sydney tweaks and reads out loud to Trent for approval before I hit "send."

> **Nora:** Hey, Brooks! I thought I had responded to you, but apparently my reply never went through. I'm so sorry! I promise I didn't ignore you on purpose! Anyways, good luck tonight. Thank you for helping make my Dad's birthday so special. We'll be there with your family cheering you on!

I pick at the hem of my shorts nervously as Trent and Sydney go back to bickering good-naturedly over who exactly it was that almost got them kicked out of the last Stormbreakers game they attended together.

Brooks

I'm tiptoeing around Jonah Bell, our starting catcher, who is dead asleep at 4:48 PM. Just like every game day, he's there, smack dab in the middle of our clubhouse training room, fully dressed in his uniform on one of the physical therapist's tables with his shoes untied.

"What would it be like?" I whisper to Miles Aguilar, our designated hitter. "To just be able to..." I gesture to Jonah's open-mouthed drooling. "Fall asleep?"

"A luxury guys like us will never understand." Miles sighs, throwing back the pre-workout drink he takes before every game. "He just shows up. Takes a nap. Does his thing."

For guys like Jonah, baseball is put into the context of the broader picture of his life. He's got a wife, two daughters, and other hobbies like reading and golf. He works hard, but he also seems to have a better grasp on how to genuinely enjoy the game. Me on the other hand? I eat, sleep, and breathe baseball. I'm generally laid-back off the field, but a perfectionist when it comes to my game. I take every minute of every game seriously, which usually pays off in my performance. I was raised by my dad to play a perfect game every single time, and I expect a lot of myself. So does everybody else.

"Maybe we should try it one of these days," Miles says with a shrug. "Seems to work for the guy."

I could never be relaxed enough to take a nap before a game. It's just not in me. Though I was lucky to have a breakout rookie season and rode a lot of highs last year, the pressure to deliver consistently weighs heavy on me now that I'm nearing the end of my second year playing for the Stormbreakers. I work as hard as I can to play my best every time I step onto the field, but when I don't nail everything exactly right, I get really frustrated. I am very intolerant of my own mistakes. My dad did a great job of pounding that into me as a kid.

Jonah gives a rousing snore and jolts awake, his eyes flying open in a panic.

"Turkey club with avocado," he says hoarsely, sitting up like a zombie. "Are there any left?"

"I don't know, man," Miles teases.

"You'd better run over there and check before Beau eats them all," I add.

Jonah flies off the table like he's being chased, ramming into the door frame with an *umph* as he unsteadily stumbles to find food.

Two physical therapists arrive, ready to give Miles and me our pre-game massages. We settle onto our respective tables, and I close my eyes as the therapist works the kinks out of my shoulders and arms.

My phone buzzes in my pocket, but I have to wait until the massage is over to check the notification. I thank the therapist, then swing my legs over the table so I'm in a seated position before slipping my phone out of my pocket.

Within seconds of opening my texts, I swear my body regains all of the tension the therapist just worked so hard to release. I stare down at the unexpected text.

It's from Nora.

"Did you just win MVP?" Miles reaches out and shoves my shoulder from his adjacent table. "You're pale as a ghost!"

"It's my mom," I lie fluidly. "Asking if she can bring me dinner. My family is coming to the game tonight."

"Ohoho!" Miles grins. "Brookie is too good for the clubhouse food now? Sheesh, man. All it takes is two years for your ego to take over. Get out of here."

He keeps up his good-natured teasing, and I take it in stride. There's a time and a place to talk to the guys about women, and pregame in the baseball clubhouse (where everyone is bound to add in their two cents) is not it.

I pile up a plate of the provided food for dinner at exactly 5:35 and eat while listening to Jonah grumble about his dry ham sandwich. I allow myself a minute while I'm chewing and nobody is talking to me to let my game-brain unlock. A single forbidden thought comes through.

Why would Nora go out of her way to give me her number at the diner, seemingly ignore me when I reach out, and then decide to respond a month later?

I don't get it.

Is she telling the truth? Maybe she really had made a mistake and thought she'd texted me back. Part of me wants to respond right now, tell her it's all good and ask her if she wants to meet up after the game. But instead, I turn off my phone completely. There's too much riding on this game for me to be distracted tonight.

Nora Foster is going to have to wait.

Nora

Brooks still hasn't replied to my text when we arrive at the stadium a couple hours later. I can't even be mad about it. I deserve a thorough waiting period after the one I put him through. Not to mention the man is about to play in a high-stakes showdown against the Utah Archers. He doesn't have time to worry about little ol' Nora from his hometown.

Although I wish he would just text me back and put me out of my misery.

Trent finds parking in a lot adjacent to Boeing Park, and then we track down my parents outside the stadium. They'd carpooled with our youngest sister, Bridget, and her new husband, Javier, to the game. After dating on and off for a couple of years, they decided to tie the knot this past spring.

"Who's ready for a Seattle Dog?" Dad calls out as we approach. "Trent, you in?"

"I don't know if I can do it tonight," Trent says. "Our marriage almost didn't survive the last game."

"Not happening, Dad," Sydney says, giving my dad a hug. "We had dragon breath for a week last time."

"Happy birthday," I say, embracing my dad. He always holds me a little longer than I think he will, like he's worried I'm not getting enough hugs and he's personally ensuring my quota is met.

"Thank you. Wish Ollie could have come, too."

"I know, your best buddy would have loved to be here. But you should be thankful you didn't waste money on a ticket for a child who wouldn't have watched a single second of the game."

"At least he would have eaten a hot dog with me."

Javier greets me with a kiss on the cheek, and I get a gawking once-over from my youngest sister.

"Wow, Nor," Bridget says, looking completely shocked at my appearance. "Bustin' out the red lipstick, are we?"

"We both know the only reason I look like this is because I was pressured into it."

Bridget, who is always impeccably dressed, laughs. "I'm glad Sydney was looking out for you. She did good work."

"I heard there's someone special you're going to see tonight," Javier says with one of his signature dimpled smiles.

"False," I refute. "I am here to celebrate Dad's birthday."

"That's not what I heard," Javier says.

"You guys are in on this, too?" I ask. "The entire family is conspiring against me. This is mutiny."

"More like strategy," Dad says with a wink. "How else am I supposed to get discounted season tickets?"

Fragrant smoke from a grill inside the stadium fills the air, and the music is already pounding against my ears, even from outside. We file through the security entrance reserved for guests of the players and an employee scans our tickets. Dad is beaming and assures Sydney that this is the best birthday gift he's ever received.

After entering the stadium, we're immediately swallowed up in the flow of the crowd. An energy pulses under my skin. It's the smell of popcorn, freshly cut grass, and sizzling hot dogs. The rumble of voices and the beat of the music blasting through the speakers. For a moment, the dread of encountering Brooks and his family again is suspended at the prospect of watching our favorite team play in person. We were Stormbreakers fans long before Brooks Alden joined their roster, and I'm reminded of how much I love being at the ballpark with my favorite people.

We're forced to file into a line to stay together, and I watch as each partnership in my family pairs off. Dad loosely links his fingers through Mom's. Javier locks one arm around Bridget's waist. Sydney clings to Trent, and his whole body leans protectively into her. He drops a kiss to her hair, and I look away.

And then there's me. Bringing up the rear. Flying solo. It hits me at random moments like this. The tips of my fingers twitch with the memory of what it was like to have someone's hand fitted to mine. Someone I loved enough to marry and spent a few happy years with.

I may not be living that reality anymore, and it's not like I don't have someone to hold, because I do. The feel of Ollie's little hand slipping into mine warms my heart and clogs my throat with emotion. But it's been a minute since I've held a man's hand, and I think I'd like the feel of it now even more than I did before.

We wander through the stadium tunnel, stopping to watch a few minutes of batting practice near the outfield.

"Is that him, do you think? It's so hard to tell from way over here," Bridget asks into my ear, craning her neck to get a look at who's up to bat.

"That's the other team, B," I say, trying to act like I'm not disappointed that I won't get to see Brooks Alden swinging away before the game starts.

We then stop at a concession stand so Dad and Javier can order their foot-long hot dogs laden with cream cheese, jalapenos, bacon, and onions.

"Good luck with that," Sydney says to Bridget. "Don't plan on kissing him for a week."

The smell of fresh kettle corn at the next kiosk draws everyone in, and though I'm not a big fan of popcorn, I buy a big bag for Trent.

"Compensation for the popcorn you lost last time," I say, and he laughs.

I hover just outside the circle of my family as they debate about where we're supposed to go, peering down the lower level of seats as the announcer welcomes the Stormbreakers to the field. My stomach swoops as my ex-boyfriend's number (twenty-eight) and name is blasted through the stadium and he runs out onto the field. He's third in the hitting lineup and even from a distance, he looks strong and athletic.

I suddenly feel the sting of our breakup all over again. Brooks Alden had been my dream, and when he'd left me to pursue all of *this*, it had broken my heart. But seeing him here all these years later makes me wonder if he would have missed out on this exact moment if it weren't for his decision to leave me behind. Maybe this is precisely where he was always meant to end up.

"Look!" Sydney gasps as we pass a little cart selling cookies. "Brooks even got his own treat! A brookie? That is adorable."

My eye is drawn, naturally, to the muscly image of Brooks in his uniform plastered onto the cart. He's smiling with his arms crossed over his broad chest, and I think he might even look more delicious than the brookie does.

"We have to try it," Mom says, crowding me in on the other side. Before I know it, I've got a warm brookie in my hand, a half-brownie, half chocolate chip cookie creation wrapped in a paper bag with Brooks' face on it.

Twist my arm.

Someone (not me) should keep the wrapper. He looks too good to throw away.

We somehow end up in the official Stormbreakers merch store, and while I'm entirely focused on not transferring the melted chocolate on my fingers to any of the over-priced t-shirts inside, my sisters are arguing over which hat we should all collectively purchase and wear for the evening.

"What do you think, Nor?"

I nearly choke on my brookie as I catch a glimpse of the price tag dangling off the hat on Bridget's head.

Wildly out of my itty-bitty diner manager budget.

"The white?" Sydney asks. "Or the blue?"

"You know," I say, busying myself with a shelf of Brooks Alden bobble heads. "I'm good. I've already got a couple Stormbreakers hats at home." Including one that Brooks brought back for me when we were dating. It's a little worn and faded, but still one of my favorites. I'd loved it too much to get rid of it, even after we broke up.

"But do you have a *white* one?" Bridget asks, placing the hat on my head. It's perfect. I love it. I think I have to have it.

A twinge of guilt hits me as I swipe my card, knowing that this unplanned purchase means groceries will be tight for me and Ollie next week. But at the same time, I rarely buy things for myself. If I'd made a fuss, one of my sisters would have bought it for me, and I don't want to be even more of a freeloader than I already am tonight. I didn't have to pay for my ticket, gas, or parking. I rationalize that it's okay to treat myself to a new hat so I can match my sisters.

"Should I call Claire?" Sydney asks me on our way out of the store, her mouth full of brookie. "She'll help us find our seats, right?"

Even though Claire has always been nothing but kind to me, I'm dreading seeing her. She was there at the diner that day. Had she seen Roman give Brooks my number? Does she think I completely ignored her brother? Oh, dear. My brookie is suddenly not sitting pretty in my stomach.

A few minutes later, we spot Claire Alden climbing up the stadium stairs towards us, smiling broadly.

"Hi!" she squeals, as Sydney practically bowls her into the surrounding crowd with a hug. "So glad you guys are here!"

"Nora," she says, jaw agape. "Is that you?"

Okay, really? You would think I am an actual toad based on the reactions everyone is giving me for putting on a little bit of makeup. I'm just not a high-maintenance girl, alright? I prefer to be comfortable when I'm chasing my child around and not at constant risk of indecent exposure every time I bend down to pick him up.

"I know, I know," I say, returning her hug. "It's a lot."

"Not at all! You're stunning!" she drops her voice low in my ear. "You might just throw Brooks off his game tonight looking as good as you do."

I laugh as she lets me go, delayed and a little too loudly, feeling my face warm. Obviously, she doesn't know I'd left Brooks hanging. Claire is a spitfire. I have no doubt she wouldn't have said that had she known.

Claire strikes up a conversation with my parents, leaving me flushed and anxious as she leads us down to our seats.

I loved the thrill of watching Brooks play when we were dating. I remember the pride I felt at being his girl, cheering him on and celebrating his wins. I knew firsthand the depth of his dedication and the pure joy he gained from playing his favorite sport. I can still taste the sweet Bubblicious kisses he'd give me and smell the sweat rising off his skin after a game. I have a feeling watching him play in person tonight is going to make my heart race and my palms sweat. But this time, I'm just another fan in the stands.

SIX

Brooks

My cleats and uniform are ready for me in my locker, having been laundered and cleaned by our hard-working staff and hung up tidily for me this afternoon. They take great care of us, and even though their consistent hard work may go unnoticed by some of the more veteran players on our team, it doesn't escape me.

I quickly dress in my white and blue home uniform, tugging my hat over my hair and lacing up my crisp white cleats before selecting my bat for the game. I toggle between a few options before settling on one that feels right for tonight. Let's hope it doesn't let me down.

Though most players were able to keep things cool all day, as we approach game time, the tension is palpable.

"Back it up, back it up," Jonah says, shaking his well-endowed rear to a song he's blasting from his speakers.

"Careful, Bell," I say. "Don't wanna split your pants before the game."

Most of us can't help but laugh at his antics. He's trying to keep us calm and help us shake off the jitters before we take the field.

At 6:23, I head out to the field with my teammates. It doesn't matter how many games I play, every single time I emerge from the tunnel into the dugout, it feels like coming home.

Kids and avid fans crowd the steps where the team funnels out onto the field, vying for autographs and pictures. It's a jumble of voices and shouts, but I see several kids single me out, their eyes bright and smiles wide. I remember how much it meant when I was younger when players would take time to sign a few cards, baseballs or to take a photo. I always try to stop and do so if I can.

"You're my favorite player," a scrawny boy with braces says to me with a grin.

"Thanks, man," I say, scratching out a signature onto his outstretched hat. "Means a lot."

I take a few selfies and then ask the one of the coaches for the time. 6:40. I take one look up at the seats behind the dugout and see my family waving wildly once I spot them. Then my eyes find her.

Nora.

She looks stunning, even from a distance. I can see her red lips from here, full and smiling. She looks right at home sitting next to my family. The sight of her here momentarily takes my mind off the nerves and everything that's riding on this game.

I'm shocked further when Nora gives me a quick thumbs-up. My heart flips. It's the same thing she used to do when she'd come to my high school games. There's no way she'd send me that little private signal if she wasn't telling the truth in her text. It must have been an honest mistake. I want to believe that. Nora knows what that thumbs-up sign used to mean to me. That small gesture gives me an instant boost. One that I didn't even know I needed.

There will be time to ask questions and get more answers from her later. For now, I've got to get out and play a great game.

I raise a hand towards my family and the fans screaming my name before loping out onto the field to play catch with Miles.

"You're smiley tonight," Miles calls out.

"What's it to you?" I yell back.

We move back to home at 6:57, lining up with the team for the national anthem.

At 7:08, we assume our positions on the field. The sharp scent of the freshly cut grass and rich smell of the dirt rises up beneath my cleats as I run.

It's game time.

Unsurprisingly, the Utah Archers come out swinging. The game is back and forth, and I've gone two for three at the plate—a nice single and a double.

We're not gonna talk about the strikeout.

The seventh inning stretch arrives, and we're all tied up. The crowd is rocking, and the excitement is palpable at the bottom of the eighth as we get two runners on base. But with two outs, Miles is up to bat next and knows he had better deliver.

"Let's go, baby!" Wesley Shaw, first baseman, hollers from my right as Miles' walk-up song, "Machika" by J Balvin, blasts through the speakers.

As Miles steps up to bat, it's pandemonium in the stadium. I'm feeling secondhand adrenaline coursing through me as I watch him get ready to hit what we all hope will be a game-changing grand slam. Beau Andrade, our third baseman, and I are chewing and spitting sunflower seeds at a record pace, hoping it will help ease some of our sky-high stress.

But, the closer the Archers decided to bring out is ruthless. Within minutes, Miles has two strikes and no balls.

"Come on!" I slam my palms down on the dugout bench in frustration. Miles looks furious as he prepares to hit again. I know there's a fire blazing underneath his skin, and he wants nothing more than to clock the next pitch sent his way into the stratosphere. This is why the fans love him. He's inhuman when the pressure's on.

"Come on, Miles," Beau mutters with his hands steepled at his mouth as if in prayer. "Come on, baby."

The next pitch is a blur as it comes in. A fastball right down the middle. I hear the satisfying crack of Miles' bat make contact and all of us seated in the dugout rise onto our feet. It's a deep fly ball, and the crowd roars as we collectively watch it whistle through the air.

"That's it!" I yell. This is the miracle we needed. Miles is going to turn the game around and give us the chance to pull ahead.

For a moment, it's as if time slows down, and I can see every inch of air the ball falls through as it lands...right into the glove of the centerfielder at the wall.

The energy in the stadium deflates in a vacuum of disappointed gasps.

But nobody is more pissed than Miles. He chucks his bat, yells something unintelligible, and then stalks off the field, his anger mounting as he enters the dugout. We all know better than to speak to him when he's this upset, so we let him pass, feeling waves of frustration rolling off of him.

Beau and I glance at each other. Now that our prime scoring position has been lost, we've got to take the field and hold the line.

At the top of the ninth inning, we're still tied.

Cortez is ready to shut it down when he steps onto the pitcher's mound. After he strikes out the Archers' first batter, the pressure in my chest starts to loosen. If he keeps this up, there's still a chance to come back and win this thing.

But then, despite an insane play by the outfielders, my old teammate from the minors, Frankie Fieldman, gets a double. He's grinning like a madman on second base despite the boos from the crowd.

The third hitter steps up to bat and whacks a perfect ground ball to Wesley at first base. Wes scoops up the grounder and touches first to get the runner out, but Frankie was still able to make it to third. Freaking Frankie.

Two outs.

I can feel my pulse pumping through my arms, down my legs, and into my feet. Even my toes are tingling. The stress is building inside me, forcing me to work to keep my breathing steady.

Frankie glances back at me and winks. I glare back, punching a hand inside my glove and getting into position as the next hitter steps up to bat.

Cortez throws a slider, and I hear the sharp snap of the ball as the hitter makes contact. It's a blur, but I'm already moving. That ball is mine.

I'm running with everything I've got, feeling the press of my cleats in the dirt, the bunching of my muscles as I throw the force of my body towards the ball. I have to slide across the field to snatch it from the ground as it bounces towards me, but somehow I get it into my glove. I barely hear the wild roaring of the crowd as I leap to my feet and turn, rearing my throwing arm back to let the ball rip to home. I jump to put as much momentum as possible into my arm, but as my feet leave the ground, my center of gravity shifts, and I feel the error before I even execute it.

The ball ricochets towards Jonah like a bullet, but I've thrown it wide. Jonah has to lunge off the plate to field the ball, and in the seconds it takes him to retrieve it, Frankie Fieldman scores.

It's like all the air has drained from my lungs. I'm shaken by the deep pang of disappointment that floods my gut.

The ball went wide.

The crowd shifts from elation and shock at what I was just able to pull off to raging anger in a matter of heartbeats. I hear the booing and cursing my name like a distant storm rolling towards me.

My father did not raise me to be the kind of guy who lets mistakes like this roll off. *Play with perfect precision, or don't play at all.* That's what he'd always say to me.

Moments like this always cut right into my center. I glance up into the stands, finding Nora and my family in the distance, and feel the mistake I just made lodge itself deep inside me.

The Utah Archers are up one, and it's entirely my fault.

SEVEN

Nora

"OH, NO," CLAIRE GASPS next to me. "This is not good."

The cameras pan to Brooks, and his handsome face appears on the big screen across the ball field. My heart glitches at the sight of him in all his long-lashed, blue-eyed, athletic glory. He's got shock and disappointment etched into every line of his features. The slant of his easy smile is replaced by a frustrated frown.

I press my hands to my heart as the crowd around us erupts into angry jeers.

"Come on now!" I say loudly, gesturing to the general mayhem around me. "He doesn't deserve that!"

"He caught the ball," Dad booms, leaning over to join the conversation from down the row. "Could any of you have done that? Didn't think so."

"Cut the guy some slack!" Sydney cries out.

But it would appear that the Stormbreakers fans present tonight are not in a forgiving mood. They're swearing and screaming at Brooks like they've each been personally wronged.

"They can still come back," Trent adds as an aside, mostly to me, I think. "It's not too late."

I want it for him. I want them to come back and win this thing. They deserve it.

I add my cheers to those of our families, hoping Brooks can somehow feel that all is not lost from his position way down there on the field.

But if the Brooks Alden before me is anything like the one I dated in high school, he's going to feel this mistake deep in his bones. He's going to absorb it into his soul and stew over it for weeks, replaying it in his mind until the right person tells him to move on, and he finally decides to listen.

Usually, I was that person. I wonder who talks him out of his perfectionist slumps now.

"Get back up, bro!" Caroline hollers. "You've got this!"

And they do, partially. Cortez successfully strikes out the next hitter, but my heart is still rapping against my chest fearfully as the inning ends.

The damage may have already been done.

At the bottom of the ninth inning, it feels like the entire stadium is holding its breath. All hope is not lost. The Stormbreakers still have the opportunity to tie the game and pull ahead.

Unfortunately, despite the booing of the crowd, the Archers' closer is in peak performance mode tonight. He strikes two batters out before Beau Andrade hitter sends the ball sailing into the outfield.

The ball is caught, and the energy leaks out of the stadium in a slow whoosh. The game is over. The Stormbreakers have lost.

My heart is heavy as I seek Brooks out on the field, wondering how he feels right now. No doubt he's just as devastated, or even more so, than the fans present.

Claire starts crying. Actually crying. And so does her mother. They stand and embrace each other, tears leaking down their cheeks.

"I'm so sorry," I say, patting Claire on the shoulder and looking between them sympathetically.

"Don't be sorry!" Mrs. Alden cries, swiping below her eyes. "We're disappointed, of course, but it's not all bad. He played a fantastic game."

"We're just relieved!" Claire says on a long exhale. "This means Brooks is done. The season is over. We'll finally get to see him again!"

I wonder if Brooks feels the same way about ending his season with this disappointing loss. Highly doubtful.

"We'll get 'em next time," Dad says, probably with great effort since he's seated right next to the family of one of the players. I'm sure his filter will come off, and my family will get an earful on the way home.

We slowly funnel towards the stairway, shuffling as the crowd moves towards the exits.

"Normally, we'd hang out for a bit and try to catch Brooks before he heads home," Claire says from behind me. "But I have a feeling he's not going to be in a chatty mood tonight. Plus, look." I follow the line of her gaze down to the field, where Brooks is being swarmed by reporters. "He's not going anywhere any time soon."

My heart pinches at the sight of him surrounded by a hungry pack of media hyenas. In another life, I would have been the one to help cheer him up after a game like this. I watch him with a pit in my stomach, knowing he's probably beating himself up right now, especially as the Archers are celebrating wildly nearby. It kills me to know that there's nothing I can do about it.

"I'm sure he would have loved to see you," Claire says.

"Had he won," Caroline adds, ever honest.

"That's okay," I say. "This was amazing. Thank you for the great seats."

"Don't thank us," Claire says with a sneaky smile. "Thank Brooks. You've got his number now, right?"

My cheeks warm. "Yep. I do."

The twins share a look that makes me feel like I've just walked into a trap.

On the car ride home, Sydney pulls up a post-game interview on her phone.

"I'm here with Brooks Alden, shortstop for the Seattle Stormbreakers, and I've got to say, tonight was wild," the reporter says. *"You made an unbelievable snag there in the eighth inning, but I've got to know, what went wrong?"*

"There's no excuse, really. I missed the throw. Simple as that," Brooks says humbly, hands on his hips. *"I tripped up and threw it wide. I'll own up to it, and yeah, I'm disappointed, too."*

"Like I said, you still made a great athletic play, something we've seen you do consistently throughout the season, but things happen, right?"

"Things happen," Brooks repeats. *"But the boys and I left it all out on the field tonight. So although I wish things would have ended differently, I can't say that we didn't get after it this season because we did. I'm proud of that."*

The reporter thanks Brooks as he turns to field more questions from the surrounding bouquet of microphones vying for his mouth.

"He could have easily pinned that on Jonah Bell," Trent says from the driver's seat. "But he didn't. He owned up to his mistake."

"That's true," I say with a sigh as Sydney swipes out of the interview on her phone.

"The noble thing to do," Sydney says, and she catches me yawning in the rearview mirror. "I hope you don't have an early morning at Delia's tomorrow. Please tell me you get to sleep in?"

"No rest for the manager." My eyeballs hurt just thinking about what time I'm going to have to wake up tomorrow to get things rolling at the diner.

"Do you ever take a day off?" Trent asks.

"Can't afford to," I say in what I hope is a light tone and not laced with bitterness. It's not entirely true. I technically could take a day off as the manager, but I choose not to. My sole income plus Nate's meager child support doesn't exactly allow for a whole lot of extra spending. Me and Ollie are happy and content with a simple life, but I have been contemplating lately how I can make our situation better without becoming a part-owner in the diner. Delia's has been good to me, but I've realized after having a kid that I don't want to be there forever.

"Have you thought about my offer to host a ceramics workshop for you at Wildwood?" Sydney offers, again. She's brought up this idea several times, but I can never seem to take her up on it with my work schedule. The cabins that she and Trent own together at Wildwood hold some kind of magic that I haven't forgotten since my stay when I was pregnant with Ollie two years ago. They're tucked away in a forest about thirty minutes west of Kitt's Harbor. "I still think it's a great idea. You could earn a little extra money, sleep over afterwards, and Trent will even make you breakfast."

"Hope you like burnt toast." Trent grins.

"You really think people would come?"

"Absolutely," Sydney says. "Need I remind you that people have been asking for a way to purchase your work for years? I also think you should do the Harvest Market coming up. I'd love to help you set up a booth."

"I could build you some shelves," Trent adds.

I look between them gratefully, feeling extra lucky that they love me so well. I think about the rush of boldness that had prompted me to text Brooks back, how good it had felt to do something out of my comfort zone and act on a whim. It hadn't gone exactly how I'd planned, seeing as I'd made the mistake of not actually sending the text, but I had felt brave nonetheless. I sit thoughtfully as Sydney fills the silence with ideas about how we could make my ceramics available to our community. Her confidence in me makes me want to throw caution to the wind and just go for it.

If I want things to change in my life, I'm going to have to start making different choices.

Maybe it's time for me to start saying yes to things that make me uncomfortable. Things that I'm afraid of. Maybe it's time for me to be brave again.

"You know what?" I say. "Let's do it."

"Really?" Sydney gasps, looking like Christmas came early.

"Yeah," I say, feeling a tingly excitement at the possibilities she'd suggested. "I want to do it."

"Okay," she says excitedly. "I'll get to work planning the workshop, and I'll book you a booth at the Harvest Market."

We share a smile, and I know she's proud of me. It won't be easy to make time for this with my work schedule, but I think it will be worth the effort.

It's only once I've been dropped off at my empty house that I notice my ears are still ringing from the noisy crowds at the game, and I've got a headache pulsing behind my eyes. One night out, and I'm officially seventy-six years old.

It's late, and I'm tired, so despite the itch in my fingers to get to work on throwing more plates, mugs, cups, and vases at the wheel so I'll have enough inventory for the Harvest Market, I decide it can wait. I usually love ending my evenings by spending an hour or two in my studio. I find that it helps ease the tension out of my body, but tonight, my bed beckons.

Unfortunately, a very handsome baseball player continues to pop into my mind while I get ready for bed. As I remove my makeup, I dwell on the fact that Brooks is probably hurting badly right now and could use some cheering up.

Not your job, Nora. He's probably got a gaggle of girls with him right now and is feeling a-okay about things. Just peachy.

Then why did he text you in the first place?

I change into a comfy t-shirt and my favorite green sweatpants and contemplate texting him again.

Before I know what's happening, I'm snuggled up in bed with my phone in my hands, a draft of a text forming without my consent. It's involuntary. It's compulsive.

I shouldn't do this...

And yet, his devastated expression keeps reappearing in my mind. Brooks was gutted tonight. I know he was. A few words of encouragement certainly wouldn't hurt. It's what I used to do for him when he was my boyfriend, and it always seemed to help him see his mistakes in the broader context of things.

> **Nora:** Hey, Brooks. You played an incredible game tonight. It was awesome getting to see you do your thing again. Oh, and if you ever want to egg Frankie Fieldman's house, I'm your gal. I've got pallets of them just sitting at the diner waiting to be put to good use.

I place my phone on its charger like a good girl, worry for twenty minutes about whether or not I should have sent that text, and then spiral into anxieties about Ollie. He doesn't cry or get upset when I drop him off with Nate and part of me wishes he would. Watching my ex drive away with my tiny best friend makes every bone in my body ache.

I slip into a half-sleep, and it takes me a few minutes to register that my phone has vibrated a couple of times. I snatch it off the charger, heart pounding as I read the notification.

Brooks texted me.

He actually texted me.
Now I'm never going to fall asleep.

> **Brooks:** Thanks, Nora. I hope you and your family enjoyed yourselves. Glad you finally figured how to properly hit send. *smiley face emoji*

I'm squealing now. Actual pig-squealing into my pillow. Relief floods through me. He's not mad. Or if he was, he's choosing to tease me about it instead.

> **Nora:** I'm so sorry! I feel so bad. My phone screen is cracked…you know how clumsy I am.

> **Brooks:** Still? Haha. It's all good.

> **Brooks:** Did you bring your son to the game? I couldn't see him, but maybe that's because he's tiny.

> **Nora:** It was just me tonight. I love having Ollie with me, but it was nice to actually watch the entire game.

Brooks: Oh, no. You saw the whole thing? You sure you didn't get up for a snack break during the bottom of the eighth? *wink emoji*

He's sending emojis. I repeat, he is sending emojis. Is he flirting with me? Oh, good gracious. I hope not. I haven't flirted in a long, long time. I'm Tow Mater level rusty.

Nora: You mean when you somehow acquired the necessary superpowers to catch that ball? Yeah, I definitely saw that. Your secret's out.

Brooks: Dang it.

Brooks: I'm sorry tonight was the game you had to see.

I feel a pang in my chest as I read over his words.

Nora: Hey, nobody's perfect, right? Mistakes happen. You still played an amazing game.

I watch the bubbles dance as Brooks types his reply, then disappear. His text comes through a few long minutes later.

Brooks: Thanks, Nora.

Do I reply? Do I let him have the last word? I can't think of anything else to say that wouldn't seem like a ploy to keep our conversation going, so I heart his text, then set my phone back on the charger and curl up under my blankets again.

A peculiar bubbly feeling is rising within me, like the sensation you get after drinking a really good, crisp sip of an ice-cold soda. And for the first time in a while, I embrace it, invite it to stay a while as I smile into my pillow.

EIGHT

Brooks

"You sure you don't want to get rid of those?" Jonah asks me as I clean out my locker at the clubhouse along with the rest of the team. He finished first because his wife is a professional organizer and came by to help him while their kids were at school.

"These?" I hold up a pair of fresh white socks I've never worn. "They're brand new."

"Dang it," Jonah sighs. "I'm pretty sure a pair of socks worn by Brooks Alden would fetch a pretty penny on eBay."

I snort, chucking the socks at him so forcefully he has to fumble to catch them.

"Not after last week's game, they won't," I mumble, not intending for Jonah to hear me, but he must because he rises from the chair he's lounging in and comes to hover over my shoulder.

"Hey," he says, prodding me with the balled-up socks. "You can't say stuff like that."

"Why not? It's true."

"You screwed up. The world knows you're human now. Capable of...humanity."

"You write that line yourself?"

"Are you really still torn up about it?"

Torn up? More like shredded.

The day after the game, I'd gotten a text consisting of several paragraphs of commentary and criticism from my dad. He was sure to tell me everything I'd done wrong in the game and listed out his suggested ways of what I could do during the off-season to ensure my "rookie" mistakes never happen again. It had made me so upset that I'd blocked his number on my phone. Should have done that sooner.

But his words found their mark and spurred me into action. I've spent the past week watching the tapes and re-working the play a thousand different ways in my mind. I've dissected it from every angle with the help of my coaches. I've lifted at the gym, worked on improving my strength and mobility, and pushed my body to its limits these past few days. While normally it feels good to meet the edge of my physical abilities, I think I've gone too far. Most of my teammates take at least a couple weeks entirely off of baseball at the end of every season, and I didn't allow myself even one day to relax after our loss. I'm exhausted.

I shove a pair of cleats into my duffle bag. "Am I supposed to be over it by now?"

"That depends on how much fun you want to have in the off-season. What are your plans?"

"Lift. Eat clean. Maintain my conditioning. Overhaul my game," I say, mentally adding to the list that I need to try to get over the mental hurdle that seems to somehow grow taller every day that goes by. Right now, it feels insurmountable. That bad play is now my identity. It's all the media has talked about since we lost. It's all anybody asks me about when I'm interviewed. I can't escape it.

And though I blocked my dad's number, it's his voice that's ringing constantly in my head. Telling me I don't deserve to play at a professional level after the mistake I made. That I'm not good enough.

That's what happens when you're raised by someone who tears you apart when you don't measure up.

"Wow," Jonah drags out with a grin. "You're a real good time."

"Aren't you going to do the same?" I know for a fact that Jonah takes his off-season routine just as seriously as I do.

"Yeah, but I plan on at least taking the weekends off to do other things."

"Like what?"

"Well, I'm gonna make time to read more books."

"Read...books?"

"Yeah. If I were you, I'd find ways to relax. Maybe talk to someone about whatever was bugging me. Then journal about my feelings."

"Journal?" I snort. The only time I pick up a pen is when I sign autographs, and even then, my hand cramps up.

"I'm going to eat lots of good, nutritious food. Play some golf. Spend time with my family. Maybe pick up a new hobby."

"Like what? Embroidery?"

"Hey," he warns. "Don't diss the stitch, bro."

I snicker.

"No, but seriously. Find something you enjoy doing off the field. Something other than working out and beating yourself up about that game."

His suggestions sound so...simple.

I'm not even sure what I enjoy doing outside of my sport. My life *is* baseball. It's always been baseball.

Well, that's not entirely true. Before I left home to play college ball, I enjoyed other things. Going to the movies or having a bonfire down at the harbor with friends. Visiting a pretty girl at Delia's Diner and sharing a hot stack of pancakes or French toast during her lunch break.

It's been a long time since I pursued any interests that didn't contribute to improving my game. Jonah's advice makes me realize that maybe I've been licking my wounds, dragging around my mistake like a ball and chain. The way my dad taught me to do.

I hate that I let him hold so much power over me. I've felt a renewed resentment towards him as I've been back in touch with Nora because he's the reason I allowed her to drift out of my life.

"It might take some work," Jonah continues. "But if you can look at this as a chance to grow in more ways than just an athlete, I think this might end up being really good for you. This might be your chance to find out what else you can lean on when the game doesn't go the way you want it to."

"How much do I owe you for the therapy session?"

He holds up the socks and grins. "Let's call it even."

Twenty minutes later, I'm closing my locker for the last time this season. My bags are packed. My work here is done...for now. Hopefully not forever. The irrational fear of getting dropped or traded has been pinging around my mind like a pinball ever since we lost that final game.

I mull over Jonah's words all the way home to my apartment. Maybe he's right. My brain has felt like it's going to explode, stuck in a constant loop of negativity and stress.

Losses like the one we just experienced always trigger my need to try to control things in my life. The same thing happened to me after my dad convinced me to break up with Nora my senior year of high school. I left Kitt's Harbor and threw everything I had into my dream of playing professional baseball. I couldn't control what happened to Nora once I was gone, but I could try to control my game. And I have. I've worked hard to excel at my sport and compete at the highest level, but all it takes is one bad play to push me back to the edge. Here I am, stuck in the same cycle and grappling for control again.

I haven't had the guts to ever take a real break from baseball. It feels dangerous. What if everything I've worked so hard to shove down and numb comes back to the surface when I stop?

Maybe Jonah's right. What I need is a new hobby. More time at home.

I avoid going home too often to avoid an encounter with my dad. His work as an airline pilot means he's away a lot, and since I've officially blocked his number, I'm starting to think that it may be worth the risk if it means I get to see my mom, sisters, and hopefully, Nora again.

I call my agent, Desi, and run my thoughts by her.

"What if you kept some structure to your work week so you still feel productive, but then spend at least part of your weekends back home?"

I'm surprised at how supportive she is of the idea. We continue to talk at length about what else I can do to set myself up for success in the new year. Alongside spending more time at home with my family, she suggests that I start seeing a therapist. Someone who can help me work through my mental blocks.

"Anything that helps your mind will help your game," Desi says, sounding relieved that I seemed to be actively looking for ways to get out of the hole I've been in. She's tried her best to keep things upbeat, but I've been in a rut, and honestly, I think she needs a break from me, too. "You're on the right track, Brooks. I'm here to support whatever you decide to do."

After we end our call, I picture how happy my family will be that I'll be around more. I can't help but wonder if Nora will be excited, too.

I had tried to forget about what happened between us, tried to not let regret break me apart by throwing myself into becoming the best baseball player I could be. But clearly, after seeing her again, I haven't forgotten what she meant to me.

Because you don't just forget about the girl who was your first love.

Believe me, I tried.

NINE

Nora

I'VE ALWAYS DREAMED OF being more than a *diner girl*.

In my heart, I'm an artist.

The house is quiet, Ollie's finally asleep, and it's just me in my studio, listening to the mellow music floating through my headphones. Trent helped build me some shelves and a worktable out of a gorgeous, natural pine. The shelves are crowded with dinnerware, mugs, vases of all shapes and sizes, and candlestick holders I've thrown at my wheel. The collection continues to grow as I work to prepare for the Harvest Market in two weeks, the first weekend in October. I put on my favorite clay-splotched apron, light a few candles, turn on some music, and sit at the wheel. The ritual soothes me from the inside out, softening the tension that builds inside me and connecting me to something deeper. The part of me that needs a little nurturing after a long day spent tending to the needs of others.

My linen apron, arms, and bare feet on the floor are speckled white, while my hands are gloved in clay. Earthy, smooth, malleable clay.

The obsession began in high school when I took a ceramics class and found I had a natural gift at the wheel. The slow coaxing of an ordinary, unassuming lump of clay into something that I could put to practical use made my heart happy. It never gets old. I've made the plates we eat off of and the mugs I drink from. The vases that hold my flowers and the cork-stopped bottles that house my oils and vinegars. I challenged myself after my divorce to process my consuming grief by transferring it into clay, turning them into something beautiful as the wheel spins rhythmically beneath my hands. My high school teacher actually lets me use the school's kiln to fire my pieces–after hours, of course.

Tonight, I'm trying to finish a collection of small salad or dessert plates. I release my foot from the pedal and the wheel stops spinning, allowing me to reach for a needle tool so I can create a more precise edge on the plate I'm crafting. Setting the tools aside, I grab the sponge again and press down on the pedal, gently pinching the edge of the plate with one hand and slowly drawing the clay upwards with my sponge in the other.

Once I'm satisfied, I dry my hands and the plate. Then I cut the plate from the bat, a flat disc which attaches to the top of the wheel, with my wire.

I smile to myself, realizing that Brooks and I share this particular tool in common (at least in name).

We've been texting nearly every day since last weekend's game. Believe me, I'm still shocked every time his name pops up on my cracked phone screen. I blink at it in disbelief, then feel a warm, tingly feeling in my stomach that makes my heart beat a little faster as I read his words.

"What do you guys talk about?" Sydney asked me earlier today over the phone. "I'm dying to know. Is he flirty? I'll bet he's flirty."

I'd blushed a little, then, remembering all over again how it feels to be flirted with by someone as charming as Brooks. He'd been the same way in high school. The most irresistible, adorable flirt. I'd had no say in the matter. From the moment we met, I'd been head-over-heels.

There's a reason Booth Six at the diner has held significance for both of us. It's where we first met.

Delia herself had started a ridiculous new protocol as she rolled out what she called "Icy Blasts," a knock-off of a popular fast-food chain's frozen treats. She required the servers to tip the ice cream sundae glass upside down to demonstrate just how thick the concoction was before setting it down on the table. I never had a problem fulfilling this requirement until the night Brooks Alden and his teammates came into the diner and sat at Booth Six.

"Okay," I'd said, nervous as all-get-out as I brought their Icy Blasts to the table. "We've got a cookies and cream blast and a strawberry blast."

The boys watched me as I turned the cups filled with ice cream upside down and then burst into laughter as my worst fear played out before me in slow motion. I watched in horror as ice cream plopped out and oozed all over the table. I was mortified.

"Oh my gosh," I gasped, attempting to scoop the mess up with my bare hands. "I'm so sorry!"

Most of the boys laughed at me while unhelpfully tossing napkins in my general direction, but not Brooks. He slid out of that booth, grabbed some rags from the kitchen, and helped me clean every bit of it up. My eyes were burning with embarrassment, holding back tears as I apologized for my clumsiness.

"Don't worry about it," he said with a kind smile. "I like my ice cream with a little table in it anyways."

Our gazes had collided then, and I'd been struck by the blue of his eyes, his crooked grin, and the swoop of dark hair that fell over one eyebrow. Oh, boy, was I in trouble.

I hadn't even noticed his friends slipping out one by one, evading the bill. Brooks paid for the spilled ice cream, despite my insistence that I'd cover the tab since I'd mucked it all up.

And then, in spite of my embarrassing clumsy moment, he asked for my number.

Fast forward nine years, and here we are. Texting again. Single...again.

I throw a few more plates to complete the set, putting them aside with the rest of the pieces I'd thrown throughout the week. Tomorrow is firing day, then I'll play around with different glazes when I have time next week. I've been building up my inventory in preparation for my first market. It was surprisingly cheap to reserve the booth, and Trent, per his own insistence, is building me a couple shelves to display my work.

I'm suddenly startled out of my thoughts by the sound of my phone ringing in my headphones. I answer the call.

"Hi, sister. I've got a question for you," Sydney says. We've already chatted on the phone earlier, but she's never patient enough to just text and wait for an answer. She calls as soon as the idea strikes her.

"I think we should limit your first workshop to eight people. Do you think we would be able to find eight wheels to rent or borrow?"

The thought of dragging a bunch of throwing wheels, messy clay, and brown-tinged water into one of the beautiful cabins Sydney works so hard to maintain makes me cringe.

"I think bringing a bunch of wheels inside one of your cabins might be really messy," I say. "I guess we could do a hand-building workshop instead."

"So, no wheels required?"

"Exactly. It would be like going back in time. We'd create something simple using just our hands and a few tools I probably already have."

"That sounds perfect! Did you set up that Instagram account yet?" Sydney asks.

"Not yet. Ollie was really determined not to go to sleep without a fight tonight." After the initial bedtime routine, the heathen had required two graham crackers, a cup of milk, and another book before he'd finally let me go.

"I still like the name Noli. Nora plus Ollie...and bonus! It also happens to be a gorgeous city in Italy! What do you think about it?"

"I like it, too," I agree. "Even though I've never been there."

"Well, not to fear, big sister. I have. What do you want to know about it? I'll be your personal Rick Steves."

My jet-setting, travel-blogging sister then regales me with tales from her Italian adventures for a few minutes while I tidy up. I can practically feel the dusty cobblestones beneath my feet, smell the tang of lemon trees, and taste the bite of fresh pesto as she speaks. I've never left the Pacific Northwest, let alone traveled to the far-reaching corners of the earth like my sister has. We're alike in many ways, but where Sydney has a penchant for wandering, I've never had the desire to venture far from home. I like it here too much.

"We've got to do a girl's trip someday," Sydney says. "I'll be your tour guide. We could find you a nice Frenchman. Or an English aristocrat."

"Yeah, because men like that would be interested in someone like me. The only cool word I know in French is *pamplemousse*, and that's only because of Carol at Brickyard Bakery. She does that grapefruit sorbet every summer."

"Look at you! You're practically Parisian."

"More like primitive."

"But wait," Sydney says slyly. "You don't need an exotic man, do you? You've already got somebody else lined up. What was his name again? Something like Rooks Falden? How's he doing, by the way?"

"Couldn't tell you," I lie. Badly. She's my sister. She can smell a lie before it's even formed in my mouth.

"Sure. Is it weird talking to him again after all these years? I know he did a number on your heart back in high school."

It's true; it had gutted me when Brooks broke up with me senior year. Though Brooks never admitted it, I'd always suspected his dad had something to do with our breakup. He'd never been supportive of our relationship, and I sensed he felt I was holding Brooks back from greatness. When Brooks was initially offered the chance to play college ball at Oregon State, I'd applied, too, thinking we could attend college together. But then I didn't get in. The odds were against us, and I don't think it took much for his dad to convince him to let me go.

I was devastated. I felt like he'd chosen his baseball career over me, and I felt horribly selfish for wanting to keep him in Kitt's Harbor.

I cried for a month when he left, feeling betrayed and confused. Ultimately, he chose what was most important to him, and it was difficult for me to accept the fact that I hadn't mattered enough for him to fight for me. In my heart, I waited for Brooks to change his mind and come back to Kitt's Harbor and claim me for himself. But six months passed, and then a year. My hope turned to disappointment, and Brooks never did come back. I had to move on.

Nate was a part of our friend group, so it was a natural progression from friends to something more. Nate and Brooks didn't remain friends after I started dating him, understandably, but Nate was a big Stormbreakers fan. I was happy when he'd told me Brooks had gotten drafted by the minor team that fed into the Stormbreakers. In leaving me behind, he'd also gone on to achieve his biggest dream of playing baseball at a professional level. It was what he wanted. How could I fault him for that?

Besides, what Brooks did to my heart is practically insignificant compared to the complete shattering I experienced when Nate broke our marriage vows. He tossed me aside for someone else after we'd promised each other forever, and the pain and repercussions of Nate's choices were incredibly intense at first. Far more intense than getting dumped by my first boyfriend.

"It's been so long since our breakup. Things are different now," I finally say. "He's still really easy to talk to. Just like he was back then."

Sydney goes quiet on the other line, as if she can hear my line of thinking.

"I'm glad you're not holding anything against him still. You both were so young. I'm proud of you, Nor. You've come so far."

"Thanks, Syd. I have no idea if I'll ever see him again, so really, I've got nothing to lose."

"Except maybe your heart."

I smile. "True."

After we've ended our conversation, I do Sydney's bidding and reserve social media accounts under the business name we'd come up with for my shop: Noli Ceramics.

One step closer to becoming the artist I've always yearned to be.

Brooks texts me just as I'm finishing cleaning up the studio.

> **Brooks:** One of my teammates told me I should start reading more books. Have you read anything lately you'd recommend?

> **Nora:** Let's see…the last book I read was a real page turner.

> **Nora:** I think it was called *The Very Hungry Caterpillar*. Wouldn't recommend reading that one unless you've got snacks on hand. Another I'd recommend is an eleven book saga

about a little blue truck and his adorable farmyard friends.

Brooks: Adding both to my list. They're probably right at my reading level.

Nora: I'd offer to let you borrow ours, but Ollie would for sure notice they were missing. Two of his favorites.

Nora: Fun fact for you. Did you know that both of us use bats in our line of work?

Brooks: Don't tell me the diner has resorted to cooking up actual bats...?

Brooks: How are they prepared? Fried? Poached?

Nora: *crying laughing emoji*

Nora: This is the bat I'm talking about. It helps me be more efficient at the wheel.

I send him a picture of one of the bats that I've just washed.

Brooks: Is it rude of me to say I'm slightly disappointed? I was hoping I'd get to tell the guys that next time I visit home I'm trying bat meat.

Nora: *puke emoji*

Brooks: All joking aside, that's awesome. You're still throwing pottery, then?

Nora: Yes! As much as I can.

Brooks: How can I order something from you? I'm in the market for a new coffee mug. My friend Miles was over the other day, and he broke my favorite one.

His friend Miles? He has to be talking about Miles Aguilar. The stud of the Stormbreakers hitting lineup.

Nora: A travesty! I could totally make you one. Just send me your shipping address, and I'll send something your way.

Brooks: I'll do you one better.

Brooks: How about I pick it up from you next time I'm in town?

My heart starts thumping as I read over his text. Up until now, there was no guarantee of us seeing each other again. Texting him was harmless. Flirtatious. Fun.

But now Brooks wants a mug? One of *my* mugs. And he wants to come grab it next time he's home in Kitt's Harbor. *Deep breaths, Nora. Be brave.*

Nora: Sounds like a plan.

TEN

Nora

October

After a wild shift at the diner on Friday, I barely have time to get home, shower, and pick up Ollie from my neighbor's daycare before heading to Alice Park off Main where the Harvest Market is held. I've shopped at the market with my mom and sisters for nearly a decade, and for the first time, I'll be selling my own products at my very own booth. Though I'm trying not to have any real expectations for how things will go tonight, the nerves have fully settled in. My stomach feels like I chewed and swallowed an entire pack of Bubblicious bubble gum.

Don't do it, Nora. Don't follow that little Hansel and Gretel trail to where thoughts of bubblegum inevitably lead in my brain.

Kissing Brooks.

A little shiver traces down my spine at the thought. I quickly turn my attention back to the smooth, cool texture of the mug in my hands instead. I've got to be present tonight. No more thinking about Brooks. Although, holding this mug is not helping. Every mug I've made since Brooks told me he wants one has been carefully and consciously crafted with the knowledge that the sweet little thing could end up being used by him. Cradled in his hands. Caressed by his lips.

Could it be you, mug seventeen with the speckled texture and the wide handle, perfect for the athletic hand of a baseball player?

Yeah...I've lost it.

I also priced a few items at twenty-eight dollars before realizing that it was Brooks' number. Now I see the number 28 everywhere I go.

I glance down to check the time. *4:28*. I suck in a gasp and shove my phone back into my coat pocket. Maybe I'm just looking for it, or maybe I've genuinely cracked.

"How does this look?" Sydney asks, gesturing to the display shelf she'd arranged for me while I was at work. Trent had made it especially for me and brought it down in his truck. I don't know what I would do without the two of them.

"It looks perfect! You're so good at these things, Sydney," I reply, scanning the park for Ollie and Trent. He offered to take him to the playground while Sydney and I finished setting up. The whole deal takes longer than I anticipated it would, and the residents of Kitt's Harbor have already started filing through the pathway lined with string lights and white tents by the time we're finished.

"My goodness!" an accented voice calls out a moment later. "She's finally done it!"

Carol, the owner of our favorite local sweet spot, Brickyard Bakery, comes barreling towards us, gathering both me and my sister into her arms for a hug.

"Look at these, Nora!" Carol gasps, admiring a row of citrus juicers I'd made. "Oh, I'm going to need one. Maybe two."

Her joy-filled inspection of my pieces fills me with a vibrant glow. I carefully wrap the items she selects while Sydney takes her payment.

"See?" Sydney says once Carol is gone. "I told you everyone would be eager to support you."

Her prediction proves correct. My hand-thrown creations are picked off one by one by old friends from high school, teachers, and neighbors. Trent eventually returns with Ollie, who's now crusted in something red and sticky.

"Uncle T gave me a treat," he says with bright, wild eyes.

"I can see that," I say, taking him from Trent.

"I'll be back," Trent says, looking furtively at the gathering crowd of people around the booth. No doubt he's going to hide out in his truck for a minute to recoup.

I hoist Ollie up on my hip and rummage through my diaper bag with my free hand for some baby wipes. I've got the container popped open and am trying to separate one single wipe from the endless string of folded wipes that inevitably comes out when I hear someone approach the booth.

I turn to glance over my shoulder, and that's when I see him. Across the way, perusing a selection of Rose Marie's famous salsas, is Brooks Alden. He's with the twins, looking tall and lean and wearing a hat, clearly trying and failing to blend in. The lines of his masculine profile are lit by the warm glow of the string lights. Between the sweep of his long lashes and the scruff on his jawline, he's nothing short of beautiful. He has no business looking so attractive while sampling chips and salsa.

He should have chip crumbs and tomato dribbles all over his chin at the very least.

So shocked am I at the sight of Brooks and his sisters, that the crinkly container in my hand falls to the ground, pulling a waterfall of wipes out with it. I curse under my breath.

"I heard that," Sydney says without looking at me.

"Shut up," I hiss, my heart pumping with nervous anticipation. What if Brooks sees me? What if he comes over to talk to me? I am completely unprepared to see him like this. With my oversized puffer jacket covering most of my outfit and my wet hair slicked back into a low bun, I look like a freaking Founding Father.

Ollie whines out *mama* in a long drawl, and I start wildly flapping the attached wipes around, trying to get one to break apart from the bunch. I whisper-swear, and I can tell Sydney's about to tell me off again, but just then a pair of bright voices interrupts my curse. Sydney notices I'm in no state to greet customers and hurries to cover for me.

"Well, if it isn't our baseball buddies!"

I wince, recognizing Claire Alden's voice immediately. Ollie decides that now is a great time to attempt to squeeze both of my cheeks together with his sticky palms. Great. Now I probably have two Ollie-sized red handprints on my cheekbones.

By some miracle, I finally work a wipe free and set Ollie on his feet. I stuff the rest back into the container before quickly swiping the wipe over Ollie's face and hands. I try to discreetly rub the wipe over my face, hoping Sydney will be a dear and tell me if I've still got an unidentifiable substance smeared all over my cheek when I turn around.

Once Ollie is situated back on my hip, I work up the courage to face the inevitable.

"Ahh, there's the artist!" Caroline says as I turn around.

Brooks is standing a foot behind his sisters at the edge of the pathway, awash in the glow of the market lights. It's like the magic of the evening collects around his edges, the smell of cinnamon and the sound of the girl playing acoustic covers swirling together all at once.

Brooks meets my eyes, and I feel like I've just dropped into another dimension. One where he and I are something to each other still. He ducks under the edge of the tent and his presence immediately fills it. He's even more handsome than I imagined when we text. Real and fully dimensional and unexpectedly *here*.

"Hi," he says softly, giving me another warm, disarming smile. I feel my stomach drop another level in my gut at the sound of his voice. It's lower and deeper, more gravelly than I remember.

"Hi," I reply, sounding dazed.

"Mama," Ollie says into my ear, snapping me back to reality. I startle and take a step towards Brooks, knocking right into the table that I forgot was there to separate me from the customers.

I'm winning tonight.

"Who put that table there?" I say, making Ollie laugh. Oh, well. Brooks already knows how clumsy I am.

"Is this your son?" Brooks asks, turning his gaze to Ollie. I nod.

I'm not sure what I expected Brooks to do when he met Ollie for the first time. I definitely hadn't pictured it happening tonight. I don't know how much Brooks knows about what happened between Nate and me, but he doesn't seem deterred in the slightest.

"What's up, Ollie?" Brooks says, putting his knuckles out for a fist bump. "It's nice to meet you."

Ollie smacks Brooks' knuckles with his own and grins up at him shyly, laying his head on my shoulder. It's only then that I realize that everyone else in the tent has gone silent and is zeroed in on the interaction taking place. My gaze flits over Sydney, Claire, and Caroline, who are all staring at us with sappy smiles on their faces. I'm surprised nobody is shedding tears.

"Thanks for coming by," I say, trying to draw them out of their stupors. "I didn't know you guys would be here tonight."

"Brooks came to visit my fourth graders today," Claire explains. "Career day. The kids were thrilled."

All heads swivel to Brooks again. "It was a good time." He glances my way, as if expecting me to contribute to the conversation, but I'm only half here. I think the rest of me is back in high school, looking at Brooks and feeling like the luckiest girl in the world that I get to call him mine.

"That's so sweet of you to come all the way out here to do that," Sydney says when I fail to speak up. The half of me stuck in the past zooms back into my body, and I startle. Sydney gives me a concerned look that reads, *What's your problem? Speak up, woman!*

"You know Claire. I didn't have much choice in the matter," Brooks replies. His eyes drift to mine, and my heart wonders if he knew I'd be here tonight.

"He did great. Pretty sure half the kids in my class now want to be professional baseball players," Claire says.

"Who wouldn't after meeting the real deal?" Sydney says. "Thanks again for letting us sit with your family for Dad's birthday."

"Of course," Brooks says. "I'm just sorry that was the game you had to see."

"Don't say that," I say, somehow finding my voice. Brooks' gaze collides with mine again. "It was a great game."

"Yeah, Brooks. Quit beating yourself up about it, would you?" Caroline says with an affectionate squeeze around her brother's shoulders. "We're all over it, aren't we, everyone?"

"Over it," Sydney says.

"Totally moved on," Claire says.

Brooks is still watching me with interest, his gaze so open and honest that I'm almost grateful when Ollie starts reaching for the ground, forcing me to set him down. But of course when I do, he immediately darts around the edge of the table and tries to make a break for it.

"Whoa," Brooks says, swiping at Ollie. "Where are you off to?" He catches him under the arms and swings him through the air playfully. "He's fast."

"You're telling me," I reply, watching as Brooks gently sets Ollie down. Ollie grins up at him. "Oh, no. You made that too fun."

Sure enough, Ollie giggles and tries to run away, and Brooks easily snatches him up and swings him in a wider arc before setting him down again.

Ollie starts pulling Brooks away from the group with each mini sprint he takes, so I squeeze past the table to get closer in case I need to interfere.

"This is amazing," Brooks says, gesturing to the tent.

"I know. I love the Harvest Market. It always makes me feel like fall is officially here."

"I was talking about your booth," Brooks clarifies.

"Oh! Thank you," I say sheepishly. "I had a lot of help."

Brooks sets Ollie down again, and before he can run away, I catch him by the arm. I clearly should have named him Houdini because he twists easily out of my grasp with a cackle.

"Why don't you two go walk around with Ollie for a little bit?" Sydney suggests. "I can man the fort for you."

Not a bad suggestion. Though, I'm docking my sister ten points for her lack of subtlety.

"Do you want to go look around?" I ask Ollie, half-hoping he says no so Sydney can't take credit for getting Brooks and I off on our own.

Ollie nods excitedly. "Let's walk," he says, reaching out a chubby little hand...for Brooks to take.

I swallow at the sudden thickness gathering in my throat as I watch Ollie slip his tiny hand into Brooks' big palm. He doesn't even know this man and is immediately so trusting of him.

"Have fun!" Claire says with a naughty wink. I hurry after Brooks and Ollie.

"Looks like Ollie is taking you for a walk whether you like it or not," I say, falling into step with Brooks on the pathway between the tents.

"I don't mind."

"Come on, Mama." Ollie reaches up and takes my hand, too, connecting the three of us together. We walk in silence at Ollie's pace for a minute, his hands gripping our respective fingers tightly.

"Hope you weren't planning on continuing your baseball career," I say. "Ollie's death-grip might cause some permanent damage to your hand."

Brooks laughs, and my heart lurches at the sound of it. It's been so long since I've heard him laugh. I used to live for that sound. It awakens something youthful and innocent inside of me. That same bubbly, sweet feeling I get every time he texts me.

"I can handle it," he says, and I finally look up to find him already staring at me.

Brooks looks totally at ease as we wander through the market together with Ollie between us. He has no idea what he's doing to me right now. How walking with him, even in this casual way, turns my world entirely upside down.

A fraction of the fear I've held onto since the divorce and Ollie's birth falls away as Brooks briefly smiles at me. It's like I've caught a glimpse of a possibility I haven't allowed myself to entertain. The possibility of finding someone who will love Ollie and me with a gentle, steady kind of love. For the first time in two years, the chance of finding the kind of love my heart so desperately yearns for feels possible.

I had thought after Brooks and I broke up and he left for good that we simply weren't meant to be. I learned to be okay with that. But memories and feelings are resurfacing, daring me to hope that maybe things could be different this time. The thought both excites and terrifies me. But I can't deny the sense of a weight being lifted off my shoulders and the unexplainable, deep need to *try*.

ELEVEN

Brooks

WHEN I'D DECIDED TO put Jonah's advice to the test and spend more time at home with my family, I knew that meant I'd have the chance to see Nora again, too. Little did I know that on my first night staying over at the twins' house, they'd successfully drag me to a public market under the guise of *supporting local artists*. And by local artists, they meant one artist, specifically. I couldn't have planned this better myself.

I may not have nieces or nephews of my own yet, but it's always a good time when my teammates bring their kids around. I find most kids to be endearingly honest and hilarious, and they generally seem to like me, too. So far, Ollie and I seem to be getting along great.

Ollie suddenly lurches towards a truck selling kettle corn, and we have no choice but to veer in that direction.

"I want some popcorn!" Ollie says breathlessly, letting go of my hand.

"Let me," I say.

"No, really, it's okay," Nora says.

"I've got it," I say again, and Nora smiles gratefully. "What do you want, Ollie?" I ask. He points to the bags of popcorn in the truck window. "Do you like the sweet or the salty kind?"

"Sweet!" he says.

"We'll take a bag of kettle corn, please," I say through the truck window. Before the bag has even fully been placed in my hands, Ollie is chanting for popcorn and reaching towards me.

"Should we find a place to sit?" I ask, gesturing to the picnic tables set up in an open area. There's a musician strumming mellow songs on her guitar and lights strung up around the seating area. The autumn air is brisk but fragrant with spices and smoke from the vendors behind us. I couldn't have picked a more romantic setting if I tried.

Maybe I should enlist the help of my sisters more often. They seem to know what they're doing.

Once we're seated across from each other at a table, Ollie immediately starts shoving handfuls of popcorn into his mouth.

"A man after my own heart." I find Nora watching me with a shy smile, and I smile right back. "You're still not a big popcorn fan?"

"Not usually," she says, pulling the sleeves of her jacket down over her hands. "Because it always gets stuck–"

"In your teeth?" I finish for her, grabbing a handful of popcorn for myself. "Yeah, I remember."

I still remember a lot of things about Nora Foster. I remember the snacks I used to pick up for her at the gas station, and the things she had strong opinions about. Like popcorn. And hats. She always did love her hats.

Now that we're seated so closely at this table, I also find it easy to recall the way her velvety lips felt on mine when we kissed, and man, did we kiss a lot.

I wonder if she remembers those parts of our shared past when she looks at me, or if I'm the only one who has held on to those fragments of us that she let go of long ago.

Nora glances at something over my shoulder and then ducks her head down, smiling.

"Don't look now," she says in a low tone. "But everyone is staring at you."

I chance a glance to my left and realize she's right. I hear my name in hushed conversations from the tables around us. I'd been so caught up in Nora and Ollie I hadn't even thought about getting recognized.

"Dang. You guys must have blown my cover."

"Don't blame us for your terrible disguise. The hat doesn't hide much."

"Really? I was hoping it would help me keep a low profile."

"It's a Stormbreakers hat. You should have at least picked something a little more subtle."

"These are the only hats I own, okay?" I say with a laugh, my hand colliding with Ollie's as we both reach for the popcorn at the same time. "After you, good sir." Ollie giggles and drops more popcorn into his mouth. My gaze catches on Nora's again, and a surge of nerves races through me. Is she testing me with Ollie? Am I passing? I hope I'm not entirely blowing this.

"Well, since my hat's not doing me much good anyways, I guess I'll just give it to you, little man." I remove my hat and plop it on Ollie's head. It dwarfs him, slipping down over his eyes.

"You look cool, dude!" Nora says, lifting the hat so he can see again. "Did you know that Brooks is a real baseball player?"

Ollie nods excitedly. "I play, too."

"You do? Let me guess...you're a real good hitter," I say.

"I throw," Ollie says.

"Ahh. A pitcher, then. Bet you can throw some solid curveballs."

He then yanks my hat off his head and slaps it on Nora's instead.

"Oh, thank you, love," she says before quickly taking it off and holding it out to return it to me. "Here."

There must be something in the popcorn because a sudden boldness gathers within me. This is my chance to let Nora know that a not-so-chance meeting at the farmer's market isn't going to be the last time we see each other. Being this close to her feels surreal. If I want my deepest hidden hopes to become a reality, I can't let her slip through my fingers again.

"You can keep it," I say, reaching across the table and carefully settling my hat on her head. She looks up at me with her wide, brown eyes, and I'm sixteen again, fitting my hat on her head before tipping her chin up to kiss her.

My fingers linger on the edges of the hat as she stares back at me from across the table. She looks gorgeous in it, with her long, dark hair twisted back into a bun underneath.

"You already gave me one of your hats," she says softly. "I still have it, actually."

Why does that knowledge make my throat knot? It's proof that some small piece of me had remained with her, even during the years we've been apart.

"You can add this one to your collection," I say with a grin, feeling my confidence grow after her admission.

"Cool dude, Mom!" Ollie says loudly, mouth full of popcorn. His little voice slices through the tension between us.

"You have to keep it now," I say. "It ups your cool factor."

"Tell you what," she says, adjusting the brim of the hat down over her brow and looking so adorable I have to swallow and resist the urge to take a picture. "I'll trade you for it."

I'm intrigued. Are kisses on the table? Because looking over at her wearing my hat makes me suddenly ravenous. We were so inexperienced when we were teenagers, but I can still remember how sweet she tasted. I'll bet she'd taste just as good now.

I'd love a chance to test this theory.

"When we go back to my booth, you can pick out the mug I promised you," she says. I shouldn't feel disappointed by her offer.

"That's not a fair trade. I didn't even buy this hat."

"Then I'm afraid I'll have to return it to you." Nora moves to pull it off her head.

"No, keep it. Please. It looks better on you, anyways. Right, Ollie?"

"Right," he agrees, reaching out for a high-five. I may not be a parent or know much about kids, but I think Ollie and I are off to a pretty good start. Nora looks up at me shyly from below the brim of the hat, and I want to lean across the table and kiss the two pink dots I see appearing on her pretty cheeks.

＊

The twins' eyebrows practically reach their hairlines when we return to the booth and they see Nora wearing my hat. Why are they still here? They don't have anything better to do than to hover around to see what happens? I try to send them a telepathic message to get lost, but they clearly don't get it because they both stay put as we enter the tent.

"Cute hat, Nora," her sister, Sydney, says.

"Make sure he signs it so you can sell it later," Claire adds.

"He tried to give it to Ollie, and Ollie pawned it off on me," Nora explains, blushing. I like it so much I'm tempted to keep teasing her just to keep that pink flush on her cheeks.

Claire kneels down and starts talking animatedly with Ollie, who offers her some of his coveted popcorn. I'm suddenly doubting our seemingly easy rapport. Maybe he's just friendly with everyone.

"Okay," Nora says, leading me to the shelf of ceramics on the left side of the tent. "You don't have to take a mug. You can choose anything you like. Are you an indoor plant kind of guy?"

"Uh...no."

"Do you like to cook? Or bake?"

"Cook? Nah. I like to eat. And drink. What's this?" I ask, picking up a tiny white dish.

"That's for jewelry," she says. I hear one of my sisters cough behind me, which coincidentally sounds a lot like the word *idiot*.

"Don't think I'd have much use for that, unfortunately. But it's lovely." I lean closer to the mugs, perusing my options and feeling an appreciation for what Nora was able to do in crafting them. I pull a tall, sandy brown mug from the shelf and inspect it, running a thumb over the handle.

"I'll take this one if that's alright, but I'm happy to pay you for it."

"No deal," Nora says stubbornly, taking the mug from my hands. I locate the sign she's got hanging up with the pricing for her items.

"I have to pay for it," I say. "It's twenty-eight dollars. I'd be betraying my number if I didn't."

Nora suddenly flushes and clears her throat, moving to the table to wrap the mug in tissue paper and package it up for me. "You're not paying for it, okay? End of discussion. There's a little card in here with care instructions," Nora says as she slips the wrapped mug into a brown paper bag. "You can put the mug in the dishwasher, but it's better if you wash it by hand."

"That must have been where I went wrong with the last one you gave me. I always put it in the dishwasher," I say without thinking. Nora freezes, her brows folding.

"Wait," she says. "You kept that? The mug I made you in ceramics class in high school?"

I swallow, feeling caught. That mug had survived up until a couple weeks ago when Miles Aguilar dropped it in my kitchen. The bugger knew it was my favorite mug and always used it when he was at my house just to irritate me. He felt awful when it shattered and offered to buy me another one, but I'd told him not to worry about it, thinking it was irreplaceable.

"That was the mug Miles broke," I say in a low voice, and it takes everything in me to meet her eyes as the truth falls from my lips. "It was my favorite."

"It was?" she squeaks, looking flustered as she adjusts the brim of my hat on her head.

"Yeah," I say. I like talking to her at this intimate volume. Makes me feel like I could say anything I wanted to right now and get away with it. "Promise I'll take better care of this one. I'll listen to you this time."

She looks up at me then, and there are questions in her eyes. Somehow what I said feels deeper than a comment on the proper way to care for hand-crafted ceramics. It feels like in accepting this gift from her, I'm telling her I won't break her heart again. I'm more careful now.

"I hope you use it well. Just keep it away from Miles, okay?"

"Will do." She hands me the bag, and our fingertips brush. She looks up at me, and I'm startled again by just how beautiful she is. She's always been pretty, but time has been good to her. Years of experience, smiling, and laughter have creased into lines around her eyes and mouth. She looks like the same Nora I fell in love with as a teenager, but she's also different in time-weathered ways.

"It's good to see you, you know, in person," I say in that same, soft tone we've been speaking in to cut the gossiping nosies out of our conversation. "It's way better than texting."

"I agree." She smiles.

"I'd like to see you again," I say, even more quietly, and Nora's eyes dart up to mine in surprise. "If that's okay."

She studies me for a moment before answering. I like the way her eyes stay locked on mine.

"I'd like that," she finally replies.

"I'll text you. Make sure when you text back, you actually hit that little button on your screen that says '*send*.'"

Nora's mouth tips up into a smile. "I thought I had, okay? I'm sorry!"

"That's what they all say," I tease. "See you soon?" I say, phrasing it like a question.

"Like...how soon?" she asks. "I'd love a little heads-up next time. So I can...you know. Put on some makeup. Fix my hair."

"No need. Just wear my hat again. It looks good on you."

I swear she'll never look me in the eye again if I keep this up. I don't even have to think before I speak with Nora. It's like muscle memory. I know how to do this. *We* know how to do this.

"When will you be back in town?" Nora asks. "You should come by the diner. You can censure my employees for what they did."

"What did they do?" I ask, confused. Nora sucks in a breath, her brown eyes growing wide.

"Gosh," she says, briefly closing her eyes. "I meant to tell you..." She sighs deeply, then stands up straighter and meets my gaze sheepishly. "So...you know how you got my number on your takeout box after you came in last time? Well...this is so embarrassing."

"What is it?" I lean in even closer, fully intrigued.

"It wasn't me," Nora admits with a grimace. "I didn't give you my number. One of my servers wrote my number on the takeout box and gave it to you without telling me."

She looks up at me almost fearfully. I don't know what she was expecting me to do in response to this, but I don't think it was to start laughing. Her shoulders visibly drop in relief.

"Wait," I say. "It was that ginger kid, wasn't it?"

"Yes, it was him. That's why I didn't text you back immediately. I thought someone was playing a prank on

119

me. There was no way it was actually *you* texting me. That would've been too good to be..."

She stops herself, suddenly very busy with folding sheets of already folded tissue paper. Her honesty is so endearing. "I had to tell you the truth. It wasn't me who was brave enough to write my number on your box. Next time you come to the diner, you can give the server who did it a thorough set-down," Nora says.

"You sure I shouldn't be thanking him?" I say with a grin. "How else would we have gotten back in touch? Maybe I should come by just to shake his hand."

She laughs. "We don't want to encourage him."

"Maybe we do." We share a laugh. I don't want to leave here tonight without ensuring she knows that I'll be back soon.

"I'm heading back up to Seattle tonight," I say. "But I'll be back next weekend...and pretty much every weekend after that until the new year. My agent thinks it would be good for me to get some space from things. Clear my head. Spend my weekends doing things other than baseball."

"Oh, really?" Nora breathes. "Where are you staying while you're here?"

"With the twins," I grit out. "They covered every inch of the walls of their guest room in posters of kittens when they heard I was coming."

Nora laughs, her nose crinkling adorably. "You're allergic, right?"

"Deathly allergic. I woke up sneezing this morning. I don't think my brain can tell the difference."

"I'm sorry, but that's hilarious," she says, and the sound of exclamations and voices interrupt our conversation. More customers are pouring into the tent, and I take that as my sign that it's time to let Nora get back to work.

"Before I go, could I buy a few more mugs?" I ask. She looks up at me in surprise. "So my teammates will stop using mine when they come over."

"Really?" she asks. "I mean, of course! Just tell me which ones you want."

She gets tied up in a conversation with an older couple I recognize as the McConnells, who run the local post office. After I select three more mugs, Sydney helps me package them up and takes my payment.

"Thank you," she says, smiling at me like I just bought their entire stock. Maybe I should next time.

Nora catches my eye, and she gives me a hope-filled smile that fills me with determination. I've got to see her again. Soon.

"See you later, Ollie." He gives me a little wave, and I like knowing that Nora's eyes are most likely following me as I retreat. My sisters finally decide to get the memo that my time with Nora is up, quickly saying their goodbyes before following me back to my car.

I brace myself for the onslaught of their inevitable, opinionated commentary. They do not disappoint.

"You gave her your *hat*? In public?" Caroline says. "I like it. Staking your claim."

Claire doesn't let me answer before she blurts out, "So, what did she say? Does she want to see you again? Did my plan work?"

They trail behind me back to my Tesla in the parking lot, chattering on and asking questions that I choose not to answer.

"I can't believe I'm going to say this," Claire says, shutting the passenger-side door. "You did well tonight. But listen to me, Brooks. You've got one job from here on out, okay? Are you listening?"

I don't even bother looking her way, knowing some wisecrack is coming whether I choose to acknowledge it or not.

"Don't you dare do *anything* to screw this up," Claire says, jabbing a finger into my bicep. "Got it?"

"Mmhmm," I say, grinning to myself at the mental image I took of Nora wearing my hat. "Got it."

TWELVE

Nora

"You've got a sunny glow about you today, Miss Nora. And you're not wearing a black polo, for once," Roman says to me with a cheeky grin as he enters the diner, sweeping past the host stand. "Would there be any particular reason for that?"

He continues past without waiting for my answer. I'm busy drawing the sections on our dry-erase chart of the diner floor plan. Each table, booth, and bar stool is numbered for reference and easy assigning. I quickly smudge out Roman's name from his favorite section (which includes most of the booths) and give him the old-fashioned bar instead. He hates the bar. Especially at breakfast.

"Hi Nora," Audrey says, all smiles. She props her chin up on her elbow and leans right over my chart, forcing me to meet her eyes. "You're looking lovely today."

"So are you. Wait, why are you saying that? Is there something on my face? Please tell me I don't have a pair of Ollie's socks stuck to my butt." I arch my neck, trying to see if I've split my pants, and nobody's bothered to tell me.

"All clear," Audrey says.

"Why are you all suddenly being so nice to me?"

"Word on the street is…" Roman suddenly appears at my side, the sound of his voice making me jump. "Somebody had the time of her life at the Harvest Market last night."

My heart jumps into my throat. Do I look guilty? I probably look guilty, though I have no reason to be.

"Somebody was also up late last night cleaning up after said market and needs her servers to get cracking before the breakfast rush begins," I say, snapping the cap of the dry-erase marker back into place and tapping the chart. "Sections are done."

"The bar, Nora? No ma'am. Not today." Roman sidles up alongside me as I move towards the kitchen. "Give me the booths back. Please?"

"Kate asked for the booths today," I lie.

"Well, surprise, surprise, Kate is late. So, the early bird gets the worm. I would have thought you'd be in more of a generous mood after last night."

I stop walking, eyeing him narrowly. "What are you talking about, Roman?"

"You know," he says, like it's the most obvious thing in the world. "Your date."

"My…date."

"With you-know-who," Audrey adds, hands on her hips.

"I don't know what the two of you are going on about," I lie, but my heart is fluttering, and I suddenly need distance from these two nosy friends of mine.

They know.

"Were either of you at the market?" I ask, dreading their answer.

"Of course we were, love," Roman says. "We were shopping and eating our hearts out all night."

"We came by your booth, but you were gone. Busy canoodling with your baseball beau. But Kate was over buying kettle corn at the food truck, and she said she saw you holding hands," Audrey says.

"We were *not* holding hands!"

"Yes, you were!" I whirl towards the diner doors to find that Kate has finally decided to make her entrance and somehow knew precisely what we were talking about.

"There was a child between us!"

"Nora!" she practically screams. "Nora, I *saw* you last night with Brooks, and oh-my-gosh-you-are-the-cutest-couple-ever!" I'm engulfed in a hug. I sigh, hugging her back and feeling entirely trapped. There's no escaping it now.

"You guys," I say, looking between these friends of mine who feel like family. "I hate to disappoint you, but it wasn't a date. We happened to run into each other, and--"

"Sparks flew, you fell back in love, yada-yada," Roman says, waving a hand through the air. "We know. We saw the picture."

"What picture?" I gasp.

Kate pulls out her phone and shows me her screen. It's a grainy, zoomed-in picture of me and Brooks, right at the moment when he'd placed his hat on my head. I'm looking up at him with wide, awestruck eyes, and he's wearing a little, affectionate half-smirk that makes my heart take a tumble.

"Did you take this picture?" I ask Kate, trying to keep my voice even.

"That depends," she says slowly.

"Can you send it to me?" I ask. I need a copy of it in my possession so I can stare at it and fantasize about Brooks giving me his hat on loop.

"You're not mad?"

I shake my head. More like twitterpated.

"Okay, then *yes*. I took the picture!" she squeals gleefully, texting me the photo. "You two are the most beautiful couple I have *ever* seen."

I'm grateful my friends desperately want me to find love again, especially after what I've been through. I know they mean well. They just want to see me happy. But my rational side feels like I'm putting the cart before the horse.

Shockingly, Roman doesn't fight me on the section assignments after doting over the photo again. I think it's because he could tell that Molly, being the diehard Brooks Alden fan that she is, was not happy about the news that Brooks had been seen with me again. She glares openly at me every time I walk past the host stand. I'm tempted to wave the photo in her face to set things straight once and for all, but Roman does the dirty work for me.

"You're too young for him, sweetie," Roman finally says to her. "Get over it."

The diner only serves breakfast and lunch, so I usually get off around four o'clock. As we're nearing closing time, the dishwashers start blasting music as motivation to get their work done. Audrey notices me sweeping the floor alone and grabs an extra broom, and before I know it, we're dancing with broom partners and scattering crumbs instead of brushing them into a pile.

It's moments like this that make me wonder if I could ever leave this place. I see these people every day. They're my family. I love being a part of something so integral to our community.

But on my drive home, I remember how it felt last night to clean off the near-empty shelves after the market was over. To know that my ceramic pieces have now been sprinkled into the homes and businesses of Kitt's Harbor. There's a deeper satisfaction rising within me that I've never been able to reach as the manager of Delia's Diner.

There's no doubt that I still need this job. I'd tallied up my earnings last night and quickly realized that I would have to scale my business considerably if I wanted it to be something sustainable. It would take a lot more hours at the wheel and many more markets for me to turn my hobby into a way to support my family.

Now's not the right time for me to say goodbye to the diner, but maybe someday that time will come, and I will be ready. In the meantime, Sydney and I have been working hard to prepare for the workshop she's hosting for me next Saturday at Wildwood. Nerves bubble through me every time I think about it. But at the same time, I can't wait to share something I'm passionate about with a small group of friends in such a magical place.

THIRTEEN

Brooks

I DECIDED TO TAKE my first appointment with the team therapist over video chat on Saturday morning from inside my car, parked in the driveway of the rambler Claire and Caroline rent on the east side of Kitt's Harbor near Old Town. They are lingering over coffee at the kitchen table when I slip outside. Caroline is busy scribbling in a notebook with a bright pink sparkly pen while Claire sits reading a book titled, *The Modern Moneymaker: How to Capitalize on Your Wealthy Relations*. Neither seemed particularly interested in where I'm going, but I make an announcement anyway on my way out the door.

"I'm taking a call with a therapist in my car," I say. "Don't bother me."

Claire glances up from her scribbling, her eyes sparkling behind her glasses, but Caroline doesn't spare me a glance. "Godspeed, brother," she says solemnly before turning the page of her riveting read.

I settle into the driver's seat of my car, swallowing down a knot in my throat as I open the app that my agent, Desi, had told me to download prior to my appointment.

"If she's not a good fit, we can find somebody else," Desi told me. "But she came highly recommended from several of your teammates."

I'm not sure what to expect but feel that this is something I need to try. Seeing Nora at the market the other night and meeting her son had made me realize, yet again, that I have a whole lot of internal work I need to do on myself. I may be jumping the gun here, but I realized that if I want to parent differently from the father I was raised by, I need to make a dedicated effort to learn how to do that. I don't have an example of what healthy fathering looks like, so I hope this process will help me in that regard.

I texted Jonah after agreeing to see a therapist, and he'd texted back: *proud of you, Brookie.* His confidence in me was what also propelled me to move forward with this, even though I feel completely out of my comfort zone.

A rush of nerves zips through me as my therapist's face fills the screen. She smiles, introduces herself as Greta, then asks me a series of questions right off the bat about my goals for therapy and what I hope to accomplish.

"There are a few things I'd like to work through," I say, scrubbing a hand over my jaw. "First of all, I get a little stuck in my head sometimes and want to get some help with that."

"Can you explain to me what that feels like?"

I let out a long breath, trying to find the words to describe the way my mind works.

"I think I'm always aiming to execute things perfectly, and when that doesn't happen, I can be pretty hard on myself."

Greta nods. "That's an easy trap to fall into as an athlete, especially when there's constant pressure on you to perform."

"Yeah, I mean, I had a pretty great season, but it ended on a really sour note. It's been hard for me to not feel like it's my fault that the team didn't progress further than we did. I feel like I let everybody down. We could have gone on to win a championship if it wasn't for me."

"Have any of your coaches or teammates done or said anything to contribute to these feelings?"

I think back to how I was treated after our loss in September. "No," I say honestly. "They were all really cool about it, actually. I guess it's mostly been the media and fans that have been coming after me."

"I'll give you one piece of advice, if you'll allow me," Greta says. When I nod, she continues. "I'm sure you've got a plan to take care of your physical health during your off-season, am I right? What does this consist of?"

"Staying fit, honing my game, eating and sleeping well."

"Right. Those are all wonderful things to focus on, but you need to give your mind as much attention as you do your body. Your mental health can really impact your overall well-being. To protect your mental health, you need to take some preventative measures. Don't google yourself. Don't read the news. Ask the people you work with not to pass on anything negative said about you from people who aren't directly in your inner circle. You can't trust the voices of the critics and disgruntled fans. They're just trying to capitalize off of your mistakes by sensationalizing them, and it will always be that way."

I mull over her advice. "I was always taught that constructive criticism can be helpful in helping me improve my game."

"It can, if it's coming from the right people. People who are in the ring with you. People who have your best interests at heart. That's the distinction."

"Makes sense. I'll keep that in mind." I think of the teammates I'm close with, my coaches, trainers, and the veteran players who took me under their wing. I'd ask any of them for advice. They're the ones I should be listening to.

"If one of your teammates made a huge mistake that cost you a game, would you be upset with them?"

"Maybe a little."

"Would you blame them for the loss?"

"No, I don't think I would," I answer. "I'd try to help them feel better about it."

"Then, you need to treat yourself just like you would treat one of your teammates: with kindness and love. The way you talk to yourself is very important. Negative self-talk can really impact the way you move through the world and has a great bearing on your relationships."

I stay quiet, processing her wisdom. I'd never thought of it that way. I hadn't been the only player on the team to strike out that night. Miles had stunk it up, too, but I would never say anything critical about his performance to him. If one of my teammates has a bad game or a bad moment, I try to let it roll off my shoulders and try not to let my disappointment show. Why shouldn't I do the same for myself when I make a mistake?

"Brooks, why do you think you have to be perfect?" Greta asks, and her question catches me off guard. "What are you afraid is going to happen to you if you're not perfect?"

I lean my head back against the headrest and think it over.

"In my line of work, everything depends on my performance. I'm being paid to play my sport at an exceptional level. I'll get dropped if I don't deliver."

"And what will happen to you if you get dropped?"

"My baseball career might be over."

"And then what? What would you do?"

I shrug, laughing awkwardly. "I have no idea. I guess I could get a coaching job or something."

"If the absolute worst thing imaginable happened to you, if your worst nightmare came true and everything you worked for was taken from you and your dreams fell apart, would you survive it?"

The thought of having my baseball career taken from me makes me sweat. Baseball is everything to me. When I'm playing well, it's insanely fun and fulfilling. I've worked my whole life to live out this dream, and if I lost it, I'd be devastated.

But would it kill me?

The more I think about it, the more clear Greta's reasoning becomes.

"Yeah," I say. "I guess I would survive it. It wouldn't be easy, but I could do it."

"That right there is the crux of the matter," Greta says. "People who struggle with perfectionism are often fueled by fear. Fear of letting others down. Fear of making mistakes. Fear of not being enough. They try to hit all the marks and think ten steps ahead in an attempt to outrun a deeper sense of unworthiness. I'd wager that you've had some experiences in your life that taught you that baseball, or how you perform in life in general, is inextricably tied to your self-worth."

I swallow. How can a stranger, someone who doesn't even know me personally, hit the nail on the head? The painful truth of her words reverberates in my chest.

"My dad," I say, and with those two words, I know that this conversation is about to take an unexpected turn.

Greta gives me a gentle smile of understanding. "Do you want to talk about him?"

No, I don't. Do I want to talk about the man who excels at two-faced, guilt-tripping manipulation? The man who raised me to believe that unless I was killing it every second of every day and putting in constant inhuman effort, I would amount to nothing? But I think if I want to be different from him, I have to talk about the hard reality of what growing up under his thumb felt like.

"It's a real can of worms," I say, feeling incredibly uncomfortable. But also knowing that if there ever was a chance for me to get some of my deepest-rooted insecurities and beliefs out in the open, now is the time.

"I love worms," Greta quips. "Sometimes taking a look into the past can teach us a lot about the present and then help us make positive changes for the future."

"Okay," I sigh. But where do I even start?

The crawling anxiety that accompanies even the thought of my dad starts to claw up into my throat, and I'm suddenly ten years old again. Already small, but often made to feel even smaller by the man whom I call father.

I sift through memories of Bill Alden, wondering if I'll even be able to articulate what the complex dynamic of our relationship is like. If you could even call it a relationship.

"My dad was always really hard on me," I say, and find an unexpected surge of anger clogging my throat and preventing me from saying more. But Greta doesn't rush in to speak again. She waits patiently. And waits some more until I'm ready to continue. "He held me to a really high standard, and if I didn't meet that standard, he was sure to let me know."

"In what way?"

"He'd lecture me. Make me work for hours so I wouldn't repeat my mistakes," I say. "He rarely had anything positive to say about me, even when I played really well or got good grades or accomplished anything. The only time he ever paid attention to me was when I messed up."

"I'm sorry. That must have been really hard, especially as a child," Greta says simply, and in that expression of empathy, I know that she's the right person for the job. I want to continue this conversation. I want to dive into things I've never processed before.

"He and I don't speak anymore," I say. "I had to essentially cut ties with him once my mom officially divorced him. It wasn't good for any of us to be around him. I still can't be around him. The funny thing is," I say with a bitter laugh, "he texted me after the last game of the season, listing off all of the things I'd done wrong and calling out my mistakes. He always expects me to be perfect at everything, but he is so far from perfect himself."

"That's usually the case, isn't it?" Greta muses. "Let me ask you this, though. Do you feel most connected to people who are perfect?"

"No, of course not."

"You like to be around flawed, genuine, authentic people?"

"Well, yeah. Doesn't everybody?"

"Then what does that give you permission to be?" Greta lets her question permeate and the answer forms in my mind like a shaft of sunlight blazing through a cloud.

"Imperfect," I say.

We spend a few more minutes chatting about how I can be more 'gentle' with myself (an entirely foreign concept to an intensely hard-working athlete like me), as she says, and ways I can handle future encounters with my dad.

"Do not engage," Greta advises. "It's not safe for you to engage with your dad. So to keep yourself safe, especially as you're healing, you can't let him get to you."

Greta wraps up our session with a call to action.

"I think it would be good for you to re-evaluate whether or not baseball makes you happy. It sounds like you have been operating from a place of fear for a long time because of your history with your father, and it might be a good time to do some soul-searching and find out if this is really the path *you* want for yourself."

I don't like the sound of this. My whole life has been baseball. But...maybe that's Greta's point.

"May I suggest," she continues. "That you do some exploring. Spend some time with your younger self–with the little Brooks you were as a child. What made him happy? What sort of things did he get excited about? I think it may be helpful for you to find some hobbies or interests outside of baseball during this off-season, so you can support not just your physical health, but also your mental and emotional health. Think of it as a chance to find more balance and approach your life holistically, so when things don't go exactly as you hope they will, you've got more than just your baseball career to lean on."

She's literally giving me the same advice Jonah had given me before. Maybe he's walked this path and gone through therapy himself. That would make sense, seeing how he seems to have a healthier relationship with the sport than myself.

"Okay," I say slowly. "How exactly should I do that?"

"That's up to you, but we have six sessions scheduled together, right? Why don't you try something new each week before our session, then come back and report your experiences to me. We can talk more about your relationship with your dad, too, or anything else that feels relevant to your progress."

I agree, feeling a little more steady with some concrete direction. Once Greta hangs up, I sit back in my driver's seat, feeling surprisingly drained. Talking about my dad is never easy, but I feel the strangest sense of relief at the same time. Finally, someone can help me work through these things I've carried on my own for so long, and that feels good.

For the first time in as long as I can remember, I want to create a full life outside of baseball. I'm not exactly sure what that might look like for me, but the possibility that Nora might be a part of it is highly motivating. I've been given the second chance I always hoped for but never felt that I deserved.

I drop my phone onto my lap and pull my hat off, running a hand through my hair. An unexpected thought hits me, and I head back into the house feeling lighter than I have in weeks.

Time to enlist the help of my meddling sisters again.

FOURTEEN

Nora

WE'RE TUCKED AWAY IN the A-frame cabin at Wildwood, where the cloud-shrouded woods are dusted in shades of gold, orange, and scarlet. Fall is in full force here at Wildwood, and I'm pinching myself that I get to teach my first workshop on the most perfect autumn evening, hidden away in the forest.

"Sydney? Will you please approve my charcuterie board?" Bridget calls out with a sigh, sweeping a strand of hair away from her eyes with the back of her hand. "I've done my best."

Sydney, Mom, and I rush over to inspect Bridget's work and gasp collectively at the sight. A picturesque variety of fruits, cheeses, crackers, breads, and jams are artfully piled across a massive wooden slab that Trent had prepared especially for tonight.

"This is stunning," I breathe, taking in the spread.

Sydney tweaks a few things before snapping some photos. Then she instructs me to light all the candles, since it's almost time for our guests to arrive. Ollie and Trent are sequestered upstairs with popcorn and a movie, but I doubt Ollie will be able to resist coming down to investigate once the evening gets underway. Uncle Trent will have no choice but to follow.

"You sure you don't want to participate?" I'd asked him earlier. Trent had given me a quick shake of the head.

"Maybe another time," he said, his eyes darting fearfully around the cabin which will soon be filled with laughter and noise and...people. His worst nightmare.

I stand off to the side as Sydney welcomes the first two guests to our eight-person workshop: Carol from Brickyard Bakery and her daughter, Nellie. They're followed by an old family friend, Cassie, my neighbor Brynn, and none other than Roman from the diner.

"You didn't tell me you were coming!" I say in surprise when he walks in. "I saw you all day today, and you didn't say a word, you sneak!"

"I wanted to surprise you," Roman says, giving me a tight hug. "I have no experience with this sort of thing, so be nice to me, please."

Roman and I continue talking as we enter the cabin, gushing over the gorgeous interior and setup that my sisters and I worked hard to create today. A warm glow flickers to life within me, watching friends chat and smile and find their places around the table. The dappled candlelight and familiar faces bring a sense of calm, and my nerves begin to dissipate.

Sydney runs back to the door to greet her friend Anika, and then she does a quick head count.

"We're just waiting on two more," she says. Before I can ask her who exactly we're waiting on, she hurries away to shepherd our guests to the charcuterie board. She hadn't shown me the final guest list beforehand.

"Start grazing!" she says, and they obey.

I'm about to grab a plate myself when a knock sounds at the door.

"Be right back," I tell Roman mid-conversation.

I lug the heavy door open, and all of the peaceful, sweet feelings that have been gathering inside me evaporate in an instant at the sight of the two people standing on the front porch.

It's Brooks Alden and his sister Claire.

Brooks looks incredibly handsome in the dim porch light. He's not wearing a hat tonight, and the sight of his unruly dark hair and smiling steel-blue eyes makes warmth pool somewhere deep in my belly.

"Hi," I finally say, looking between the siblings. "Come on in." I move robotically behind the door to make room for them to pass. Claire enters first, but it's Brooks who makes the entryway to the cabin suddenly feel far too small. I can't help but stare at him, looking more polished than I've ever seen him in a black wool coat, jeans, and boots.

"Hey," he says, and my pulse skitters at the sound of his voice. Is this going to happen to me every time he speaks? Maybe I'll build up an immunity to it with time. Eons of time.

Brooks sidles through the door into the entryway, and before I know what's happening, he's tugged me out of my hiding place behind the door and into his arms for a hug. Every nerve ending in my body sputters to life as he circles his strong arms around me, one looping around my shoulders while the other skates across my low back. I don't even have to think about how to settle into him. I've done it before, but this feels different. He's taller, broader and stronger now.

I tuck my chin as he pulls me close, my cheek dipping against his chest. The heady smell of him envelops me as I tentatively slide my fingertips across the ridges of his back until they curve around his waist. I remember this. The feel of the planes of his chest against mine, the cords of his muscled arms pulling me closer. I'd forgotten how good it feels to be held by someone. I have to resist the urge to close my eyes and snuggle into him for as long as he'll let me.

All of this takes place in just a few seconds, but we must linger longer than is normal (I wouldn't know...I haven't hugged many men since my divorce) because I hear Claire give a little giggle from behind me. Brooks slowly traces his fingers down my arms and then releases me, making my skin ache as soon as we break apart. He shoots me a charming half-grin, lodging more arrows into my already punctured heart.

Hey, whoever is in charge of the general flow of time, can we rewind the tapes and do that again real quick? Thank you so much.

"This place is amazing," Brooks says, looking up at the peaked ceiling of the cabin.

There's an uncomfortably long pause before I pull myself together and realize that it's my turn to speak.

"Oh, thank you. My brother-in-law built most of the cabins on this property. It's one of my favorite places."

"I can see why," Brooks says, lifting the lapels of his coat so he can remove it. I shouldn't eye him like a feral wolf who hasn't eaten in days as he does this, but I think I do. The man is impeccably built, and I have no qualms about getting a front-row seat to his disrobement.

"Here," I say, reaching for his coat. He hands it to me, and I hang it on the rack by the door with the others. I turn around to find him watching me. Claire has conveniently left us alone together in the entryway, and though I see some curious eyes peering in our direction, we're far enough away from the group to have a private conversation.

"I thought I told you to give me a heads-up before we saw each other again," I say. As if I'm disappointed in the slightest that he's here.

"I would have," he answers slyly. "But I thought I might be barred from entry."

"Why's that?"

"I was worried I might be the only man in attendance tonight. I'm going to bring down the vibe of this whole thing."

"You're in luck. My friend Roman is here, and Ollie and Trent are upstairs. If the feminine energy gets to be too much, you're welcome to join them."

He genuinely looks relieved. "Okay, good. There's my backup plan if I set something on fire or break something."

"That's my job, remember?" I say. We share a low laugh, glancing sideways at each other. Gosh, it's good to see him.

"I'm glad you're here," I say, feeling nervous as I let the honest truth leave my lips. "I had no idea you had an interest in ceramics."

"I don't, to be honest. But I've been advised to try some new things, and when Claire told me about your workshop, I figured I might as well give it a shot. This is my chance to learn from the best."

"So, what you're saying is if you don't create an impeccable masterpiece tonight, it's entirely my fault?"

"Yes. That's exactly what I'm saying. Don't let me down, Nora," he says, giving me a playful nudge with his shoulder as we move closer to the group. Would he notice if I slowed my walking down to the pace of a slug? I'm not ready for our conversation to end. I like the way his arm brushes against mine as he swings it at his side.

"I don't want to keep you," he says, gesturing to the table. "Go do your thing."

"Thank you. I expect great things from you tonight."

"Bringing my A-game." He grins, and the tilt of his crooked smile causes more memories to resurface. There was once a time when he'd smile at me like that and I'd respond by kissing it right off his face.

I wonder if he remembers the heart-melting effect his smiles used to have on me.

Twenty minutes later, I've handed out lumps of clay and hand-illustrated instruction cards, finished my demonstration, and am about to make my rounds to help everyone get things started. We're supposed to be making mugs tonight, so they will each need to craft the body of the mug along with a separate handle. It's fairly straightforward, and so I allow them to get started on their own, offering to help if they get stuck. Of course, this is right when Ollie appears at the top of the stairs with a very reluctant Uncle Trent trailing behind.

"Mama, I need a snack," Ollie calls loudly, his feet thumping twice on each stair as he descends.

"I'll get you something," my mom says, rising from her seat. I send her a grateful look as she scoops Ollie up and takes him over to the charcuterie board.

Roman clears his throat and raises his hand like the star student I'm sure he was. "Excuse me, Miss Nora? I'm in need of a little assistance."

I help Roman separate pieces of his clay and show him how to hollow out the larger piece with his thumb. He picks up one of the sample mugs I'd brought along.

"Can you just make mine for me? There's no way my mug is going to end up looking like yours."

"That's the beauty of it! Yours will be completely unique to you," I say, letting him take over his clay again.

I stop to assist Nellie and Carol next, but for the most part, everyone else looks to have a grasp on things...except for Brooks. He's staring at the instructions, brow furrowed, looking deeply confused.

I stop between Claire and Brooks, resting my hands on the back of Claire's chair.

"How are things going?"

Claire has already shaped the body of her mug and is rubbing a wet sponge over the rim to smooth it out. "I think I'm off to a good start."

"Yes, you are. It looks great. How about you, Brooks?"

"Uhhh..." he says, looking boyish. "I'm a little lost."

"What can I help you with?" I reach down and rub my thumb on the lip of his...I'm not exactly sure what shape he's going for here. "Maybe if you take some water on your fingers, like this," I say. "And use one hand on the outside to keep it steady while you slowly widen the walls of your...um...cup?"

"Don't sugarcoat it. It's somehow morphed into a bowl."

"Well..." I say, stifling a laugh. "I mean, it could still work as a very large mug."

145

"I think it wants to be a bowl."

"Hey, soup mugs are a thing, right? If that's what you're wanting to do, you can add more depth here and draw the edges up like this..."

My voice trails off as Brooks suddenly traps my hand beneath his where I've got it settled on the outside of his mug. He uses his other hand to do as I instructed inside the mug, his fingertips pressing against mine. I think I forget how to breathe as he slowly coaxes the clay beneath his fingertips.

"Like that?"

I slide my hand away, my fingertips tingling. "Yes, exactly. You've got the right idea."

"Let's see if he can execute it," Claire says, crafting a near-perfect handle for her mug.

"Shut up," he mumbles, hunching back over his clay with a renewed determination.

I realize that most of the table has been watching our interaction with great interest, and I don't blame them. If I had an excuse to sit and stare at Brooks Alden, I would, too. Pretty sure Nellie snuck a photo of him when he wasn't looking. Do I blame her?

"So," Brooks says, promptly abandoning his clay and settling back in his chair. "Have you ever taught a workshop like this before?"

"Nope. This is my first," I say. "Can you tell?"

Apparently, everyone else is listening in on our conversation because Carol chimes in enthusiastically. "Oh, come on, Nora. We've been trying to get her to do something like this for years. Her work is really something, isn't it?"

"It is," Brooks agrees. My face flushes. "What was your name again?"

Carol eagerly introduces herself and her daughter.

"Is your bakery the one on Main Street?" Brooks asks.

Carol lights up, and Nellie positively beams as Brooks starts chatting with them about the story behind their business and how it came to be.

"I can't believe I've never been," Brooks says, nudging his sister. "We'll have to come by."

Carol looks like she might weep at the prospect of Brooks setting foot in her bakery.

"We'll treat you to anything you'd like. On the house."

"Now, that's an offer you cannot pass up," I say. I love Carol's chocolate croissants like nothing else in this world. Trent brought some to me when I was in labor, and I swear that's what got me through.

"I recognize you," Brooks says to Roman. "From the diner, right?"

Roman shoots a sly glance my way before sliding his eyes back to Brooks. "Yes, sir. That's me. Nora's favorite employee."

"That's right," I say. "He's everyone's favorite." Brooks and I share a glance, and I arch an eyebrow. "He's very...intrinsically motivated. He does a lot of things without me asking." Understanding dawns on Brooks' face.

"I do what needs to be done," Roman says with a wink.

Brooks' clay remains untouched for a while, and he seems perfectly content with chatting with my friends around the table instead of working on his mug. I catch him sneaking glances my way when I'm assisting others, and I like the way his eyes linger on me while I work. He finally enlists Claire to help him finish, and she does a great job at redeeming his sorry, shapeless mass of clay.

After everyone deems their work to be finished, I instruct them to carve their initials on the bottom of each piece. "After I fire these pieces, I'll add a glaze of your choosing, and then I'll have them ready next week for you to pick up at the diner."

I glance over the table and feel a sudden surge of emotion well within me. I'd been so lost in the work and fun of tonight that it had flown by so quickly. I'm sad it's already over.

"Thank you for coming," I say, surprised to feel tears welling in my eyes. "It means a lot to me that all of you are here, supporting me." I try to blink the tears away, but then I see Ollie hauling down the stairs again with Trent on his heels, and this time I let him come to me. He's my safety net. He's what I need in vulnerable moments like this.

Everyone begins to clap for me, and Ollie beams, thinking the applause is for him. He joins in, and I think the smile on my face might become permanent as I look into the faces of these wonderful friends who showed up for me tonight.

My gaze dances over Brooks' face, and the unabashed admiration I find in his expression makes my heart stutter. He gives me a little thumbs-up, and a tear slides down my cheek. I quickly turn away before the flood begins, but that little sign of support from him was a reminder of how we'd been there for each other in a past life.

Brooks showed up for me tonight, too, and he's got no idea how much that means to me.

FIFTEEN

Brooks

PATIENCE IS NOT A virtue I naturally possess, especially when it comes to Nora. After the workshop is over, I stand restlessly with Claire while she chats with Nora's mom and sisters. It's testing my limits, having to wait for a chance to speak to Nora. Preferably alone.

As much as I want her full attention, I force myself to wait until everyone leaves before stealing her away. She's still talking with a few women lingering in the entryway while Ollie tugs at her arm and clings to her legs. I decide to try to distract Ollie by stepping into his line of sight and pretending to be shocked when he looks my way.

"Hey, Ollie!" I whisper-yell, waving to him. "Remember me?"

Ollie buries his face in Nora's leg again. Without missing a beat in her conversation, she palms the back of his head and begins stroking his hair. She must be used to multi-tasking with Ollie climbing all over her constantly. I'm not really sure how she does it. Must be a mom thing.

I stay where I am, feigning surprise every time Ollie peeks back at me from behind Nora's leg. He starts giggling and makes a sudden dash towards me. I catch him under the arms

149

and swing him around just like I'd done at the market, and his laugh grows wilder.

"You think you're fast, don't you?" I say.

"I *am* fast! Like a race car!" he says in a gruff voice.

"Not fast enough!"

"You slow!" he taunts after I set him down. "Slow like a slug."

"Like a *slug*? Oh, now you're in for it."

I chase him around the coffee table in the living room, and he clambers onto the couch to escape me. He taunts me with various insults about how slow I am, making me laugh, too. I don't even notice that Trent has approached behind me until I back into his broad chest. The man is huge. I have to look up to meet his eyes as I move out of his space.

"Oh, hey," I say. "Trent, right?"

He takes my proffered hand in a vise-like grip, not cracking a smile.

"You built this place?"

"Yeah," Trent says, picking Ollie up as he reaches for him. "Sydney did all the decorating."

"It's amazing, man."

"Thanks."

Not much of a talker, this guy. I watch Ollie nuzzle into his shoulder with the familiarity of a father and son. Trent then levels me with a threatening stare. The dude is wildly intimidating. "These guys mean a lot to me," he says, gesturing towards Nora. "So if you're planning on sticking around, you'll be seeing more of me, too."

At first I feel mildly threatened, but I realize he's preemptively sending me a clear message. He's protective of his sister-in-law and nephew, and I get it. I'm sure he's watched them go through some pretty tough times. He doesn't want me messing around with them, which is something I would never intentionally do, but he doesn't know me. Yet.

"Well," I reply with a smile. "You guys seem like a really close family. She's lucky to have you looking out for her."

He grunts, opening his mouth as if he's going to say something else but stops when he realizes that the cabin has emptied out. Nora's standing nearby, listening in.

"Playing nice, Trent?" she asks, giving him a loving pat on his arm as she joins us. Trent glances over at me, still assessing. He's not going to be an easy one to win over.

"I was just asking him about the cabin," I say, not wanting to throw Trent under the bus.

"Trent is our in-house handyman. He can build anything." Nora looks up at him proudly and takes Ollie from his arms. Ollie immediately scrambles to the floor and taunts Nora.

"You slow, mommy," he says, pointing to me. "And he slow, too."

"You're ruthless," she says to Ollie, charging at him. He screams as she picks him up and flops down onto the couch with him in her arms. "Do you know who you're talking to? Calling slow?"

"You slow like a cow."

"A cow! How *rude*!"

She tickles Ollie until he wriggles free from her grasp and races up the stairs. "Come on, Uncle T!"

"Are you okay to watch him while I clean up?" Nora asks. "I can put him to bed in once I'm done."

"I can put him to bed," Trent says. "Are his pajamas in his backpack?"

"Yes," Nora replies. "Thank you. You're the best."

I watch Trent trudge up the stairs after Ollie. He gives me one last skeptical look before disappearing up the landing.

"Don't mind Trent. He's not much of a people person," she says. "He's very protective of me and Ollie."

"So I gathered," I say with a grin. "I'm flattered, really, that he thinks I'm a threat."

"Are you not?" she asks, a teasing tilt to her smile.

"You tell me," I counter.

"I don't know where Ollie comes up with his insults," she says, changing the subject. "He knows how to hit you where it hurts, doesn't he?"

"He's awesome. Such a funny kid."

"Maybe he's onto something, though, calling you slow," Nora teases. "You took forever making your *soup* mug tonight."

"Hey, now," I say as we slowly meander toward the front door. "Lay off me. It was my first time, okay?"

"You did a great job. Thanks to Claire, it ended up being–"

"Acceptable?"

"I was going to say beautiful."

"You're a gifted teacher. I think I may need another lesson from you, just to make sure this first triumph of mine wasn't a fluke."

Nora's eyes widen in surprise. "Really? You liked it enough to want to do it again?"

"Why not?"

"Are you being serious?"

"Maybe," I say. "Or maybe I'm just looking for an excuse to see you again."

Nora gives me a timid smile, and I see the hint of a blush on her cheeks. Just the reaction I was hoping for. I may not get another chance to shoot my shot with Nora, so I'm going to take it.

"I had a really good time tonight. It was fun seeing you in your element," I say. "I like being around you."

Nora blinks, and for a moment, I catch the slightest flicker of emotion behind her soft smile. It was there and gone so quickly, I almost didn't catch it. Hesitation. Doubt. Maybe even fear.

"I like being around you, too," she finally says softly, glancing over my shoulder, as if she's worried someone might have heard. "But I haven't gotten to know anyone, really, since my divorce. I'm not really sure how to do this."

"If it makes you feel any better, I haven't dated in a long time, either," I admit. "But I think we could figure it out. I mean, we've done this before, right?"

"That's true," she says with a coy press of her lips. "But life is so different now. We're not in high school anymore."

Don't I know it. I feel the weight of this moment and don't want to screw it up. Nora deserves honesty, so that's what I'm going to give her.

"How about we make a promise?" I venture.

"What kind of promise?" she asks with a curious smile.

"The honest kind. I'll be completely honest and upfront with you, even if it is super awkward, and you can be totally honest with me. No games."

"I like that."

153

"Look," I say, edging a little bit closer so we're nearly standing toe to toe. Nora has to tilt her head up to look at me. "I know things are different now, and it might be a little bit of a learning curve for both of us, but I'm willing to try to make something work, if you are."

Nora slips her hair behind her ear nervously, her gaze darting away from mine. Her thick, dark hair is down tonight, and man, if that doesn't make me want to knot my fingers in it and kiss her like I used to.

"You know what," I say, the wheels spinning in my head. I don't want to scare her off, but I need her to know upfront that I plan on putting everything I've got into this unexpected chance I've been given with her. "I've got an idea. Hear me out. I just started seeing a therapist." Nora's eyebrows arch ever-so-slightly. "Don't act surprised. You of all people know I've got plenty to work on."

"Don't we all?" she says. "I see a therapist, too. She knows more about me than my own mother."

"Look at that. Something else we share in common, along with an affinity for ceramic mugs and the greatest sport of all time. You still like baseball, right?"

She gives a half-hearted shrug. "I don't know," she teases. "You kind of ruined it for me for a while, not gonna lie."

"Ouch," I say with a wince, placing a hand over my chest. I may be joking, but Nora was directly impacted by my choice to make baseball my life, and that reality sits heavy with me.

"I'm just being honest. It's what you wanted!"

We laugh, and I'm encouraged by her playfulness.

"Anyways," I continue. "My therapist encouraged me to find some new hobbies outside of baseball. Apparently, I've become too obsessed with my performance, and that's not necessarily a good thing."

"Is that why you came tonight?" she asks. "You wanted to try something new?"

"No, actually. I came here tonight to have an entire table of strangers stare at me *while* I try something new and then take pictures of me when they think I'm not looking."

Nora laughs then, full-on, and pleasure swirls through me at the sound.

"So, here's my idea," I say. "Like I told you at the market, I plan to be here in Kitt's Harbor on the weekends. What if we meet up while I'm here and try something new together?"

"Sounds like something *my* therapist would recommend, honestly."

I wait for Nora to mull things over, resisting the urge to sell her on it further. Despite my desire to give Nora every possible reason to give me a chance, maybe she needs me to take things slow.

"I like it," Nora says. "Sounds pretty fun."

"*Pretty* fun? Don't get too excited on me."

"It sounds like the most fun thing I'll ever do in my life!" she jokes, spreading her hands out to emphasize just how thrilled she is.

"That's what I like to hear. I've got five weeks of therapy left. What if we spent the next five Friday nights together?"

"Friday nights?" she repeats. "That would work. Ollie goes to his dad's every other weekend, but we could hang out after he goes to bed on the Fridays I have him."

I'm reminded that there's another man in Nora's life already, one that I used to call my friend. Jealousy courses through me at the reminder of Nate, but it quickly dissipates as I realize that I'm the one standing here with Nora now.

"That works for me," I say. Her arm is hanging free at her side, so I close the inches between our free hands, dancing my fingertips across the back of her knuckles. Her brown eyes pop up to mine, and she glances down at our hands, her fingers lifting to brush mine again. I want to make sure she's getting the message loud and clear. I turn my palm and trace my index finger down the back of her palm before looping my fingers loosely between hers. She takes several breaths, her gaze downcast, before she looks back up at me. Holding her hand is like slipping on my favorite worn baseball glove. Warm and familiar. I tighten my grip, liking the feel of her palm against mine as much as I did back when she was mine.

"Do we have an agreement?" I say in a low tone. "Five Fridays. Getting to know each other."

"Again," Nora whispers, a slow smile growing on her lips.

"Again," I repeat. I drag my thumb over hers, and her breath hitches. I'd give anything to close the distance between our lips and kiss her right now, to give her something to hold onto until next week when we see each other again, but I don't want to move too fast. Besides, I guarantee my sister is beadily watching our every move.

"I'd better get Claire home," I sigh, reluctantly loosening my grip on her hand. "Are you staying here tonight?"

Nora nods. "Ollie's so excited, though, he probably won't sleep much." She smiles then, and I can see emotion swimming in the corners of her eyes. "Thank you for coming tonight. It meant a lot to me that you were here."

"I wouldn't have missed it," I say, mirroring her smile with one of my own. "Thank you for helping me broaden my horizons. Be thinking of more new things you want to try with me." Nora's mouth curves up, and I realize how that sounded. "I didn't mean it like that."

"Of course not."

"But, I mean, if you want to try new things with me like *that*, I wouldn't say no..."

"Claire?" Nora chokes out. "Your brother says it's past his bedtime."

I lower my lips to her ear and whisper. "See, there you are talking about bedtime. If I didn't know better, Nora, I'd think you were trying to turn our arrangement into something entirely inappropriate."

She giggles, turning her face up towards mine. We're standing so close that the tips of our noses nearly brush. Her brown eyes widen, and her pink lips barely part as her gaze dances over my face. A slow smile tugs at my mouth, and I don't bother to move away from her.

"That's not what I meant, and you know it," she protests. I resist the urge to kiss her and, instead, pull her to me in another hug. She folds into me effortlessly.

I like the idea that I could be someone to her. Like I used to be.

SIXTEEN

Nora

First Friday

Our over-the-water deck seating area is officially closed for the season, but that doesn't stop me from seeking refuge outdoors on Friday afternoon after my shift. It was an uncharacteristically slow afternoon at the diner, and after making myself a pumpkin chai, I head outside to get some fresh air. This unparalleled view of the harbor is part of what keeps me here at Delia's. I love looking out at the stretch of ocean surrounding the dock, listening to the sounds of the waves gliding up the pebbled beach and watching the grey mist retreat beyond the coastline. Breathing in the briny scent of the sea and distant woodsmoke always calms me. It's a mild autumn day with clear skies, so I settle into my chair, drawing one knee up to my chest and resting my chin on it.

Brooks is coming to pick me up at seven tonight. *Tonight*. I've felt like I've got a cloud of starlings swirling in my stomach all day.

He'd made a good argument after my workshop. How could I have said no to spending five Fridays with him? The prospect was sparkling and irresistible. But now that our first agreed-upon Friday has arrived, I'm nervous as all get out.

Ollie is at his dad's this weekend, and although I thought it would help matters to have him out from under my feet, it hasn't. I miss him even more knowing that I don't have my wingman, my best buddy, to act as a buffer between me and my fragile feelings. I could have used someone to hide behind tonight.

I relish a few precious minutes of quiet contemplation before my co-workers decide to interrupt my tranquility.

"So," Roman says, plopping himself down in a chair across from me. "What are you wearing tonight?"

"Please take pictures!" Kate pleads.

"Is he taking you to dinner first?" Audrey asks.

I look between my friends, circling the lid of my coffee cup with my index finger and watching the steam twist into the humid air.

"Oh no," Roman says. "We've overwhelmed her."

"How are you feeling?" Audrey asks, leaning closer.

"Part of me is floating somewhere up there," I say. "Above the clouds. It feels like I'm dreaming. But then the other part of me is scared out of my mind."

"Why?" Kate says. "Brooks seems like an absolute sweetheart."

"He is," I admit, and the swirling in my stomach intensifies. He really is. "I'm so out of practice. I haven't dated anyone in ages. What if I'm bad at it? What if he tries to *kiss* me?"

"He-llo! Kiss him back!" Roman cries.

"It's just been so long since I've been...courted."

Roman snorts. "Courted? What are you, a spinster in the Regency era? Goodness, honey. Brooks has gone to great lengths to get you back. The least you could do is let him kiss you!"

"Let's look at the facts, shall we?" Audrey interjects. "Brooks texted you immediately after Roman gave him your number, and he didn't hold it against you when you ghosted him."

"That's true," I admit.

"Then, he whisked you away at the Harvest Market," Kate adds.

"He even came to your workshop, Nora," Audrey says with a pout. "He is precious."

"Precious!" Roman echoes. "You have nothing to worry about with that man. He is a walking green flag."

"See, that's how I felt about him when we first dated. But when he left Kitt's Harbor, I felt like he chose his career over me. I'm scared that he's going to do the same thing all over again when spring training starts up in February."

My friends grow quiet, looking at each other in turn.

"Nora," Roman says, reaching across the table for my hand. "You've got to give him a chance to prove to you that he's changed. He's not the same young buck who dumped you all those years ago."

"I know," I sigh. "But it's hard not to worry about the future. Especially with my track record."

"Maybe you should share your worries with Brooks. Clear the air right at the start," Roman suggests. "Play a little Truth or Dare. If things take a turn and clothes start flying off, all the better."

Kate smacks Roman's arm. "She's worried about him *kissing* her, Roman. Not seducing her."

"She's a *mother*, Kate. She knows full well how babies are made."

I swallow. Nope. Not going to let my mind drift in that direction. It would never come back to me. Forever lost to the wind.

"Roman's got a point," Audrey says. "It wouldn't hurt to lay things out for Brooks right from the get-go. Talk to him about how things ended the last time you dated and walk through how things are going to be different this time."

"We did agree to be open and honest with each other," I say. My therapist encouraged me to expect that from everyone in my life after what Nate did. Especially men I might potentially date.

"Cheers to honesty," Roman says, raising his cup in the air. "And to Betty–may she never lead you astray,"

I snort. "You mean Beverly?"

"Whatever. The old bat who listens while you talk about your issues."

"Thank you for the advice," I say with a laugh, giving Roman's hand an affectionate squeeze. "You're the ones who got me into this mess, so it's the least you could do, really."

"We had no choice, honey. There's just something special between you two. It's undeniable," Roman says.

That's how I'd felt when Brooks and I were young and still in the blush of first love. Things may not have worked out the first time, but after seeing him at my workshop, there was no denying the tangible tether that still exists between us. I'd been in a giddy haze for hours after he left. Maybe it had always been there, a tiny string linking us together, even across the time and distance. Who am I to deny the undeniable now?

I swipe some lip gloss over my lips and drag my fingers through the roots of my hair, trying to give it a little more volume. I tug the hem of my deep green sweater down, turning in the mirror to make sure it covers my legging-clad rear. I'd texted my sisters a picture of my original outfit and had then changed four more times until I was given the sisterly stamp of approval. Apparently, there are rules now about how many colors one can wear at the same time, and I was breaking all of them.

Brooks and I agreed to take turns planning our Friday activities, with Brooks heading up the plans tonight. Lucky for me, our activity warrants comfy clothes I can move in. Right up my alley, much to Sydney's dismay. For once, she deemed it acceptable for me to wear leggings in Brooks' presence.

At 6:59, I hear a knock at my front door. My heart feels like it's being yanked right outside my chest. *He's here.*

I take a deep breath, wishing once again I had Ollie here with me as I move towards the door. I realize as I'm doing so that Brooks is the first man to come calling in two years. And no, Tommy Collins doesn't count. Maybe I am a spinster, like Roman said. Twenty-seven and already on the shelf.

But the way Brooks looks at me as I swing open the door, his blue eyes bright in the glow of the porch light, makes me think otherwise. He gives me an easy smile, one that surely would look perfect on the big screen at Boeing Park, and my stomach drops into my toes. Suddenly, the neckline of my sweater feels suffocating, and this doorway is too small.

"Hey," Brooks says, his eyes traveling down my frame in a slow, appreciative assessment. "You look great."

He says it so casually, so guilelessly, that I have no choice but to believe him. A sweet warmth slips down my limbs and through my body, like wax dripping down the sides of a yellowed beeswax candle.

"Thank you," I say, still half hidden behind my door. I move aside and allow Brooks to step across the threshold.

He immediately pulls me towards him with one strong arm around my shoulders. I slip into his embrace, and my hands bunch against his firm chest. There's a heightened awareness of the points of contact between our bodies. The soft feel of his sweatshirt against my chin. The cool texture of his jacket under my fingertips. The toe of his left sneaker against my right foot. I flatten my palms against his chest and appreciate the fact that he has filled out in all the right, masculine ways since we were seventeen.

"You ready to go?" Brooks asks, pulling away with a quick glance down at my hands still resting on his chest. I drop my hands and adjust the hem of my sweater just to keep them busy.

Brooks steps back out onto the porch, and I appreciate just how good he looks tonight, especially with his hair styled and not peeking out from under a baseball hat. I think I may have to tug at one of those dark swirls of hair at the base of his neck just to see if it feels as soft as it used to.

"Yeah, I think so," I say, snatching my house keys and wallet off the entryway table before tucking them into my coat pocket. I suddenly feel the looming sense that I'm forgetting something. I pause on the porch steps, patting my pockets as my brain draws a blank.

"You sure?" Brooks asks with a teasing smile. "We can do something else if you're not excited about what I've got planned."

"It's not that," I insist. "I just feel like I'm forgetting something."

"Let's see…" Brooks says, lumbering down the porch steps. "I'm here. Check. You're here. Check. Rollerblades are in the car. Check."

"Okay, yeah. You're right," I sigh. It always feels so weird when I leave the house without Ollie. My hands feel empty without the diaper bag, water bottles, and snacks…SNACKS.

"Oh!" I gasp. "I remember what I needed to get. I'll be right back."

I slip back inside the house and run to the pantry, grabbing two Fruit by the Foot. I hold one out to Brooks, who is looking like an ad for an athleisure brand, standing casually with his hands in his jogger pockets on my porch.

"For you," I say, presenting him with the snack with a ceremonial swish.

"No way," he says, and a grin splits his face. "These are my favorite."

"I know," I say. "I remember. They're Ollie's favorite, too."

"My guy!"

"Remember that one time before play-offs, junior year, I think, when you stress-ate like ten Fruits by the Foot? Wait…Fruit by the Foots…whatever they're called. These things." I flap mine in the air for emphasis.

Brooks laughs. "I forgot about that."

"You were so sick, you almost had to sit out the game." We meander down the porch steps, and he glances over at me with a smile that nearly makes me trip and fall flat on my face.

"I can't believe you remembered that. Wanna know something funny?" Brooks opens the passenger-side door for me. "I used to eat one of these before every game. It was part of my ritual. But one of my New Year's resolutions this year was to eat less Fruit by the Foot and more...actual fruit."

"And how's that going for you?"

"I was on track until the Wild Card series. Then, I binged an entire box by myself later that night, after we lost. Made me so sick."

I laugh as I slip into his Tesla. After he shuts the door behind me, I pull on my seatbelt and take a quick inventory of his car. It's pristine. Not a rogue french fry, sticky juice spill, or sour milk stain to be seen. My car constantly looks like the snack aisle imploded inside it and smells like bacon...and probably diapers. Brooks' car smells fresh, like he's just gotten it cleaned, and I can see my reflection on the massive LED screen on the dash.

"I can leave these here if you're not going to eat yours," I say. "I don't want to throw you off your nutrition goals."

"Oh, believe me, I'm going to eat mine. And I'm going to enjoy it." He hands it to me as he backs out of my driveway. "Can you open it for me?"

"Right now?"

"Why not? You've dangled temptation in front of me. How am I supposed to resist?"

166

I unwrap both snacks and hand him one. He unrolls it with one hand and takes a bite, pulling to break a piece off from the long strand.

"Oh yeah," he says. "So good."

"So," I ask between bites of strawberry-flavored roll-up. "Why rollerblading?"

"Why not?"

I get a hit of Brooks' cologne as he readjusts in his seat and palms the steering wheel. Oh me, oh my. Long gone are the days of cheap aftershave from the Walmart deodorant aisle. Whatever he's got on smells expensive—like it's made from the tears of mermaids in the Mediterranean.

"Admit it. You chose this activity because you know I'm a klutz and you wanted to challenge me with something that requires both balance and coordination. Neither of which I possess."

"You'll be fine," he says, glancing over at me with a grin. "I'll be right by your side."

That's exactly the answer I was counting on. I don't intend on releasing him from my grip the entire night.

"I used to rollerblade as a kid, actually," he says. "So, it's technically not something entirely new, but I haven't done it in a long time."

"I've never rollerbladed in my life. If I go down, I'm taking you down with me."

"Bring it on," Brooks says with a smile. "I have to admit something to you. I thought that Kitt's Harbor still had a roller-skating rink, but apparently, there isn't one anymore."

"I could have told you that. It closed right after we..." I almost said *broke up.* Oops. "After high school," I amend.

"I knew I should have asked you beforehand."

"You had an entire week to plan this, didn't you? Plenty of time to ask the resident expert."

"Hey, come on. I had a lot of ideas, and it took me until yesterday to narrow it down to just one," he says. "We've got a bit of a drive ahead of us because the closest roller-skating rink is in Port Angeles."

My stomach swoops. "No worries."

"It's actually the only roller-skating rink on the entire Olympic Peninsula," he says. "I figured it would give us a chance to talk more. You know, get to know each other again."

A nervous surge floods through me as I realize that I'm going to be trapped in close proximity to Brooks for the forty-five minutes it will take us to get there...and forty-five minutes back. That's the longest I've been alone with a man since I was...well...married.

I finish off my Fruit by the Foot and stare nervously ahead, building up the courage to initiate the conversation we need to have tonight.

SEVENTEEN

Brooks

THE TANGY FLAVOR OF the Fruit by the Foot coats my mouth and sticks to my teeth: a lasting reminder that Nora Foster might remember just as much about me as I do about her. Her gesture makes me wonder if some small part of her always hoped that we'd somehow find our way back to each other.

"How was your day?" I ask. "When I texted you this afternoon, you said the diner was slow?"

Nora jolts out of her blank stare out the car window. "Oh, yeah. It was so slow. But that's nice sometimes, honestly, just to have a change of pace. How was your day? Did you...work out? Or train? Or whatever it is you do in the off-season."

"All of the above. I'm actually working with a trainer, a retired MLB player, at a gym three days a week with a couple of the guys on the team. Then, I had a meeting with one of my sponsors in Port Angeles. They're opening a new store there in a couple months."

Nora sits up straight. "Wait, you were already in Port Angeles today?"

"Yeah, for most of the afternoon."

"Then you had to come all the way to Kitt's Harbor to pick me up? I could have met you there."

"I wanted to pick you up."

"Well, thank you," Nora says softly. "That's a lot of driving for you."

"I don't mind. Really."

She gives me a shy glance that makes my chest constrict. I like seeing her here in my passenger seat. It reminds me of the drives we'd take back when she was my girlfriend. But she's so much more quiet now. Like the Nora I knew, but with the volume turned way, way down.

"I was talking to my co-workers after my shift," Nora says. "And they gave me some advice." She shifts in her seat nervously. "Okay, I'm just going to say it. This is me keeping up my end of the honesty pact."

"I'm all ears."

"I'm really nervous about tonight, Brooks," she says with a sigh. "My friends told me I need to just tell you my concerns and get them out into the open."

"Solid advice."

"Yes, I thought so, too. We need to speak about a few things before things go any further."

She sounds earnest, and I agree. That's why I orchestrated an activity that would involve driving together so we could have some uninterrupted time to talk.

"Okay," I say. "What would you like to address first?"

"I don't even know where to start," she sighs, and in my periphery, I see her glance out the window.

"How about I start with a question for you?"

"Okay."

I'm emboldened by the shadows around us and the fact that I don't have to look directly at her when I ask questions I've wondered about for many years. "Why are you still working at the diner?" I ask. "Because I remember when we were..."

"Dating," she supplies. "We might as well call it what it is. We dated."

"Right. So, back when you were my girlfriend..." I swear Nora freezes at the word and doesn't blink for a solid ten seconds. "You had different dreams. I'm just curious to know what changed."

She spends another long minute in silence before speaking.

"It's comfortable," she says. "The diner has always been comfortable for me. I like Kitt's Harbor. I never really wanted to leave. I think I needed something predictable and easy and safe after you broke up with me, so I kept my job at the diner and never left."

Her honesty hurts. I swallow down the regret of letting her go all over again.

"I'm sorry, Nora," I say, glancing over at her. She meets my eyes. "I'm sorry about what happened."

"You have no idea how badly I wanted you to come back and say those words to me," she says quietly, looking down at her lap. "After you left, you looked so happy at school, living out your dreams. I was heartbroken that you moved on so easily."

My grip tightens on the steering wheel.

"It wasn't easy for me to leave you, Nora." She lifts her gaze to catch mine. "I questioned my choice every day those first few months in Oregon. But then, my sister told me that she'd seen you with Nate, and I was..." I laugh, and it tastes bitter. "Jealous. Insanely jealous. But I knew I'd made my choice, and I couldn't back out of it."

"I've always wanted to know," Nora says softly. "Did you break up with me because your dad told you to?"

It's my turn to sit in the uncomfortable quiet as I'm forced to wrestle with the truths of our past. She doesn't know the reality of what I faced after I'd allowed my dad to manipulate me into ending our relationship. She needs to know the truth.

"Yes," I finally say. "I shouldn't have listened to him. But I did. He thought our relationship would only get in the way of my career, so he told me I needed to make the hard choice and let you go." It feels good to get the truth out in the open between us, as hard as it is to face it. "I messed up. I let him control me, just like he always had before and like he still tries to do from time to time."

"I thought so. He never liked me, did he? The rest of your family has always been really nice, but your dad..." she trails off, and I know exactly what she's implying without her having to spell it out.

"Yeah," I say. "He's...complicated. We don't speak anymore."

"I wondered. I never really see him around town, and he wasn't at the game, so I figured things between you must be...not great."

"I started putting some distance between us once my parents divorced."

"I'm sorry," Nora says simply. "You deserve better than that."

"You deserved better, too," I say, wishing I could pull the car over and take her face in my hands to emphasize the depth of my regret. "I'm sorry, Nora."

"It's okay," she whispers, reaching for my hand across the console. I drop my fingers between hers and pull our palms flush together. It feels perfect. Like our hands imprinted years ago and still hold the memory of our shared touch. "I thought if it was what you wanted, who was I to get in the way?" she continues. "I had to come to terms with the fact that you weren't coming back. I had to move on."

We share a glance in the darkened cab of my car. There's a beat of silence, the whir of the passing traffic filling in as the only sound. The reality is that there is another man present in her life. However reluctant she may be to keep him in it, he's there. He's the father of her child.

"I've got a hard question for you. You don't have to answer it if you don't want to," I say. "What happened with you and Nate? I'd be lying if I said I wasn't jealous that he was the one who you chose to marry, but I thought you wouldn't have done it if you didn't really love him."

"I did love him," she says. "And he loved me, too. Until he decided he wanted someone else."

Anger mounts inside me at what Nate did to Nora. "I just don't get how he could have been unfaithful to you. It makes no sense."

She shakes her head with a sad smile. "He changed, Brooks."

"How could he have changed that much?" I say, then realize I need to curb my emotion. She doesn't owe me an explanation. "You don't have to tell me any details, but if you want to talk about it, I'm listening."

"Okay," she says, then lets out a long, slow breath. I know this can't be easy for her to talk about, but I want to know what happened.

"Things were really great for a few years, but then Nate got a new job at a different insurance firm in Carleton Point. His new position required him to be at the office a lot more. That's when he started growing distant," she finally says. "He always made it sound like he had an endless amount of work to do, which I would never understand, because I had a job I could clock out of at four PM every day." Nora sighs. "I had early mornings at the diner, and he had late nights at the office. We barely saw each other. I should have seen it coming, but it still shocked me when I found out that he was having an affair with someone he worked with."

"How did you find out?" I ask, hoping I'm not overstepping in doing so.

"I picked up his phone to look something up, and I found their text messages. I still can't even say her name," she says, taking another deep breath. "Once I confronted him about...*her*, he didn't even try to deny it. He told me he wanted out of our marriage because he was in love with her."

My heart feels like it weighs a thousand pounds.

"And you were...pregnant at the time?"

"I found out I was pregnant right after that. Great timing for my marriage to fall apart, right?"

"Man," I grit out. "What he did was unbelievable. I know there are no words sufficient for this, but I'm so incredibly sorry." She gives my hand a squeeze as if she's trying to ease me off the ledge.

"I know," she says simply, with a little smile. "I did my best to love him well, but that wasn't enough for him. Sometimes I wonder if marrying him in the first place had been a mistake.

But then I remember that if I hadn't married him, I wouldn't have Ollie."

My heart is thundering in my chest, filled with anger towards Nate. Anger towards myself. If I hadn't left her, maybe she wouldn't have had her heart broken so badly. Twice. It's hard not to feel partially responsible for the turns her life has taken. Like maybe I could have prevented all of this from happening if I hadn't listened to my dad.

But then again, she's right. Ollie is a gift. He wouldn't be here if things hadn't gone the way they did. I'm not sure I trust myself to talk more about Nate right now and not let my anger show, so I ask her a different question.

"Has it been hard raising Ollie on your own?"

"I'm not on my own," she says. "My family has really stepped up and helped me so much these past two years. Sydney even gave me part of her income after Ollie was born so I could spend more time at home recovering before going back to work at the diner. My mom takes care of him several days a week, and my neighbors and friends took really good care of me. They still do. I'm lucky to be surrounded by good people who love me. Actually, now that I'm thinking about it, maybe they just love Ollie."

"Ollie's awesome, but you are…" I struggle to find adequate words to describe Nora and all that she is. "Even in the short amount of time we've been talking again, it's evident to me that you're an amazing person. Just like you always have been."

Nora looks at me then, and when I return her gaze, she's watching me intently.

"You've been through a lot, Nora," I say. "But you're better for it. I can see it in everything you do. You work so hard to take care of Ollie and everybody around you, so tonight, I want to take care of you."

She squeezes my hand, and I can feel hers shaking beneath my grip. She sniffs, and I realize that she's crying.

"Oh, no," I say. "I'm making you cry on our first date? Things aren't looking good."

"It's not our first date," she laughs.

"You're right," I say, glad we can acknowledge the relationship we had in the past.

"I'm not upset, I'm just..." she says with another sniffle. "I appreciate you being so open about things with me. I need that, especially after what happened with Nate."

"I get it," I say. "You can trust me, Nora. I'm going to prove that to you. You can always ask me about anything, and I promise I'll never hide anything from you."

She lets out a shaky breath. "Okay."

We drive in silence for a moment before Nora speaks up again. "Have you been happy with your choice?" she asks.

I pause before answering, wondering if she's asking me about all the ways I regret leaving her. Or maybe she just wants to make sure I've still found some kind of fulfillment without her, the way she did. Because some part of her always cared for me. "I thought I was pretty happy, but after the way this last season ended, I'm questioning whether I've really got a grasp on what's supposed to make me happy. That's what I'm trying to figure out."

"I've felt the same way since my divorce. It turned my life upside down. Made me question everything."

"So, how did you get through it?"

She lets out a tired laugh. "I'm still getting through it. Every day I'm getting through it. There doesn't seem to be an end in sight. That's the funny thing about grief. It sneaks up on you when you least expect it and stifles your happiness and strangles your hope. There are things that help, for sure. Like going to therapy or being around loved ones. I think my favorite coping mechanism is trying to stay busy. Usually with work."

"Same."

"But that only works until you're off the clock, right? Then I try to distract myself from being sad by doing things I enjoy, like throwing pottery."

"What happens when you run out of distractions?" I'm afraid of her answer. Like Nora, I never stop moving. I don't want to know what happens if I choose to sit with the feelings I keep numbing and shoving down.

"I think those moments where you allow yourself to really process your grief are necessary. They're so painful, but that's what you need sometimes, you know? You have to let yourself grieve the full weight of what you've lost."

"I don't want to do that," I say with an uncomfortable laugh.

"I don't either. But I do it anyway, sometimes. And then I usually feel better because I know that hard feelings pass. They're not permanent. And I know I'll be able to get through it when the grief comes again. My therapist told me to try and remember that each day is just a moment, and that tomorrow will be better."

"Tomorrow will be better," I repeat.

"You have to take things one day at a time because if you start to think too far ahead, you get so completely overwhelmed that you want to...give up."

"So why haven't you?"

"Ollie," Nora says without hesitation. "I need him. He needs me. He's the motivating force behind everything I do."

My thoughts turn inward, and I ask myself what my motivating force is. I don't have a child or family to care for, so does that mean my motivation in life is just to serve myself? That doesn't seem right. Maybe that's why things have felt so unmanageable. I'm so busy worrying about myself and my mistakes and my problems. My life seems shallow and self-serving compared to Nora's. Her experiences have given her a depth I lack. I suddenly feel like a student, like she's the teacher with all the life experience, and I'm sitting at her feet, ready to learn.

"What about you? How do you cope with loss?" she asks. "You can't win every game, right?"

"My losses are nowhere near as great as yours. Baseball is just a game," I say, and it feels like a revelation.

"That doesn't matter. A loss is a loss."

"I don't lose well," I admit. "It's something I need to work on. You know how I am. I stew on things and beat myself up. Pick my mistakes apart."

"Just like your dad used to do?"

"Yeah."

"Maybe that's what you're really grieving," she suggests. "The fact that you can never please him, even though you want to so badly."

I'm suddenly antsy. I don't want to talk about Bill. It makes my blood boil under my skin just thinking about him.

"Maybe," I say finally, not wanting to bring my dad into our intimate conversation. At least not yet. Nora gets the memo because she gives my hand a squeeze.

"Thank you for talking with me and asking the hard questions," she says. "I need it. I hope you know that you can talk to me about things, too. Anytime."

"Thanks, Nora," I say, shooting her a smile. "I'd like that." I lift our joined hands up. "And I like this."

Her lips lift in a shy smile, and she adjusts her grip in my hand. "Me, too."

"Wait," Nora says as my trunk opens to reveal the rollerblades in the back. "You didn't buy these just for me, did you?"

I flick the receipt out of sight and pull the box containing Nora's rollerblades out. "No, of course not."

"These are brand new!" she gasps. "You didn't want to rent blades inside?"

I wince. "Absolutely not." I'm sure the fact that I make really good money has crossed her mind before, and I don't want this to seem like an attempt to flaunt my wealth. I decide to paint myself as the poster child of OCD instead. "Just think about it for a second. Would you want to wear rollerblades that have had hundreds, maybe even *thousands*, of other people's sweaty feet inside them already?"

Nora wrinkles her nose. "Well, no, when you put it that way."

"Here," I say, handing her one rollerblade I've unwrapped. "Try this on. Hopefully you still like yellow."

"How did you remember that?" She scoots up into the bed of the trunk next to me and tugs off one of her sneakers, revealing bright pink socks covered in yellow smiley faces. I grin at the sight.

"I remember a lot of things," I say.

She pauses, brushing her hair back from her face and giving me a curious smile. "Like what else?"

"How deep do you want to go tonight, Nora?"

"We've already gone pretty deep already," she points out, tugging the rollerblade on over her sock and snapping the buckles into place. "I'm curious to know what you remember about us."

"You go first," I say, leaning against the side of the car and crossing my arms.

"Fine. I remember how hard you used to be on yourself. Clearly, that hasn't changed."

I tilt my head in acknowledgement.
"I remember that one time we skipped fourth period...Mrs. Gibson's class, I think? And went to Tony's to get pizza instead. But then, your car wouldn't start, and we had to call your mom..." she trails off with a giggle.

"She was so mad at us," I say, laughing at the memory.

"I remember that you don't like ice in your water." She purses her lips, and I nod. "And that you're very particular about the cleanliness of things."

"Correct on both accounts."

"And I remember..." She suddenly ducks her head, looking embarrassed.

"What?"

"Never mind."

"Come on. Don't leave me hanging."

She toys with the ends of her long, dark hair before looking up at me. There's a flicker of the memory there in her brown eyes, and without her saying a word, I know exactly what she's going to say.

"When you bought my dream prom dress with all your savings because my dad had lost his job, and we couldn't afford it."

I slide my hands into my pockets and look down at the yellow rollerblade dangling off one of her feet.

"You looked so pretty in it," I say softly, lifting my eyes to meet hers. "I had to."

Another thread pulls taught between us as we recall the shared memory. One of the many moments that had made us both certain that even after graduation, we were going to be together for a long, long time.

"And here you go again," she says, lifting her rollerblade into the air. "Buying me things."

"Does it fit?"

"Perfectly."

"I had to guess at your size, so you can be honest if they're too tight or too big."

"No, they're perfect," Nora says, reaching down to unsnap the buckles.

"Here," I say. I cup the wheels of the rollerblade with one hand and help her slide it off her foot. My other hand settles around her calf, and I feel the warmth of her skin through her thin leggings.

"Thank you," she says, and my gaze flicks up to hers. She's so pretty. Still the prettiest girl I've ever known. I reluctantly slide my hand off her leg to place the rollerblade back into the box.

Never in a million years did I think I'd be with Nora again, casually talking about the past we'd shared while easing into what could be our future. I'd thought she was gone for good.

But she's not. She's here. She's smiling down at her yellow rollerblades like I just handed her the world, and something tilts inside me.

Maybe she is what my life has been missing. She's the missing piece.

EIGHTEEN

Nora

IT'S DARK AND LOUD inside the skate rink, and it smells like a fine mixture of sweat and bodies and greasy cheese. Brooks sneakily buys our passes while I use the bathroom, and after placing our shoes in a sticky cubby hole that probably hasn't been cleaned in a decade, we find a bench to sit on so we can put on our rollerblades.

"I'm telling you now," Brooks says. "If you need a hand to hold onto, I'm your guy."

I nearly hiccup at his words and busy myself with my adorable new rollerblades. I think I just found my new favorite pastime. I don't even care if it takes me three years, I'm going to figure out how to use these puppies. I will not be wasting the precious gift he just gave me. Heck, I might even start requiring all my servers to wear skates at the diner like the good ol' days.

"You're assuming that I'm going to need your help?" I fire back. "Watch me. I'm going to be flying past you like Twinkle Toes over there." I gesture to an older gentleman zipping past who's wearing skin-tight green sequined leggings and a neon-yellow tank, revealing an inappropriate amount of chest hair.

"I suddenly feel underdressed," Brooks says. He looks incredibly attractive in his fitted grey long-sleeve t-shirt and jeans, but I'm not quite brave enough to tell him that. Maybe I can convince Twinkle Toes to slow down and capture a photo of us so I can stare at it later.

"You could have borrowed some of my leggings," I say, reaching down to pull on my second rollerblade. "My collection has quadrupled since becoming a mother."

Brooks's lips curl up in a cheeky smile, and he glances away. I'm jealous of his eyelashes. Men shouldn't have lashes as thick and long as he does.

"What?" I ask flatly.

"You'd like that, wouldn't you?" he replies in a low, gravelly voice that does funny things to my pulse.

"Like what?"

Suddenly his mouth is pressed right up against my ear. "Wanna know something I remember about you?" he whispers. My breath snags in my throat as his lips brush over the whirl of my ear.

My voice comes out scratchy. "What's that?"

Brooks pulls away and lets out a little snicker before pressing his mouth to my ear again. "I remember how into me you were every time I wore my baseball pants."

I jolt away, sliding two inches down the bench. "Brooks Alden!"

He gives a one-shouldered shrug, looking smug. "I don't blame you. They make my butt look good." I blink, open-mouthed. "Your words, not mine," he says with a slanted smirk that makes my heart flip a U-turn, tires screeching.

"You can't say things like that to me!"

"I'm the *only* person who can say things like that to you," he says with a confidence that makes me shiver. He stands up and extends a hand towards me. "Just as a precaution, I'm going to skate right next to you this entire evening just to make sure you're not checking me out while I'm skating."

I laugh as he tugs me to my feet, then let out a little *eep* as my blades slip beneath me on the carpeted floor. Brooks moves lightning fast, grabbing my elbows to steady me.

"Would you quit thinking about my baseball pants? We haven't even stepped out onto the rink yet."

"You're terrible," I say, tossing my hair out of my eyes to look up at him. I'm firmly determined to not let my gaze stray anywhere near his butt, no matter how badly I want to, especially now that he's mentioned it. Because, yes, okay? Brooks wears the heck out of baseball pants. There. I said it.

He smiles at me, his eyes dipping to my mouth as he loosens his grip on my elbows. "You like it. Or at least, you used to."

Mercy me. I still do.

◆

"Somebody needs to tip the DJ," Brooks says on our third slow turn around the rink. "He's playing some bangers."

"What DJ?" I laugh because there's definitely nobody spinning the tunes here tonight, but Brooks is right. The amount of Pitbull, Kesha, and Flo Rida in this rotation is incredible.

"I liked your walkup song," I say. "Getting Started, right?"

"Oh, yeah?" he says with a grin. "You a fan of Aloe Blacc?"

"Well, I wasn't until I heard that song blasting through the stadium when you stepped up to bat," I admit. "That alone may have converted me."

"I'm losing you, Nora," Brooks says playfully, giving our joined hands a tug as we round a curve in the rink so we're skating side by side again.

"If you would just slow down a little, maybe then I could keep up!"

Brooks points at two little kids up ahead of us. "Gear up. We're gonna pass those slow pokes in t-minus five seconds."

"What!" I cry, trying to yank my hand away as Brooks starts picking up speed. "We are not taking down children just so you can feel like you're winning!"

He clamps down on my hand so I have no choice but to start lengthening my strides to keep up. We're both laughing, and I'm breathless, and the party music is bumping through my body. I haven't felt this light in ages.

"That's right!" Brooks raises a fist in the air as we successfully pass the kids.

"Your competitive streak is still going strong, I see," I say. "As well as your good sportsmanship."

"How else do you think I got drafted?"

"My dad was so proud when he heard you'd be playing for the Stormbreakers."

"I'd better get my crap together before next season," Brooks says, and I get a tiny glimpse of the fear he buries so well. The anxiety that fuels his work ethic. "Can't let Mr. Foster down again."

"You didn't let anybody down," I say, or yell, rather, because we skate right under one of the speakers. "Nobody's perfect, Brooks."

He gives me a sidelong glance, and his grip on my hand tightens. I'm feeling pretty confident on my skates now, but I'm not about to let him see that. I want him to think I'm an invalid for the duration of this entire evening so I can keep my hand firmly locked inside his big, strong one. It feels so good. His skin on my skin. I haven't been touched by a man in a long while.

"When you're playing a sport at my level, everybody still expects you to be."

We skate in silence for half a lap around the rink, and I think about what it must be like to have that pressure hanging over you every time you have to do your job.

"Is it worth it, do you think?" I ask.

Brooks is quiet for a moment. "I used to think so. I've always loved the game."

"But you don't anymore?"

"It's different when it's your livelihood. I could get traded or my contract could expire or any number of things could happen to me if I don't perform well."

"But you're just one player," I point out. "You're not carrying the weight of every game by yourself. That's what your teammates are for."

Brooks dips his head slightly. "True."

"At the diner, for example, as manager, I'm making schedules, doing payroll, updating the menu, you know, that kind of stuff. But there's no way I could run the entire restaurant by myself. I've got servers, the kitchen staff, busboys, a hostess who hates me..."

"Hates *you*?" Brooks says. "I don't buy it."

"It's your fault that she hates me. She sat you at your table the last time you came in and thought it was love at first sight. Once she found out that me and you were...you know..."

"Seeing each other?"

"Is that what this is?" I say, giving him a nudge with my shoulder and trying to keep the thrill his words sent through me hidden. "I thought I was just helping you fulfill your assignment from your therapist."

"No," Brooks says, gently pulling our joined hands across his body so I move closer to him. "We're definitely seeing each other."

My pulse is bursting through my skin. But I try to maintain a cool exterior and offer a sigh instead of screaming. "Well, in that case, Molly is going to murder me."

Is this real life? I, Nora Foster, am actually seeing the man I once thought would be my forever? If someone had told me about the twists and turns my life would take to get me here to this moment, I think I would still agree to all of them, if in the end I get a chance to *see* Brooks again.

"What were you saying?" Brooks asks, and the smile he throws me tells me he knows full well that he derailed my train of thought.

"I think the point I was trying to make was that we all work together to make sure the diner is successful. Just like you and your teammates do every time you play."

"I see your point." Brooks takes three smooth strides before speaking again. "You wanna know something?"

"Hmm?"

"Every time I'm with you, I forget about losing that game," Brooks says. "I forget about baseball. When we're texting or talking or hanging out, I feel like I can just let go and enjoy myself."

A warmth floods through me as I realize that since I stepped out onto the rink with Brooks tonight, I hadn't been worrying about Ollie. I hadn't been burdened down by financial concerns or stressing about the diner or paralyzed by fear of the future.

"I feel the same way," I say, bringing my other arm up to grip Brooks's forearm. Good golly. His arms are so thick.

"Thanks for coming with me tonight," Brooks says, and I look up at him, melting under the warmth of his kind smile. "Now..." he says, leaning closer. "Race you around the rink."

He lets go of my hand and takes off in a wildly athletic sprint in his rollerblades, leaving me and everyone else in the rink in the dust.

After deeming the pizza at the rink to be inedible, we walk a couple blocks down the street to find somewhere to grab dinner.

"This place looks pretty good," Brooks says, stopping outside a pub that's buzzing with people. We glance over the menu before stepping inside to get a table.

Brooks greets the hostess at the stand, and I glance furtively around as the entryway seems to grow quiet. I see people starting to stare at Brooks in recognition and hear his name hissed in whispers as the hostess leads us to a tiny two-top in a back corner of the restaurant. Brooks acts completely oblivious to it all, but people are being far from subtle as we pass by. I even see someone raise their phone and snap a picture of him from the bar.

Once we're seated, Brooks' smile widens as he looks at me from across the table. I shift in my chair as a server drops two glasses of water on our table. "Is it always like this?"

"Like what?" Brooks takes a sip from his glass, looking nonplussed.

"Everybody's looking at you."

"Maybe they're looking at you," he counters. "I would, if I didn't know you."

"And why is that?" I say, proud that the rust is slowly fading from my long-dormant flirting abilities.

"Because," he says softly, leaning towards me across the table. "You're the most beautiful girl in any room."

I smile down at my napkin as I smooth it over my lap, my heart rapping against my ribs.

"Excuse me." Both Brooks and I glance up to see a mother and her son have approached our table. "We're so sorry to bother you, but my son is a huge fan of yours and we wondered if you could sign something for him."

"Of course," Brooks says with a broad smile, reaching out for a high-five. "What's your name, my man?"

"Theo."

"You like baseball, Theo?" A nod. "Do you play?"

"Shortstop," Theo says shyly. "Like you."

"You keep it up, okay?" Brooks says, scribbling his signature on the napkin Theo proffers. "Thanks for saying hi."

Theo beams, and his mother asks for a picture. I offer to take one of all three of them, and she then thanks Brooks profusely for making his day. Brooks waves as Theo retreats, and I wonder if moments like this would be the norm if I were to become serious with Brooks. Would people recognize me? Or Ollie? Does he ever get to eat meals out in public without being interrupted?

There's a lot I still don't know about the life he leads.

"You're not bothered by kids, are you?" I say.

"Nah," he says. "A lot of the guys on the team have kids I see pretty often. We have a good time when they're around. Probably because I still am one myself."

"Do you want kids of your own?" I ask, and Brooks' blue eyes shoot up to mine. He knows my question is about more than just a hypothetical future. I have a son. That's not something either of us should take lightly.

"Of course I do," he says with a tilt of his head. "That's part of the reason I'm seeing a therapist. I need help now so I can be the kind of father I never had."

I love his answer. I love his honesty.

"Me and Ollie are kind of a package deal," I say.

"I know," he says with a smile.

"And that doesn't scare you?" I ask.

"Not at all," he says with that same confidence he seems to carry so naturally. I find it so incredibly attractive.

"So, if we're going to be, as you say, *seeing each other*," we share a smile, "Ollie needs to be able to know and trust you, too."

Brooks eyes me from across the table before reaching out to take my hand in his. He drags his thumb over my knuckles.

191

"I will do whatever is required to earn your trust," he says, and my pulse flutters. "I broke it once, and I don't plan on ever doing that again. We'll take things as slow as you need. One Friday at a time."

I'm breathless at the knowledge that Brooks is trying to win me over.

"Thank you for understanding," I say. "I'll take care of the plans for next Friday."

Brooks grins. "Looking forward to it."

Our food arrives a few minutes later, and we eat quickly, clearly both starving after our escapade at the skate rink. Our server drops off the check before we've even finished our meal.

"He's super eager to get us out of here, isn't he?" I say, reaching for the bill.

"I've got it," Brooks says, swiping it away.

"You've already treated me tonight. I'm happy to buy you dinner."

Brooks looks at me like I've just suggested something completely ridiculous. "Not happening, Nora. I told you I was going to take care of you tonight."

I don't put up too much of a fight because, honestly, I can't really afford to eat out much and I appreciate being taken care of. Especially by Brooks. He's been nothing but sweet to me tonight, and I'm a little high off the feeling of being cared for so thoughtfully. Part of me wants Brooks again, so badly that I want to defy all logic and make him mine right now before someone else does. But there's still the reality of my situation, and the fact that we come from two very different worlds. While I'm used to pinching pennies and parenting, he's accustomed to the lifestyle that comes with the paycheck of a professional athlete.

Brooks is the kind of guy who goes all in. I wish I was more like him, but getting my heart broken, first by him, then by Nate, has made me cautious. I appreciate his willingness to let me figure things out on my own time. It's what I need, and it's what's best for Ollie.

On our way out of the pub, we sidle past the bar. I hear a rough voice call out, "Hey!" and turn to see a big, burly man wearing a Stormbreakers hoodie slide off his stool and lumber towards us.

"You're that rookie kid, aren't you?" he slurs. Brooks angles himself in front of me protectively. I peer around his shoulder. When Brooks doesn't answer him, the man holds out a hand and lets out a wheezy laugh, swaying on his feet. "Just wanted to personally thank you for costing us the Wild Card this year."

My heart sinks as I watch Brooks' shoulders tense and his hands clench. For a second, I think he may slug the guy, but instead, he slowly takes the man's hand and shakes it before letting go.

"We'll get 'em next year," Brooks says flatly, masking any emotion he might be feeling. "Have a good night."

The man returns to his buddies at the bar, launching into a detailed retelling of the play that's haunted Brooks since that game last month. I reach for Brooks' hand once we're outside, holding onto him tightly as we walk back to the car.

Once we're safely inside, I say, "Are you okay?" Brooks doesn't respond. "I'm so sorry about that. That man was an a–" I catch myself. "A jerk. I can't believe he said that to you."

Brooks gives me a quick, forced smile as he starts the engine and pulls on his seatbelt. "He's not the first."

"You're kidding me."

"Stormbreakers fans are very dedicated."

"That's ridiculous! Nobody should be able to talk to you like that."

"They're entitled to it," he says with a smile. "They're out on the field with us, batting and catching balls, right? They're practically on the team. At least, that's what they think."

I study Brooks' profile as he takes us out of downtown Port Angeles and back towards the freeway entrance. If I didn't know his tells from the years we were together, I would think he'd already shrugged the snub from the drunk fan off and forgotten about it. But it's there in the subtle clench of his jaw. The tense way he's gripping the steering wheel. He's going to stew on this one for weeks if I don't try and help him nip it in the bud.

"Hey," I say, leaning over the console. "Let's not let that idiot ruin our night."

Brooks shakes his head in awed disbelief. "There's no way he could. This was the best night I've had in a long time."

"Me, too. Thank you again, for the rollerblades and for dinner."

"You're welcome," he says gently, glancing briefly in my direction.

I've got to keep him talking. Keep him distracted so he doesn't drop into that endless swirling sinkhole of self-doubt and perfectionism that he's trying so hard to get out of.

"So, I just remembered something else about you and me," I say, ignoring the blaring red light in my brain telling me to keep my mouth shut. This is not the time for me to listen to fearful warnings ringing in my mind. Brooks needs reassurance. He needs my boldness.

"Really?" Brooks says, easily matching my flirtatious tone. "What is it?"

I place my elbow on the console between us and rest my chin on my hand. My nose is inches from his cheek, and the scent of his cologne further emboldens me.

"Do you remember," I say in what I consider to be my sexiest voice, moving my lips closer to his ear. "The game we used to play at stoplights?"

Brooks doesn't look at me, but I watch the subtle shift of the edges of his mouth, the tilt of his chin, the deepening of his gaze as he stares out at the road ahead. He's silent for a beat, and I worry that I may have been a little *too* bold in bringing this part of our past up tonight.

I realize that the car is rolling to a stop before I can do anything about it, and within seconds, Brooks has taken one hand off the wheel and turned his face towards mine. We're a breath away from each other, the glare of the stoplight casting the cab of the car in a red glow. I swallow, entirely losing my nerve as his gaze stops at my mouth, and his lips slant into a tilted, confident smile.

"You mean when I used to kiss you at stoplights like this one?" he says, his voice a gravelly rumble in the space between our bodies. He reaches up, and his fingertips graze over my cheekbone, tucking a strand of hair behind my ear.

I see the colors shift in his eyes as the light turns green, and Brooks reluctantly drags his gaze away from mine. I practically slam back into a forward position in my seat, heart pounding against my ribs.

"Yep," Brooks says, and I don't dare look over at him. "I remember."

NINETEEN

Nora

THE FOLLOWING MORNING, MY employees are endlessly curious about my first Friday evening spent with Brooks. Maybe it's the lack of sleep and the fact that I'm partly delirious, but I find myself unable to mask the happiness I'm still carrying. It's spilling over into my walk, my smile.

"Did he kiss you?" Kate asks eagerly as she spins past me, balancing plates loaded with steaming stacks of pancakes and artfully assembled eggs Benedict.

"Don't answer that," Audrey says, hands full of a stack of bills ready to be processed.

"None of your business!" I say, biting back a grin. Brooks didn't kiss me, but I wanted him to. Desperately.

"Tell that to the smile you can't keep off your face," Roman hisses into my ear from behind. I swat at him as he saunters past.

I get lost in the mindless task of stuffing paper napkins into the metal dispensers, which is technically Molly's assignment today, but I decide to be a saint and help the poor thing out. I can see the panic-sweat shine on her pretty pink cheeks from here. The line near the host stand is growing longer and longer and the diners are in no rush, lingering as they do every Saturday morning.

Verl and Sue McConnell stop me on one of my rounds. "That mug I bought from you is my absolute favorite," Sue says emphatically. "I reach for it every day and think of you."

I can't possibly express to her what that means to me, but I try, fighting back the swell of emotion it conjures up to know that she is using something I crafted with such care.

As the morning wears on, my mind easily slips back to thoughts of a sturdy hand clasping mine, laugh lines deepening around striking blue eyes, and a mouth so irresistible it's truly a miracle I didn't claim it for myself last night.

Being with Brooks unlocks something long tucked away in the deepest chamber of my heart, freeing sun-washed memories from another time when he occupied my thoughts as much as I'm allowing him to now. Everything about last night felt...good. So good I want to relive it in my mind all day long.

He'd somehow ignited a flickering desire within me while still making me feel entirely safe and at peace. A bubbling, contagious kind of happy. I shouldn't be surprised, really. Even as a young girl caught up in the fire of her first love, that's how he always made me feel.

"Nora?" Audrey's voice cuts through my musings, and I look up. She's got a suspicious grin on her face. "There's someone here who wants to talk to you."

"If it's Tommy Collins again, tell him I'm busy." I half-duck behind the counter fearfully. "I can't handle him asking me out again, Audrey. I've run out of excuses."

"It's not Tommy. It's somebody else. He's waiting for you in Booth Six."

My heart takes those words and runs ten miles with them.

"Booth Six?" I ask, craning around Audrey to try and get a peek at who Molly must have just sat there. The booth had been occupied for most of the morning.

Audrey gives me a little push out of the prep area. "Go!"

I straighten my apron and tighten my ponytail, weaving through the crowded dining area. The side of Booth Six I can see is unoccupied, so I don't get a full view of its occupant until I'm standing fully in front of it.

An undeniably attractive man wearing a grey hoodie is scanning the menu with his lower lip caught between his teeth. He's clearly trying to hide most of his face from view with a black baseball hat pulled low over his brow, but I'd recognize that mouth anywhere.

"Is there something I can help you with, sir?" I ask. His eyes flick up to meet mine, and the smile that spreads over his face at the sight of me makes my pulse stammer.

"Yeah," Brooks says, pretending to further contemplate the menu. "Can I get a smoothie? Or a protein shake?"

"Hmmm..." I give him a faux grimace. "I'm sorry, sir. I'm afraid you won't find anything here that's not made with butter and excessive calories."

"In that case," he replies, setting down the menu with a sigh. "Ma'am..." His eyes dance. "I'll just take five minutes with you."

"Five minutes?" I counter, placing a hand on my hip. "You sure that's all you want?"

Brooks' eyes do a slow drag down my body and back up to my face before he smiles.

"You know I could never be satisfied with that," he says, and I hope nobody in this restaurant can see the blush burning up the back of my neck right now.

"Here you are," Roman's cheerful voice cuts in behind me, and so does a steaming cup of coffee as he slides it to Brooks across the table. I catch his eye over my shoulder, and he winks at me.

"Join me?" Brooks says, gesturing to the bench across from him.

Roman doesn't wait for me to answer and instead practically shoves me into the seat. "Sit down, honey. Get off your feet for a minute. I'll make sure nobody burns the place down."

"Thank you," Brooks says, raising his coffee in salute towards Roman as he bustles away. "I like him. He makes things happen."

I pull my lips in to hide my smile. My foot bumps against Brooks' under the table as I try to scoot into the far corner and hopefully out of view from any prying eyes.

"He's the one who wrote your number on my box, right?" Brooks asks. I nod. "He's getting a massive tip."

We share a smile.

"You didn't tell me you were coming in today," I say.

"Was I supposed to?" Brooks says, taking a sip of his coffee. "Mmm," he hums appreciatively. "That's good."

"It feels unfair," I continue. "You're always showing up and surprising me, but I never know where to find you."

"Easy fix," Brooks replies, setting down his coffee. "I'll text you my sister's address. Come by anytime. I'm sure they'd love the chance to interrogate both of us at once. Or you could come see me in Seattle sometime. I've got an apartment in the city near the stadium."

The thought of showing up at Brooks' apartment alone makes my insides quiver. No, no. I could not be trusted to be alone with him behind the firmly closed doors of his living quarters.

"You sure you don't want to order some food?" I ask. "I can have Max make you your omelet just the way you like it."

"I just finished a run," Brooks leans forward, resting on his elbows. "I only came here to see you."

Warmth floods through me as he looks me over with a soft affection. I sink further into the corner of the booth, determined not to be seen blushing and fidgeting by anyone in this diner.

"It hasn't even been twenty-four hours," I tease. "Did you miss me that badly?"

"Yeah," Brooks says, his expression open and eyes truthful. "Yeah, I did."

There's that honesty of his that disarms me every time. My brain has officially short-circuited. There will be no more taking orders or remembering requests for the remainder of the business day today. Or tomorrow, for that matter.

"I wanted to get my daily dose of Nora this morning. Thought it would help me stay on track."

"What's this about a daily dose? I thought we were casually hanging out for a few Friday nights?"

"Tell me," he says, adjusting the brim of his baseball hat. "Did you think about me after I dropped you off last night?"

I swallow. Did I *think* about Brooks? That would be the understatement of the century. I tossed and turned in my bed like a fish flopping on a deck. I was wired after the night we spent together. It hadn't been long enough.

"Maybe," I reply coyly.

"Then tell me you're not glad to see me."

"I *am* glad to see you."

"Then, I would think our standing Friday dates can continue, but if we both are on the same page, we can see each other as much as we want."

"Here we go," Roman's voice cuts through the tension between us, and I sit up, not realizing I'd been leaning across the booth towards Brooks like he's a magnet. Roman slides a plate of French toast onto the middle of the table. "Eat up, sweetheart. I haven't seen you eat anything all day, and I know how you get on an empty stomach." Roman grimaces at Brooks to convey just how awful I get when I'm hungry before dancing away.

"Have some of this, please?" I beg Brooks. "There's no way I can eat it all."

"I'm not sure *anyone* could eat all of that food. Who set the portion sizes at this place? This is obscene." He reluctantly takes my proffered fork and knife.

I watch Brooks fork a bite of French toast into his mouth, waiting to gauge his reaction.

"That is sinful," he says, shaking his head.

"I thought you would like it," I say, feeling pleased as he goes in for more. "But what will your trainer say?"

"Forget my trainer. Where you at, girl? Help me out."

I dig into a piece of fluffy, syrup-soaked bread with my fork. A few short minutes later, our plate is practically licked clean.

"Hope you have nothing planned this afternoon. Get ready to hibernate," I say.

Brooks eyes me from across the booth. "What are *your* plans for the rest of the day?"

"Grocery shopping. Cleaning my house. Then, my sister Sydney is coming over tonight to paint one of my bathrooms."

"You guys need help?"

"It's a small bathroom," I say, not really answering his question.

"Then, it wouldn't take very long to paint it." He pushes his plate away and crosses his arms over the table. "I could help."

"That's very kind of you," I say. "But Sydney is using some new technique she saw on the internet and wants to test it out in my house first before she does it in one of the cabins. I don't think I'll be helping her much at all."

"Well, in the future, I'd be happy to help you with things like that. Put me to work," he says, disarming me with another smile. I most definitely will. The thought of Brooks working on my house is so tempting that I may just go home and break something, just so he can come fix it.

"Did you have anything planned for tonight?" I ask.

"Well, not tonight," he says. "But apparently, my dad is back in town. He invited my sisters and me over for dinner tomorrow."

"Oh," I say. "I'm guessing you don't want to be there?"

"No. I don't." The honesty in his voice makes my chest ache. There's so much hurt hidden there.

"Then don't go," I say with a shrug. "I'm sure the twins would understand."

"It would be easier to provide an excuse if someone, say, you, perhaps, were free tomorrow night. Then, I could tell my sisters that we already had plans."

"Are you trying to use me to avoid seeing your father?" I tease.

"No, not at all. I'm trying to find any excuse I can to spend more time with you."

First, he shows up at the diner, brightening my whole day. Then, he offers to help me paint my bathroom. Now, he tops it off with a comment like *that*?

I think my list of favorite things now only consists of one thing...Brooks Alden.

"Well, tomorrow is Sunday," I say. "I have to go pick up Ollie from his dad's."

Brooks rolls his lips together, and his eyes darken at my mention of Nate. "Right. I'm so sorry, I wasn't thinking..."

"But," I hear myself saying, and my hand makes a hesitant path across the table to land on Brooks' arm. "If you wanted to come with me to pick him up, I'd be fine with that."

Something shifts in Brooks' expression, and his eyes take on a determined cast. He layers one of his warm, strong hands over mine, and his fingertips dance over my knuckles.

"They live half an hour away in Carleton Point."

"I can come pick you up, and we can go together," he says.

The idea of having Brooks by my side when having to face my ex-husband is relieving. Nate and I really don't speak much, except on the days when he has Ollie. Our custody agreement stipulates that he sends me updates on

204

how Ollie's doing so I don't worry too much about him. I never anticipated that Nate and Brooks would ever come in contact with each other again, and I'm not entirely sure how either of them might behave. Nate was something of a fan of Brooks...but I doubt he'll see him that way once he finds out about us.

"I'd like that," I say, and Brooks squeezes my hand in his reassuringly.

"Nora?" A gruff voice asks from above. I turn to find Tommy Collins staring down at me from his impressive, lanky height. My grip on Brooks' hand tightens, and he looks at me curiously.

"Oh," I say, feeling flustered at being caught sitting with Brooks by the ever-persistent, blindly oblivious Tommy. "Hi, Tommy. You remember Brooks Alden, right?" We'd all gone to high school together, but Tommy was in the grade above us. I glance over at Brooks to find him watching me with an amused smile.

"What's up, Tommy?" Brooks says, and though his tone is light, I detect the slightest hint at unfriendliness. "Long time no see."

"Yeah," Tommy stammers, rubbing one hand behind his neck. "Yeah, it's been a long time." Tommy looks down at our joined hands, and I know I've got to use this to get Tommy off my back. For good.

"So are you two...uh..." Tommy gestures between us. "Are you two dating?" I shoot a panicky glance at Brooks, not wanting to mislabel our relationship in front of someone else. Tommy gives me a hurt look like it was my job to personally update him on such things.

"Yep," I say quickly, and Brooks arches one eyebrow, questioning. "We're dating." I widen my eyes at him to non-verbally tell him to roll with it, and he smiles, lifting his chin in understanding. Tommy is not going to take this news well, but it needs to be conveyed. "It's a recent thing," I continue.

"Very recent," Brooks says with an amused quirk of one eyebrow. "So, help me out here, Nora. If we're dating that would make us...what, exactly?"

One side of his mouth slips up in a cheeky grin that makes my belly swoop. He's playing along while simultaneously setting me up to define our relationship.

"We are..." I say slowly, trying to keep from laughing. "A...couple?"

"We're a couple," Brooks repeats, looking highly pleased at my answer.

"You're a couple," Tommy repeats dejectedly, looking like he may actually shed tears at the receipt of this depressing news.

"Yes. We are," I say brightly, hoping Tommy will get the message.

"Thanks for stopping by," Brooks says, a slight edge to his words that makes it very clear that I am off-limits. Tommy is harmless, but I love how easily Brooks claimed me as his own.

Tommy swipes a finger under his nose, glancing away. "This is a blow to the ego, I admit," he says with a bitter laugh. "But I can't compete with...with..." He waves a loose hand at Brooks and then sighs in defeat. "Can I get a picture with you?"

"Sure," Brooks says, shooting me a look that says he's highly entertained by all this. He waits patiently while Tommy fumbles for his phone, which is appropriately encased in a Stormbreakers logo pattern.

Tommy leans awkwardly over Brooks' side of the booth, and I snap a picture of the two of them.

"Good luck..." he says as I hand him his phone back. He gives me a lingering, dejected glance. "To the both of you."

Brooks doesn't let go of my hand, even after Tommy is well out of sight.

"Thank you," I breathe a sigh of relief. "He might actually leave me alone now."

"He'd better leave you alone," Brooks says, a flash of possessiveness in his eyes. "Because according to you, we're a couple now."

"You forced that out of me!"

"No, I didn't," Brooks says with a satisfied smirk. "You defined our relationship as exactly what you want it to be."

"Brooks–"

"Don't worry," he says, leaning across the table towards me. "I won't tell anyone."

"But Tommy will!" I whisper-yell. "Everyone's going to think that you're my..."

"Your what?" he says, lifting his chin, daring me to continue.

"Stop it!"

"Your boy toy? Your friend with *benefits?*"

"You'd better keep your voice down!"

He lifts a hand and drags his thumb across my cheekbone and down my jawline. I swear I forget how to breathe as he says, "I'll be whatever you need me to be, Nora."

TWENTY

Brooks

WHEN MY SISTERS HEAD to dinner at my dad's on Sunday night, I'm relieved to drive in the opposite direction toward Nora's place instead. She lives a few blocks away from the house I grew up in, down the street from Kitt's Harbor Elementary, where Claire teaches. The houses look relatively new on her street, a series of cohesive bungalows all featuring low-pitched roofs and wide, open front porches. The trees are shorter in this part of town and the landscaping still looks fresh. Nora's house is a greyish green with white trim and a deep blue door. It almost looks like it belongs beachside down by the harbor.

Before I can get out of the car to knock on her door, Nora comes bounding down the front porch steps. She smiles and gives me a little wave, and I can't tear my eyes away from her.

She's wearing my hat.

But it's not the hat I gave her at the Harvest Market. It's a faded blue hat with an old yellow Stormbreakers logo...the one I gave her in high school.

I come to my senses just as she's rounding the front of my car and quickly hop out to intercept her. My fingers circle one of her wrists, and I yank her gently towards me.

"Slow down, girl," I say, holding her at arm's length so I can get a good look at her. Her brown eyes sparkle as I drag my gaze down her body, taking in her crewneck sweatshirt, jeans, and high-top sneakers before flicking back up to that dang hat. "Where do you think you're going?"

"Hi to you, too," she says with a timid smile that I return easily.

"Nice hat." I can't believe she still has it.

"Thought you might like it."

I do. I like it way too much. Someone needs to remove her from my presence immediately before I do something wild like yank her towards me and kiss her like my life depends on it. But I don't want to rush her into it. I've got to wait until the right moment, even if it kills me.

I reluctantly release her before opening the passenger-side door of her car. She thought it would be easiest for me to drive her car, since Ollie's car seat is already secured in the back seat. It's smaller than mine, and I feel like a giant trying to clamber into the driver's seat.

"Okay, shortie," I say, my knees nearly hitting my chin. I have to move the seat back about a foot before my long legs can comfortably reach Nora's pedals. She laughs at me as the seat slowly edges backwards.

I take a long moment to check her out again as she's buckling her seatbelt. I'd like nothing more than to tangle my fingers into her hair and make out with her right here in her driveway.

"The neighbors are watching," Nora says, quickly glancing up at me before staring straight ahead out the windshield with what can only be her attempt at a poker face. She's failing. I see that smile tugging at the edges of her mouth.

"What?"

"The neighbors," Nora repeats, gesturing nervously out the car window. "They're watching us."

I glance outside, and sure enough, her next-door neighbor is out front with her kids. She gives me a small wave which I awkwardly return.

"That's Brynn. She runs the daycare Ollie goes to out of her house. She was at the workshop, remember?"

"That's right," I say, putting the car in reverse to back out of the driveway. "And we care about her seeing us together because...?"

"You clearly don't know how much moms like to talk." She sighs. "There are a few moms in the neighborhood who are big fans of yours. I don't want any of them near you."

I like the competitive edge in her voice.

"The only mom I'm interested in," I say, glancing her way, "is you. You've got nothing to worry about. Especially after that little stunt you pulled with Tommy yesterday."

"Thank you for going along with me," she says, sounding relieved. "He's harmless but so determined."

"He'd better stay away from you. You let me know if he doesn't," I say. "And in my defense, I can't be expected to play it cool when a beautiful girl walks up wearing my hat." I catch her smiling behind her hand as she turns to look out her window. "You'd better hope we don't hit any red lights."

The look she gives me then is priceless. A curious mixture of fear and desire that makes my blood hum.

She types an address into the maps app on my phone, and I follow the directions to the highway. "Carleton Point, right?"

"Yeah," Nora says, pulling the sleeves of her sweatshirt down over her hands. "That's where Nate's new wife is from. I'm glad they live far away, honestly. I never have to worry about running into them."

Nora turns to stare out the window, no doubt lost in her thoughts.

"Hey," I say, reaching over and laying a hand on her thigh. Her eyes dart down to my hand on her leg before they bounce up again to meet mine. "I'm here for you. I know this can't be easy."

She sighs. "It's so hard. Every time I have to hand Ollie over to them it breaks my heart." She gives me a little sad smile that makes me want to buy her a puppy or take her to Disneyland just to cheer her up. "You'd think I'd be used to it by now."

"How could anyone get used to seeing their ex with the person who tore their marriage apart? It's messed up."

"It's not just that. It's knowing that she's Ollie's stepmom. His *other* mom. Feeling like I have to compete with her as a mother, too, is so hard. I already lost my husband to her. Now I feel like I'm losing my son to her, too, just because I have to share him. I don't want to share Ollie," Nora says, and there's anger simmering beneath her words. "They don't deserve him."

"They don't," I agree. "So, why do they get to have him?"

She sighs, resting her head back on the headrest. "Because I allowed them to. I was very accommodating and as kind as I could be during the divorce proceedings. I was so pregnant and tired, and ready to just be done with it all."

I give her leg a little squeeze, which seems to make Nora remember that my hand is there. She flips my palm upward with gentle hands and starts tracing her thumbs along the lines of my palm.

"You seem worried," I say. "Why don't you tell me what's on your mind?"

"You sure? You might get a little more than you bargained for."

"Lay it on me. I don't mind."

I stay silent, feeling the tender press of her fingers into the knots of my palm as she gently works them out.

"I'm worried about Ollie. I worry that one day Ollie will want to be with *them* more than he'll want to be with me because they have a nicer house, and they buy him cool toys all the time. I worry that they'll outshine me and push me out of my son's life."

A drop lands in the center of my palm, and I realize Nora's crying. My own throat knots as I glance over and see her, head bowed, dripping tears onto my open hand.

"Ollie loves you," I say. "You're his mother. There's a bond there, a real relationship that will last far longer than any cool toy will."

"I hope so," Nora says, and I close my hand around hers and thread our fingers together.

"Just so you know," I say firmly. "After you told me what Nate did..." Anger is burning in my chest, and I swallow to keep it down. "I was so upset and angry. It makes absolutely no sense. You're amazing, Nora."

She sniffs, swiping at her eyes with her free hand. "It was the biggest blow to my confidence when I found out he was cheating on me. I still struggle with feeling like I'm never going to be enough for anybody ever again because clearly..." She lets out a bitter laugh. "I was not enough for him." She glances over at me. "I always wondered if maybe I wasn't enough for you either. If I had been, maybe you would have stayed."

My grip on her hand tightens, and I have to focus on the road for a moment to let my thoughts settle before I speak.

"It breaks my heart that you feel that way, Nora," I say softly, meeting her gaze briefly before looking back out the windshield. "I was an idiot to let you go in the first place. But I'd like to think that if we'd stayed together, we would have still been together now. Unlike Nate, who made the choice to break his promises to you and throw away his family. He's something else," I sigh. "I could never take you for granted the way Nate did. You might have to hold me back when I see him because I'd love to just..." I slap a palm on the steering wheel. "Deck him right in his nose."

Nora laughs. "Wouldn't that be a sight."

"Don't test me," I growl. "I might just do it."

"I can't say I wouldn't like to see you give him the ol' Alden throwing arm right to the face."

"Worst-case scenario, I've got a bat in the trunk," I say, and we both laugh. Nora leans over the console to rest her head on my shoulder. I haven't seen Nate since we were buddies in high school, but whatever respect I had for him before is long gone. I don't think Nora's bringing me along so I can teach Nate a lesson, but I wish I could.

"What Nate chose," I say, loving the weight of her head on the curve of my shoulder, "is a cheap imitation of the real thing. It won't last. It can't. It's not built on trust and honesty and fidelity like real love is. And you, Nora..." I wait until she lifts her head to meet my gaze before continuing. "You deserve the real thing."

Her eyes are still watery from her honesty earlier, and I watch as she blinks more tears away before resting her head against me again. "I know."

Nate Elliot steps out of his Range Rover at the park where he and Nora usually meet, looking like he's aged twenty years since I last saw him. The man has shoulder-length dark hair and an unnaturally muscular frame. He was never a big dude back in the day, but for him to be this jacked? Steroids are the only explanation.

Nora told me I could wait in the car, but there's no way I'm about to sit here and let her converse with this poor excuse for a man all by herself. I get out of the car while Nora's busy unbuckling Ollie from the car seat in the back of Nate's SUV.

"He said he wasn't hungry. Heidi made him a nice lunch, and he wouldn't even touch it," Nate is in the middle of saying, his back to me, one hand on his hip while he lets Nora do all the work of getting their son out of his vehicle. I allow the car door to shut loudly behind me, causing Nate to glance back at me over his shoulder.

The double take happens in slow motion. There's even a terribly unflattering open-mouthed gawking that immediately follows. His reaction is a thing of beauty.

"Brooks?" Nate asks incredulously, turning fully to face me.

He reaches out a veiny hand for me to shake. There's no way in hell I'm about to take it.

"Nate," I say darkly, crossing my arms over my chest in clear dismissal of his gesture.

Nora lifts Ollie out of his car seat, and he immediately throws his arms around her neck.

"Mama! I miss you!" he growls through clenched teeth. He's squeezing her as hard as he can, and she's got her eyes closed, holding him equally as tightly and whispering in his ear.

When Nora finally turns and sees me facing off with her ex-husband, she gives me a censuring look. It might have been more effective if she wasn't wearing my hat and holding a cute kid. Better luck next time, sweetheart.

I continue to stare Nate down. He glances at Nora then gestures towards me with an insincere smile that reveals his perfectly cut, blindingly white teeth. The man for sure has veneers, too. His new wife clearly influenced him to change nearly everything about his appearance. What a winner.

"What is this?" Nate asks, gesturing between me and Nora.

"What is what?" Nora replies coolly.

"What's going on with you guys?" Nate asks. "Did you win a day with a Stormbreakers player, or something?" He lets out a little awkward laugh.

No one joins him.

"We're together," I say flatly, and Nate's mouth drops open in surprise.

"You...and...and...Nora?" he stammers. Like what I've just suggested is impossible.

"You'll probably be seeing a lot more of me," I say with what I hope is an intimidating smile that conveys the message that he'd better not do anything to mess with my girl. Or Ollie.

"Really?" Nate says, suddenly looking angry. "Well, if that's the case, and you're going to be involved in any capacity with my son, I have the right to know about it."

"*Our* son," Nora says curtly. "And no. You don't. You forfeited any right to knowledge of my relationships when we signed the divorce papers, Nate. We're not doing this right now. Not in front of Ollie."

"If I'd known he was going to be here..." Nate says, looking flustered.

You what, Nate? Go ahead and finish that sentence.

"Have you just been waiting for this?" Nate says, taking a step towards me. "To cut in as soon as Nora was available again?"

My fists clench at my side. "You mean, was I waiting for you to screw things up so I could see Nora again? Maybe. You did a great job of making that happen for us."

Nate scowls, a vein in his thick neck popping. What can he say? Ollie must sense the tension between me and his dad because he launches himself out of Nora's arms towards me. I'm surprised by his sudden lurch in my direction, but hey, I'm used to catching airborne objects. I catch him before he falls and toss him up in the air.

"Hey, little dude!" I say as I set him down on his little feet. "I like your shoes, bro. You've got good style."

"I like your shoes, dude," he echoes enthusiastically, giving me knuckles.

"Maybe we should trade, then," I suggest. "You give me yours, and I give you mine."

Ollie squints up at me, grinning. "No!" he insists. "Mine are too small."

"Are you sure?" I squat down at his level. "Let me try them on."

Ollie starts edging away, and I pretend I'm going to snatch his shoes right off his feet.

"What is your intention with Nora?" Nate cuts in, his voice sharp and demanding. Too bad it cracks like a pubescent halfway through Nora's name. Who is he to ask me a question like that? He swooped in and claimed Nora after I left Kitt's Harbor, which was reason enough to hate him, but then he broke her heart. I slowly rise from my crouched position and face Nate, watching one of his eyes twitch as I rise to my full height.

"What is my intention with Nora?" I say slowly, cocking my head to one side as if contemplating his question. "You know, I'm not sure that's something I could discuss in detail with little ears listening in." I give Ollie a little pat on the head.

The tips of Nate's ears turn red, and Nora purses her lips, trying not to laugh. Ollie starts jumping up and down, reaching for me. I gather him up easily.

"But if I had to answer your question," I say, lifting Ollie up onto my shoulders. "I'd say my intention is to take care of these two. In whatever capacity they need me to."

Like you failed to do. The message is unspoken but rings out loud and clear.

"Let me get Ollie's bags for you, Nora," Nate says tersely. Finally, the useless man is stepping in to help.

Nora arches an eyebrow at me, and I give her my best innocent face, mouthing the word, *what*?

While Nate's got his backside sticking out of his car, huffing and puffing trying to wrestle the bags out, I take off with Ollie bouncing up and down on my shoulders. His little hands are clamped around my neck so tight, but the sound of his laughter ringing through the park makes it worth it. We trot around for a minute while Nate puts Ollie's things into the backseat of Nora's car.

Nate peels out of the parking lot without saying goodbye to Ollie, looking back at me out his window with his designer sunglasses on.

"I'm sorry about him," Nora says with a tired sigh as we begin the drive back to her house. "He was not very kind to you. Not that I expected him to be."

"Well, I wasn't exactly a peach, either," I say. "But now that I've experienced the full magnitude of his idiocy, you're not going anywhere near him unless I'm there, too. I'll try to be more civil next time."

I'd been partially dreading an encounter with Nate, wondering how things would play out when he learned that I was back in Nora's life again. He may not be happy about it, but Nora was right. He forfeited his right to Nora's choices when he chose to be unfaithful to her. His involvement with Ollie appears to be pretty surface-level, and it makes me wonder if he would be open to changes in their custody agreement that would allow Nora to have Ollie more often.

If he genuinely wants to keep Ollie every other weekend, I could handle that if Nora chooses to keep me around. We would never be friends and I could never respect him again, but I could be the bigger person and be civil in our future interactions for Nora and Ollie's sake.

Nora gets a sly smile on her face and leans across the console. She slips her arm through mine and tips her chin up.

"Thank you for sticking up for me," she says, her breath tickling my ear. "I really appreciated that."

"You're welcome," I reply in an equally low tone.

"It was...very attractive," she says, and her soft lips brush against my earlobe in the most tantalizing way.

There better not be any red lights on this drive home, or Ollie's gonna get a front-row seat to a showing of *Brooks Alden Kisses Nora Foster with the Passion of a Thousand Fiery Suns*. Sure to be a box office smash.

I glance back at him in the rearview mirror and can't help but smile. I knew I was attracted to Nora, but there's something deeper, a sense of warm belonging, growing within me every time I'm with her. I didn't realize what I was missing until now. The thing that Jonah has that keeps him grounded and keeps the ups and downs, the inevitable wins and losses of a career in baseball in perspective.

Family. One of my own.

TWENTY-ONE
Nora

WE STOP AT A drive-through to grab tacos for dinner before Brooks takes us back to my house. He then gets Ollie out of his car seat, unprompted, and follows him into the backyard while I gather up Ollie's things and our food from the car. A peculiar sensation wriggles through me as I watch them play together from the window over my kitchen sink. There's an effortlessness to having Brooks around that I'm both intrigued by and terrified of. It feels so easy. He fits right in with us like he was always meant to be a part of our story.

Past experience has taught me that when it comes to men, things can change on a dime. I'm hesitant to lean into the joy of these moments with Brooks, afraid they're going to haunt me later when he leaves. What if he forgets about us once he's busy playing baseball again? I'm already certain he's going to be hard to say goodbye to, even after the short amount of time we've spent together. I don't want to let him go, and I'm not sure what to do with that knowledge.

I bring the food out back along with a blanket given to me by Trent's grandmother, Fran, on Ollie's first birthday. It's overcast and cool tonight with dark clouds gathering overhead, but there's no sign of rain yet. Brooks is seated cross-legged inside Ollie's sandbox, digging him a massive trench with a tiny, pink plastic shovel.

"Is this deep enough?" he asks Ollie before smiling over at me. Ollie leans over to inspect Brooks' work and deems it to be satisfactory, so Brooks continues.

"Your food is going to get cold," I call out. "Come eat!"

It takes me another five minutes to persuade Ollie to break away from his construction project to eat his dinner. After they wash their hands inside, Brooks sprawls out on the blanket beside me, one muscled arm angled behind his head, with his face upturned towards the cloudy sky. He closes his eyes briefly, and I admire his strong jaw and the firm line of his lips. He pops one eye open and grins at me before rolling onto his side. My mouth is a mirror of his. Every time he smiles, my mouth involuntarily curls up in response.

"So, tell me about these tacos," Brooks says, reaching for his takeout box.

"They're Ollie's favorite. Right, Ollie?"

"I like chips," Ollie says, salsa dripping down his chin. "You like chips, Big Dude?"

"Big Dude?" I laugh.

"He's Little Dude, and I'm Big Dude," Brooks explains. "And I love chips, too. Can I try some of yours?"

"Sure!" Ollie exclaims, picking up his bag of chips and plopping himself down practically on Brooks' lap. The two of them demolish the chips before I'm even able to try one.

"Thanks for saving some for me, guys," I tease. They look at each other guiltily, and Ollie giggles.

It's hard to not feel happy as we eat together, sharing food and laughing at Ollie's silly antics. He's glad to be home with me. I can tell.

Brooks doesn't seem in any rush to leave, and I'm not eager for him to go either. We're unbothered by the chill in the air that turns the tips of our noses and cheeks red. Even as the sky begins to darken, we work to finish crafting a sandcastle, complete with a surrounding moat. It's only when I see Ollie yawning that I take him inside to give him a bath and put him to bed.

"Say goodnight to Brooks," I prompt, and Ollie surprises me by rushing over and clinging to Brooks' leg.

"Night, Big Dude," he says. Brooks palms Ollie's hair, glancing up at me with a crooked smile. My heart splits at the sight.

"Night, Little Dude. Sweet dreams."

"I'll be right back down," I say to Brooks as I usher Ollie upstairs. It doesn't strike me until Ollie's sloshing around in the bath that I left Brooks alone and completely unattended. He's got free reign of the downstairs level of my house right now. I hope he's not snooping through my drawers or inspecting anything too closely. Suddenly I'm racking my brain, trying to remember where I put that Brookie wrapper from the Stormbreakers game. Hopefully, nowhere Brooks will see it.

"Big Dude read a story?" Ollie asks hopefully as we settle into the rocking chair in his room with a stack of books.

"Oh, honey," I say. "He's downstairs."

"I go get him!"

"No, it's okay..." But before I can stop him, Ollie is tearing out of his room and yelling for 'Brookie' to come upstairs to read him a book.

"You don't have to," I say as Brooks appears on the upstairs landing, his hand clasped in Ollie's.

"I'd love to," Brooks says without the slightest hint of hesitation, and *hello*. If that isn't the most attractive thing I've ever heard in my life. His fingertips graze my elbow as he passes me in the doorway to Ollie's room. "If you're okay with it."

I stand there nervously, watching Ollie instruct Brooks to sit in the rocking chair before climbing onto his lap. He's completely comfortable around Brooks and his easy trust in him makes me feel a hesitant sense of relief. I want to trust him as easily and completely as my son does. I fight back feelings of worry that Ollie is getting too attached to Brooks too soon. But how could I possibly try to stop Ollie from being his loving, pure-hearted self?

"Now, I should warn you," Brooks says, glancing up at me with a grimace. "It's been a long time since Big Dude has read a book."

"I want *Little Blue Truck*," Ollie says, sliding a book out from the stack.

"Excellent," Brooks says, shifting Ollie on his legs so he can hold the book out in front of him. "This one came highly recommended, am I right?"

I nod, leaning against the doorframe as Brooks begins to read.

Who knew that a story of a little blue truck and his farmyard friends could sound so entirely different when read aloud by the right man? Watching Brooks gently hold my son while reading him a bedtime story is enthralling. My heart thumps against my ribs as layers of fear I've carried for so long begin to dissipate.

I'm worthy of a love like this.

I've always known that Brooks was a good man. It's there in the lift of his smile and the warmth of his gaze as he glances up at me over the pages of the book. I'm reminded of our conversation in the car last night. Brooks apologized for letting me go, and he's proving in his actions that he realizes the gravity of his mistake.

I want to believe him. I want to believe that he wants me just as badly now as he did before his dad interfered. I want to let him in. Maybe it's my turn to show him that I'm willing to completely set the heartbreak we both experienced in our past aside and take a step into the dark with him. If Brooks doesn't try to kiss me tonight, then I'm going to have to kiss him myself.

Ollie wheedles two more books out of Brooks before I intervene and insist that it's time for him to go to bed.

"Love you, my boy," I say from the doorway. "Goodnight!"

He comes out three more times before finally staying in his room and falling asleep. I take a deep breath at the top of the stairs, blinking up at the ceiling and willing myself to find calm before I face Brooks again. *I'm safe. I can trust him. I need to show him that I'm willing to try.*

I find him in the semi-darkness of my studio downstairs, hands clasped behind his back, admiring my shelf of completed and partially-finished ceramics.

"You made all of these?" he asks when he hears me enter. I nod. "Amazing."

"This is where I usually end up after Ollie goes to bed," I say, joining him at the shelf and feeling a fresh wash of nerves at his sudden nearness. We've been together all evening, but there's been an anticipation growing within me that is reaching its peak now that we're alone. In the dark. In my studio.

"This is your space," he says, hands still clasped behind his back. I wish he'd let them swing free so I can slide my hand into one of his again. I like feeling the scrape of his calloused palms against mine. The strength of his hands and length of his fingers.

"Yes," I say softly. "I come in here, light a few candles, and sit at the wheel for as long as it takes for the stress of the day to melt away."

"Sounds relaxing. Could we do it together?"

"You want to?" I ask, surprised. We hadn't talked about any additional plans for tonight.

"Why not? I need a re-do after my first attempt."

"Oh!" I gasp, reaching up to pull down his soup mug he made at my workshop. "I forgot! I meant to give this to you last night."

He takes the finished mug from my hands, and our fingers barely brush in the exchange. "Wait a second," he says, twisting the mug in the air to inspect it from all angles. "Did you tamper with this, Nora?"

"Why do you ask?"

"Because it looks way better than I remember."

"I may have trimmed it up a bit before firing it," I admit.

"I knew it." He sets it aside with a laugh. "Could you teach me how to use the wheel?" he asks. "This could count towards trying something new, right?"

"It's not even Friday!"

"If I wasn't here, is this how you'd be spending your night?"

"Probably."

"Then don't let me ruin your plans. Show me what to do, and I'll do it."

Listen here, Nora, I tell myself. *Do not read into that statement.*

Fifteen minutes later, candles have been lit, music is softly playing from my phone (I don't own a proper speaker), and Brooks is seated at a stool in front of my wheel, looking up at me expectantly. He's wearing one of my aprons, and I think it's his best look yet.

He's set up with a nice piece of clay that I had already wedged last night. I pull up an adjacent stool and explain the basics of throwing clay at the wheel.

"The pedal is here," I say, gesturing so Brooks can locate it with his foot. "The harder you press down, the faster the wheel will spin."

He tries it a few times and nods. I gather my materials and show him how to use a wet sponge and his fingertips to gently guide the clay into the beginnings of a shape.

"Do you know what you'd like to make?" I ask, trying not to be entirely distracted by the press of his shoulder against mine and the length of his strong legs on either side of the wheel.

"Maybe a bowl?" he suggests.

"Great," I say, encouraging him to start spinning the wheel. Our work is slow, and Brooks is deeply focused on getting it right.

"My therapist says I try too hard to be perfect," he says after pressing too hard and causing his clay to become uneven.

I reach over to help correct his error. The smell rising off his skin where his shirt falls open at the neck is delectable.

Brooks leans back and presses down on the pedal, allowing me to lift the wonky side of the bowl to an even height once again. "You can't worry about getting things perfect here at the wheel. That's the nature of making something with your hands. It's going to have imperfections and flaws, but that's what gives it character. That's what makes it unique."

Brooks continues to shape the bowl, stopping so I can make minor corrections and guide the shape into what he wants it to be.

"This is relaxing," he says softly. "I get why you enjoy it so much."

I sit back, watching the hunch of his wide shoulders and the curve of his profile, the length of his arms and the subtle movements of his strong hands as he molds the clay. There's something terribly intimate about watching him work here in this quiet, candle-lit space of mine. Another piece of my armor burns away as he shifts on his stool, taking up the space beside me that had felt so achingly empty for so long. Brooks's presence is so beautifully unexpected and deeply welcomed. I swallow down a gathering knot of emotion in my throat.

Eventually, he declares it finished and glances over at me for approval.

"Beautiful," I say. I help him remove the bat from the wheel and use a stretch of wire to free the bowl. He follows behind me, helpfully following my instructions in an almost-perfect silence. It's like a hazy golden spell has been cast over this moment and neither of us want to break it by speaking too loudly or by saying too much.

I'm struck by the powerful awareness I have of everything he does. My brain registers every subtle movement he makes, his hovering closeness and every lingering glance we share as we clean up. He washes his hands first, and I follow. I'm washing my hands in the sink, pumping foamy soap onto my palms when I feel him draw in behind me. My heart is thundering now, my breathing growing shallow. I turn off the water and wipe my shaking hands on my apron, not daring to meet Brooks' eyes in the darkness.

He stays there, inches behind me, waiting for me to turn around. When I don't immediately move, he lays the pads of his fingertips on my arm and guides me around to face him. I slowly lift my eyes, intending to meet his, but instead, my gaze finds his mouth, which is drawn into the slightest shadow of a frown.

"Nora," Brooks says, and his breath dusts over my face. He angles his head, looking over me in concern, and his big hands land firmly on my hips. "I don't want to rush you."

My whole body is humming when I finally raise my eyes to meet his. His face is half-lit in the dim glow of the candles burning, but the intensity of his blue gaze lands somewhere deep in my belly. I slowly trace my hands up his forearms and find a gentle grip on his biceps. His hands flex in response, his grip on my hips tightening.

Brooks ducks his head, the tip of his nose nudging mine. My lips part in anticipation, and my eyes gently fall closed. He draws me closer by my hips with a confidence that makes my heart pump even faster. My hands explore the curve of his taut shoulders before joining behind his neck.

"I want to kiss you," he breathes against my mouth. "I've wanted to kiss you all day. Ever since you walked out wearing this hat." He reaches up and slides the hat off my head, gently setting it on the side of the sink behind me. My eyes flicker open, and he gently glides his fingers into my hair, brushing it away from my neck.

"I'm not a very patient man, but if you're not ready for this, I can wait."

"I don't want to wait," I breathe. "After you left, I waited for you. I thought maybe you'd miss me enough to change your mind. I wanted you to come back for me."

"I should have," he murmurs, and a shiver lances through my spine at the look in his eyes. I've seen it before, but it's tinged with a masculine strength and confidence that Brooks didn't have when he'd kissed me all those years ago. "But I'm here now. Can I kiss you?"

I dip my chin in the slightest nod, and the corners of Brooks' mouth turn up in a relieved smile. His eyes are assessing, discerning. My heart is in my throat as he tilts my head up and catches my mouth with his.

His lips take mine in the sweetest, most gently assuring kiss, his hands holding me securely against him. I breathe him in, remembering this. The warmth of his mouth and the grip of his hands. Feeling the safe encircling of his body around mine. He kisses me again, and I melt into him as he brings both of his hands up to securely frame my face. The strength in his hands unravels me further, and I grip his wrists tightly on either side of my head, wanting more. Needing more.

Brooks tugs at my bottom lip with his teeth, parting my lips so he can deepen the kiss. I taste him, and candlelight shimmers behind my eyes. His kiss is heady, laced with shared memories. I drop one hand where I can feel his warm pulse flickering under the skin of his broad chest. He takes his time with me, as if he's ensuring that I'm satisfied by every press of his mouth on mine, every caress of his hands. This kiss is as much for me as it is for him.

I'm dazed and weak when his lips drift from mine to press into my cheekbone. My jawline. My forehead. I circle my hands around his torso and lay my head against his chest, never wanting to move. Never wanting to be released from this safe haven he's provided for me tonight. We linger there, and I let him hold me. I haven't been held in so long, and being firmly locked in his arms is nothing short of healing.

Time bends while I'm in his arms, and before I know it, he's bidding me goodnight with a gentle kiss on my forehead. "I'd better go," he says, and I want to beg him to stay, but I know he's right.

"See you next Friday," he says, smiling up at me from the bottom porch step. As I watch him duck into his car and drive away, I still feel the press of his mouth on mine and the warmth of his hands on me. A truth strikes my bones with a surprising clarity.

I could easily, readily love Brooks Alden again.

TWENTY-TWO
Brooks

"WHAT ARE YOU SMILING at, Brookie?" Miles asks, nudging me with his shoulder as he passes. We're lifting at the gym, which has become a daily ritual for all of us so we don't lose our conditioning. I'm supposed to be spotting Beau, but Nora had texted me and I couldn't wait any longer to read it.

"Wouldn't you like to know," I say, quickly returning my phone to the pocket of my shorts.

"We would, actually," Beau says, replacing the bar on the rack and clapping his hands together as he sits up. "You're up."

I load up my weights and lay down on the bench. Jonah, Miles and Beau hover annoyingly around me.

"What's her name?" Miles asks with a quirked grin.

"Does she have a sister?" Beau asks.

"Is she marriage material?" Jonah points to each of us in turn. "That's the only question that really matters, gentlemen."

I puff out a painful laugh and focus on completing my set. But the boys continue to speculate above me, lounging around instead of continuing their workout.

"I'll bet he's got a hometown honey he's been secretly seeing," Miles says in a loud whisper. "That's the only explanation for it."

"Explanation for what?" I say in a strained voice, exhaling to press the heavy load once more.

"Your transformation," Beau says, drawing out the word obnoxiously.

"Y'all are cracked," I mutter. But they keep it up until I've finished my set and have set the bar back down.

"We're going to find out sooner or later, Brookie boy," Beau says with a click of his tongue. "Might as well set the record straight. How hot is she, on a scale of one to ten?"

Now, I'm not a shallow man. But after kissing Nora last weekend, I think she may just have shattered the scale.

"Off the charts," I finally say, smiling to myself as I take a drink from my water bottle.

"Come on, man!" Miles says, slapping me on the back. "Be a homie and show us a photo!"

"I ask again..." Beau says. "Does she have a sister?"

"You're not going to shut up about this, are you?"

"No," the three of them say in unison.

"Fine," I say, as we move together to our next circuit. "Her name is Nora."

Beau whistles. "Beautiful."

I eye him narrowly before continuing. "She and I dated in high school. We've recently reconnected, and...."

"Now when you say 'reconnected,' do you mean, like–" I slap Miles upside the head before he can continue.

"It's not like that," I say, feeling the need to defend Nora, not even myself. "She's got a son."

"Ding, ding, ding!" Jonah chimes. "Marriage material."

"Where's the father?" Beau asks.

"Pretty much out of the picture," I say, and just thinking about Nate makes my blood hiss. "He has custody every other weekend but doesn't seem to want much more involvement than that."

Beau clamps a hand on my shoulder. "And that's where you come in, I take it? Insta-Dad?"

"I guess so," I say. I may not have any personal experience when it comes to parenting, but I'm highly motivated when it comes to learning a new skill. I know it's something I could put my heart into if I was given the chance.

"She's the one who made the mugs I gave you," I admit, and this leads to Miles pulling his mug out of his gym bag.

"Why did you bring that with you?" I ask with a laugh.

"This goes everywhere with me," Miles says. "Everything tastes better when drinking from this mug. Be sure to tell her I said that."

"When do we get to meet her?" Jonah asks.

Bringing Nora out to meet the team seems like a serious move, and I don't know if she's ready for that yet.

"I'm not sure I want her hanging around you fools. You'll make me look bad."

Miles scoffs. "You don't need help with that. You do that all on your own, player."

As the conversation shifts and we resume our workout, I mull over the idea of bringing Nora to meet the guys. She would like them, and they would definitely smother her. But merging our worlds would make things feel very...real. That might be a way for me to give her a glimpse of what life with me might look like. A life where we could learn to strike the balance between baseball and everything else that's becoming more important to me.

We've still got four Fridays left in our deal. Guess we'll have to see how things shake out with a little more time.

"How's therapy going for you?" Jonah asks me. I probably shouldn't, but I feel an automatic surge of embarrassment that he brought this up in front of the other guys.

"Oh, did Jonah get you talking to Greta?" Beau says. "She's great."

I blink over at him in surprise. "You see her, too?"

Beau gives a little shrug. "We've all got our problems. It helps to have somebody to help you process them."

"Who's this?" Miles asks, lifting Nora's mug I'd given him to his mouth. He's legit drinking water from it.

"Greta," I say. "She's the team therapist."

"Hmm," he hums. "All three of you talk to her?" We nod.

"Have you found it helpful?" Jonah asks me.

"Definitely," I say, not wanting to delve into things that are too personal for me to share with these guys in this setting. "I'm learning a lot, actually."

"About what?" Miles asks curiously.

"How to mentally prepare myself for games," I say. "Being okay with mistakes. Dealing with people I don't like."

Miles clicks his tongue against his teeth. "Alright, don't gatekeep, y'all. Somebody give me this woman's number."

We linger at the gym for a while, and I realize that I have more in common with these guys than I thought. We've all walked through hard times, done things we regret, and have relatives who make life difficult. I never would have known about some of the things they've gone through, and talking about our shared life experiences makes me feel even less alone.

Second Friday

After finishing my workout at the gym, I meet with what we players call a "swing doctor": a professional who can help me rework my natural batting patterns and identify where I can improve my hitting performance at a micro level. I've always been told I've got a naturally beautiful swing, but my sessions with Greta have inspired me to approach everything as if I'm a beginner. Like I'm learning things for the first time.

"Adopting a beginner's mindset will help you gradually progress, both in your relationships and on the field. You won't feel such intense pressure to perform perfectly if you're telling yourself that you're allowed to be a forever student of the game," she told me yesterday.

I've taken pieces of different swing philosophies from teammates, coaches, and trainers over the years I've been playing professionally, but I felt ready to approach next season with a clean slate. The session was grueling but also really fun. It's like a weight is slowly being lifted from my shoulders every time I step up to the plate. I'm enjoying myself again, and I'd been satisfied with my efforts even though they weren't perfect.

After taking a virtual meeting with one of my sponsors in preparation for the upcoming holidays, I shower and change before driving back up to Kitt's Harbor to see Nora. She's got Ollie this weekend and, as promised, took charge of our plans for the evening. Honestly, I couldn't care less what we're doing, as long as I get to touch her, hold her, and kiss her again. That kiss in her studio short-circuited my brain last Friday. I don't think I'll recover until I get another taste of her. Maybe I'll never recover. I'd be fine with that.

When I arrive, I'm surprised to see a Subaru Outback already parked in her driveway. My questions are answered almost immediately as the door swings open and Nora welcomes me inside. I sweep her into a bone-crushing hug.

"I missed you," she says breathlessly into my ear, and I want to hold her forever. But then I lift my gaze and find her sister and brother-in-law are standing in the living room with Ollie, watching us. Sydney is grinning from ear to ear.

"You remember Sydney?" Nora says, and her sister extends a hand towards me.

"Good to see you again," I say, feeling slightly disappointed that Nora hadn't warned me that we weren't going to be alone tonight.

"And Trent."

He's got Ollie scooped up in one strong arm and still manages to crush my hand with the other, offering a clipped greeting. He's clearly still not warmed up to me.

"I've enlisted their help for our activity this evening," Nora says, her brown eyes sparkling. She looks gorgeous, dressed in a denim jacket and jeans.

"Should I be nervous?"

"Very," Sydney says with a wink. "Let's get on the road while we still have good light?"

We carpool down to the harbor where the sun is just about to drift below the horizon. Sydney pulls a bulky camera out of her car and several lenses. Ollie even has his own little camera—one that she had given him, I gather.

"Nora asked me if I would teach you some photography basics," she explains, adjusting the settings on her camera. "Have you ever used a DSLR before?"

"I can't say that I have."

"That's okay. I'll teach you everything you need to know."

The October air down by the water is salt-tinged and cold. I steal Nora's hand, grasping it tightly as we pick our way down the rocky beach to the waterline.

"Photography, huh?" I ask her. "Is this just an excuse for you to take an excessive amount of photos of me so you can stare at them when you miss me?"

"So what if it is?"

"I'm all for it," I say, squeezing her hand. "As long as I can take some of you, too."

She gives me a sly side-eye. "Did you miss me this week, Brooks?"

I pull her hand back and bring us both to a stop before sliding my mouth near her ear. "Of course I missed you. You're all I've been able to think about."

Nora's gaze crashes into mine, and charged tension stretches taut between us. Her lips curl up into a smile, and for a second, I think she may close the gap between us and kiss me right there in front of her family...but then Ollie scurries towards us, and she looks away.

"Cheese!" he cries, lifting his little camera up. I wrap an arm around Nora's shoulders and lean my head against hers, drawing her close. I hear the beep of the button on Ollie's camera, but from his height, he probably only captured our legs in the photo.

"Get down here, you two! We're losing the light!" Sydney calls out. We comply, joining her down by the water.

"Okay, stand here. Act like you like each other," Sydney instructs, with Trent and Ollie hovering behind her as she starts taking photos. Easiest photoshoot I've ever done.

"Come look at these!" Sydney gasps, showing us the display of her camera. She clicks through a few photos, and I love the way Nora is looking at me. Her easy, bright smile says it all. She's into me and happy I'm here. I'm gonna need all of these pictures sent to me immediately, along with several prints to take up residence in my apartment.

"Do you see how I positioned the two of you in the shot here? This is called the rule of thirds." Sydney then explains about a whole bunch of things in her camera settings like the aperture, f-stop, and white balance. I'm taking mental notes and find her lesson genuinely interesting. She then drags Trent in front of the camera with Ollie on his shoulders and hands Nora the camera. She explains how to best pose ones' subjects, how to frame them to best capture the landscape, and then she lets Nora snap away.

"We're good. Right, Ollie?" Trent finally says, pulling Ollie down off his shoulders and following him down to the water's edge.

"Look, Uncle T!" Ollie gasps. Trent crouches down, carefully bending over to inspect the rock Ollie has picked up.

"You're up, Brooks," Sydney says, pushing me out in front. "You're used to this sort of thing, right?"

I laugh, gazing into the camera lens like I've been coached to do on the few brand and commercial shoots I've done. Though I'm never completely comfortable in front of a camera, I've learned to fake it pretty well.

"Oooh-whee!" Sydney screams. "Do you see that Blue Steel, Nora? I hope you got that shot. You're a natural, Brooks. Move in closer, Nora."

"Yeah, Nora. Come closer."

She steps towards me, raising the camera up to take more photos. After she and Sydney deem my modeling to be sufficient, we then switch places. I receive some brief instruction from Sydney before she skips off to join her husband and Ollie.

"What do I do with my hands?" Nora asks, raising them awkwardly.

"Just pretend we're the only ones out here," I say, snapping a few photos. "Nobody else is watching."

She hugs herself, clearly uncomfortable being shot by herself. I lower the camera and move in closer.

"Just look at the camera the way you look at me," I say, and I'm pleased to see a blush deepen the color on her cheeks. I raise the camera up again and look at her through the viewfinder. She glances out at the water and then back at me, and the hesitant smile that rises on her lips makes my chest ache.

"You're a babe," I say, trying to make her laugh. "Stunning. Gorgeous." She giggles, and I take a few more pictures.

Ollie wanders over with a handful of rocks he's collected, and Nora bends down to admire them. I take photos of the two of them, then turn the camera on the distant forms of Sydney and Trent, walking together further down the beach.

I turn the camera out to the ocean and snap a few shots of the ribbons of color stretched along the skyline.

I wander a ways down the beach, taking photos, pausing to note the way the fading sun glitters on the surface of the water, the barnacles that tack the posts holding up the dock. There are so many intricate details that I wouldn't have noticed had I not been actively looking. Something about having the camera in hand makes me more sensitive to the beauty around me. One beauty, in particular. I could shoot photos of Nora all day. I turn back and take a few more of her from a distance.

Sydney gathers Nora, Ollie, and I together for a few more photos. There's a deep tug in my gut again as I stand there on the beach with Ollie in my arms and Nora leaning into me. We feel like a solid unit, the three of us. Something complete and infinite.

Once the sun has dipped below the ocean and Sydney deems the "golden hour" light to be long gone, we pile back into our cars and head back to Nora's house.

Trent offers to put Ollie to bed, but Nora looks up at him skeptically. "Are you sure?"

"I've got it," he insists, tucking Ollie under one arm like a football. "Your work isn't finished yet."

He's right. Sydney then opens her laptop and begins loading all of the photos into the editing program she uses. I'm glued to the screen as she flicks through the photos, teaching us a few basic editing techniques.

"Here," she says, sliding the laptop to me. "You edit this one."

It's one of the photos she'd taken of Nora and I, and it's phone background-worthy. Nora's got her head tipped up to look at me, and I'm gazing back down at her, smiling broadly. Our hands are tangled together, and her hair is lifting in the ocean breeze.

I hunch over the laptop, adjusting the toggles to play with the exposure, colors, and white balance in the photo. Sydney watches me work and occasionally offers suggestions, and when I sit back and slide the laptop back toward her, she looks impressed.

"You sure you've never done this before?"

"First time," I say, raising my hands in innocence. "But I like it."

"Did you take all of these?" Nora says, clicking through the photos until she lands on one I'd taken of her and Ollie.

"Yeah," I say, suddenly feeling sheepish. I hadn't meant to fill Sydney's memory card to the brim. I'd been enjoying the process.

"These are great photos, Brooks," Sydney says approvingly. "Really."

"Thanks," I say, glancing shyly at Nora, who is looking at me like I've just done something really remarkable.

"Greta will be proud," she says.

After Sydney uploads all of the photos to a shared folder and gives me and Nora access, she and Trent say goodbye. Trent glances back at me before hopping into his truck, and he gives me the slightest nod and raises a hand in my direction. I take it to be bro-code for passing whatever test he was running to determine whether or not I was worthy for Nora. After tonight, I think he approves.

I linger in the doorway, not wanting to leave Nora again. Feeling like I'll never have enough time with her.

"I've got batting practice with some of the guys from the team tomorrow morning," I say, lacing my fingers through hers and tracing my thumb over her knuckles. "So, as much as I'd love to stay longer, I'd better head home."

She draws her bottom lip under her teeth, looking disappointed. "Okay." She suddenly gets a mischievous gleam in her eyes, reaching up to toy with the buttons on my jacket.

"There's something I've been curious about," she says. "Do you still chew Bubblicious?"

"Who wants to know?" I tease.

"The girl who used to kiss you in high school. You always tasted like Bubblicious."

"Well, in that case," I say, "yes, I do. But only on game day. So, if you like it that much, you're going to have to come to one of my games."

"You'd kiss me at a game?" Nora says with a tilted smile. "In front of all those people?"

"I'd kiss you anywhere."

I slowly back her into the wall and cage her in with one arm over her head, bending my head down to find her mouth.

Nora kisses me back hungrily, her hands bunching the front of my shirt, traveling the length of my torso and exploring the ridges of my back. This kiss is breathless. Nipping and tugging, grasping and catching. I kiss her with questions, she readily kisses me back in answers. I don't want to leave her. I don't want to break apart. When we finally do, she knots a hand into the hair at the back of my neck and brings my mouth back down to hers again. Who am I to deny the woman what she wants? I delve in for more, feeling like I'll never be satisfied. I'll never grow tired of her.

"Brooks," she finally mumbles against my mouth, her fingers locked into my belt loops. "You're too good at this."

"Mmm," I hum, catching her lips again in a slow, languid kiss. "Is that going to be a problem?"

"Yes," she whispers, pressing her forehead against mine. "I can't walk into my studio without thinking about you, without wishing you were here." She trips a trail of kisses across my cheek, and my heart thunders in my ears with every delicate press of her warm lips. "And now you've ruined my front entryway, too."

"There's still several more rooms in your house. I'm happy to ruin the rest of them for you."

She laughs, her hand tightening in my hair. She kisses me once more, and I know she's giving me the sign that it's okay for me to go. I sigh and reluctantly shove away off the wall, freeing her from the press of my body.

"This week while I'm away," I say in a low voice, "you think about which room you want me to kiss you in next, and let me know."

A slow smile grows on her plump, swollen lips. "All of them."

TWENTY-THREE
Nora

November

Third Friday

I've lived in Kitt's Harbor my entire life, and not once have I felt the particular urge to throw myself into the frigid ocean in the dead of winter. So, when Brooks suggested we take a night dip in the harbor as our activity for our third Friday evening spent together, I was underwhelmed.

He brings me my favorite Chinese takeout to the house to butter me up before reiterating that no, this activity is not negotiable. I argue that I'm questioning his sanity in wanting to do this, but he's determined as ever to push us both further out of our comfort zones.

"I promise I'll warm you up afterwards," he says once we finish dinner, looking far too excited about that prospect.

"What if I get frostbite? What if I lose one of my toes?" I speculate.

"I'll still like you," he promises. "It can't be that dangerous if my therapist suggested I try it. She said I'll probably like the benefits so much that I might start to crave it. Crave the cold."

Unfathomable.

I change into a swimsuit, layering my favorite hoodie and sweatpants on top. I jam a pair of thick socks into my old, wooly slippers I only ever wear outside in the winter. Between the puffy parka and the knit beanie warming my head, I look like an illustrated character in a folk art painting in my hodgepodge ensemble. We drive down to the harbor after dark, which is only around six in the evening, and I stare at his shadowed form as we bundle out of the car.

"Where's your coat?" I ask Brooks, looking disapprovingly at the socks he's got tucked into a pair of slides.

"I think I left it at your house."

"Turn around! You're going to need it!" I think my paranoid mom side is showing.

"I'll be fine," he says with a confident grin. "We do ice baths every so often in the clubhouse. It's no big deal."

"No big deal," I mutter, slinging the towering mass of towels I'd brought along into my arms before following Brooks down the pebbled beach. It's drizzling. The wind is biting. And now I'm going to have to strip down and jump into the ocean because Brooks wants to check this act of insanity off his new experiences bucket list.

When we reach the water's edge, Brooks begins peeling off his sweatshirt. Of course there's not a wetsuit or rash guard in sight. The flash of his bare chest I can make out in the dim evening light is spectacular.

"The faster we get in, the faster we can get out," he says, huffing out a breath that billows around him in the cold. He glances over at me, still fully clothed and in denial. "Need me to help you out of your clothes?"

"No!" I snap, reluctantly shrugging out of my coat and yanking my sweatshirt off over my head. I watch Brooks slip his thumbs into the waistband of his pants and slide them down his thighs, feeling a shiver course through me that's got nothing to do with the wind pecking at my exposed bare skin. He's standing there in nothing but a pair of tight black boxer briefs, jumping in place like he's about to head out onto the baseball field, all sinewy muscles and smooth skin. Meanwhile, I'm looking like a plucked chicken in a black one-piece swimsuit.

"You ready?" he asks, looking utterly thrilled at the prospect of throwing himself into the freezing ocean. He's insane.

"Please don't make me do this," I beg.

"You have to!" he yells playfully, clasping my hand in his and giving it a lively shake. "Ready?"

"No!" I scream, but I know it's futile.

"Three. Two...one!" Brooks takes off running, and I have no choice but to crunch down the beach after him. He lets out a whoop as we crash into the dark foaming surf. My scream gives out as the water engulfs my legs. I can't feel my toes. May they rest in peace at the bottom of the ocean. Every inch of my legs stings as we shuffle further into the sea. Brooks releases my hand and dives fully under the water, as was the agreed upon deal.

I squint my eyes shut, wanting to cry and run back to shore instead of following his lead. But I'm already here. I'm already wet. I've done harder things than this before, and I came out on the other side stronger for it. I may as well submerge myself in the deep.

Before I can talk myself out of it, I launch myself into the black, swirling water. The cold hits me and squeezes every bit of air out of my lungs. It's consuming. Every thought, every feeling is siphoned from my being. The only thing that exists is the complete, devastating cold.

I surface, dragging in a ragged breath as Brooks' fingers grasp my wrist. He pulls me forward and together we stumble out of the water, gasping for air.

I'm shaking. It feels like the sea shrunk my body, sucking every needless bit of me into its depths. My blood is humming in my veins as I quickly dress and hobble back to Brooks' car, losing a slipper once along the way and having to clumsily retrieve it.

Brooks ensures I'm safely tucked inside before he hurtles into the driver's seat. He moves jerkily, first starting the engine, then blasting the heat. He begins rubbing warmth into my limbs and then his in turn. We don't speak for a solid three minutes as our minds and bodies regain sensation. My skin is prickling, my eyes are stinging, but as I look over at Brooks, dripping icy water from his dark hair and lashes, I'm shocked by how perfectly clear and calm my mind feels.

"That," he says, racked with a full-body shiver, "was crazy."

I agree. Somehow, every worry plaguing my mind, every heavy thing weighing on my heart, has disappeared. Lost to the deep.

It feels amazing. *I* feel amazing.

"You did it," Brooks says, pressing a cold kiss to my cheek. "You did it."

A sudden surge of emotion rises behind my eyes, and I'm surprised to feel hot tears threading down my face. "I don't know why I'm crying," I bubble.

Brooks gathers me into him, and I sob into his damp shoulder, both of us shivering and shaking and entirely alive.

I cry for a solid few minutes, and Brooks doesn't say a thing. Just holds me to his chest until the shaking begins to subside and my breathing levels once again. It feels like the final spidery threads that have been clinging to my heart for over two years have just been shaken off. Cut loose. Set free. I've been renewed and cleansed in a way I hadn't anticipated. It's like everything heartbreaking that happened between us before has been left behind in the water, and we've been made new.

"It feels good, doesn't it?" Brooks whispers, pressing another kiss to my temple.

"So good." I sigh, sinking into his shoulder, still clinging to him like my life depends on it. "You're not going to believe this."

"What?"

"I think I would do that again."

Brooks leans in and kisses me, a long, slow pull.

"That's my girl."

It only feels right to let ourselves into Delia's Diner after our dip in the harbor. I don't have ingredients to make hot chocolate on hand at home, but the kitchen at the diner sure does.

I let us in the door and flick on a couple lights, leaving most of the dining area in darkness.

"I feel like I'm breaking all the rules right now," Brooks says, wandering the diner with his hands in the pockets of his sweatpants. He pauses to look at our wall of fame, where framed portraits of celebrities and well-known local patrons smile down at him.

"We're missing your photo up there," I note.

"If you're going to put me on that wall, I'd better be front and center."

I snort. "I've got the perfect photo to put up there."

"One of the pictures Sydney took of us?" he asks.

I shake my head, sliding my phone out of my coat pocket. My fingertips are still slightly numb, but I manage to open the photo Kate took of us at the Harvest Market last month. I still love it.

"Remember this?" I say, and he leans closer. "This is my favorite photo of us."

We share a knowing smile, and he presses a kiss to my temple. "My girl in my hat. Never gets old."

I send the photo to him before stowing my phone. "Table for one?" I joke.

"I'd like a booth, please," he replies.

"I would be happy to seat you at your favorite booth, but I need your assistance first. Right this way." I lead him to the beverage prep area and flick on more lights before opening the fridge. "Okay," I sigh. "Milk. Chocolate. Whipped cream?" I glance back at Brooks to gauge his preference.

"Is that even a question?"

Once I've got the ingredients assembled on the counter, I start by steaming the milk. We invested in a giant espresso machine several years ago after a customer complained about our "average" coffee. I practically became a barista trying to perfect our recipes and wow people with some more-elevated drinks.

"I'm completely out of my element here," Brooks admits, hovering over my shoulder.

"You don't cook?"

"Not really. I pay a nutritionist to prep most of my meals for me, and on game nights, I eat dinner at the clubhouse."

"What do you guys usually eat?"

"A little bit of everything."

"Let me guess. They keep a stash of Fruit by the Foot on hand just for you?"

"Not after my New Year's resolution," he laughs. "Maybe I'll have to ask the staff to bring them back next year. For good luck."

Brooks watches me work, picking up random cooking utensils and placing them back.

"We'll have to cook something together sometime," I say. "Although, most days I eat at least one meal here at the diner and end up bringing home leftovers because I'm too tired to cook." I drop a generous portion of thick bittersweet chocolate into the bottom of a large metal cup filled with milk and combine the two.

"Is that it? No secret ingredient?"

"Close your eyes," I say, but he doesn't listen, peeking at me through half-shut lids. He watches as I add brown sugar, vanilla, salt, and a hint of cinnamon into the cup.

I split the hot chocolate into two oversized mugs on saucers and top them both with a generous helping of whipped cream and a dusting of cinnamon. "Now they're finished."

Brooks takes his plate with both hands, walking slowly. I catch him licking the whipped cream out of the corner of my eye, but when I glance his way, he looks back at me innocently.

We wander straight to Booth Six, with me stopping to snag two spoons along the way, without saying a word. But this time, instead of sitting across from each other, Brooks waits for me to slide into the booth before settling in right next to me.

"Honest review," I say after Brooks takes a careful sip from his mug. "Go."

His eyes widen and then close in contentment. "This is the best hot chocolate I've ever had."

"You're only saying that because you just emerged from the harbor like a sea monster."

"I'm not!" he insists, digging into his whipped cream with his spoon. "It's really good."

I take a sip of my own and have to agree. This is exactly what my body and nerves needed after our polar plunge.

"Can I ask you something?" Brooks asks. I hum in assent as I sip my drink. "Would you ever quit the diner?"

I set my mug down and glance around at my second home. "If I had another sure way to provide for Ollie, then yes. I would. I really haven't had the time to search for another job since he was born."

"What about Noli?" Brooks asks, looking at me intently. "Would doing something like that make you happy?"

"Maybe. But I wonder if turning it into a business might ruin the magic of it for me. If my income suddenly depended on how many ceramics I could create, would that suck the fun out of creating them? It seems like that might be what happened with you and baseball. You used to love playing the game just for the fun of it."

"A valid point."

"You'll be proud of me, though. I signed up for the holiday market in a few weeks. I've been trying to build my inventory back up after the last one."

"I wish I could offer you my assistance, but I don't think anyone would buy my sub-par pieces."

"Yes, they would. People would buy anything with your name on it."

"Not true."

"It is true! You even have a delicious brookie named after you at the stadium!"

"That's not a hard sell," he laughs. "People would buy those whether or not my name was attached to them."

"I don't know...I bought it purely because your face was on the wrapper."

"I know," he says with a wicked smile.

"What do you mean *you know*?"

"I found the wrapper in your kitchen last weekend. In the drawer to the left of your dishwasher." He licks his spoon, taunting me.

"You rummaged through my *drawers*?" I say, an embarrassed flush crawling across cheeks.

"Of course I did. When I drop you off, I'm personally ensuring you tack that wrapper to your fridge."

"I can't believe you!"

"I'll make it up to you," he says, setting down his mug. "Next time you come to one of my games, I'll make sure they let you have unlimited brookies. All you can eat."

I toss my head back and laugh, and he laughs with me. But actually...that sounds like satisfactory compensation for his nosiness.

"Maybe that's what we should do next Friday. Try to recreate your famous brookie. Bet they'd give you the recipe."

"You're probably right. I'll ask for you."

We both take long sips from our mugs, huddled together and finally feeling warmth spread through the close space of the booth.

"Would you ever quit baseball?" I finally ask, feeling as if I already know the answer. The sport is his lifeblood. I can't picture Brooks without it.

"Maybe," he says, turning contemplative. "If you'd asked me that question two months ago, I would have said, '*never.*'" He grins. "But Greta, and you, honestly, have helped me see things in a different light. I'm realizing that if I lost baseball, it would suck, but I'd ultimately be okay."

"Of course you would," I reply. "I had to ask myself similar hard questions during my divorce. If I lost my house, my job, my child, and my marriage, would I really be able to pick myself up again and keep going?" I stare down into the dregs of my hot chocolate. "And I realized that yes, I would. I couldn't give up. And neither should you, no matter how many disgruntled Stormbreakers fans you might encounter."

Brooks smiles, a soft thing that makes my heart pound.

"You've helped me a lot, you know," he says, his blue eyes fixed intently on me. "Spending time with you and Ollie has helped me remember that there is so much more to life than baseball."

"Yeah, like changing diapers and folding laundry and the occasional superb hot chocolate."

"Exactly. And after what you conquered tonight, I'm even more proud of you," Brooks says. I turn to face him, and he tilts his head admiringly before stretching an arm over my shoulders and easing me close. "You didn't run away. You dove right into that water like it was nothing."

"I've never felt cold like that," I murmur, grateful to be safe in the warmth of Brooks' arms. "Except..." I clear my throat, feeling the surprising desire to share something with him that very few people in my life know about.

"After Ollie was born, I..." I pause, trying to wrangle my thoughts. "I had a hard time. The combination of Nate being unfaithful, bringing our child into the world without him and having to figure out how to take care of a helpless little baby on my own was...overwhelming."

"I can't imagine," Brooks murmurs gently.

"My sister Sydney was living with me at the time, and she and my mom really stepped up and helped me figure things out with Ollie. But even though they were there, I felt more lonely than I ever had before."

Brooks clasps my hands firmly in his, looking for all the world like he wants to go back to that time and save me from it, even now.

"I struggled with postpartum depression," I say softly. "It was the scariest thing I've ever been through."

"What was it like?" Brooks asks.

"Like drowning in the cold depths of the sea and not knowing if I'd ever find the surface again. It was surviving. Every day. Just surviving. Even talking about it now is really difficult."

I find myself recalling the way hot tears had spilled from my eyes after our dip in the ocean and realize that I had unknowingly healed some part of myself that still needed healing from that dark time after Ollie was born. I felt the sting of the cold, the enormity of it, but I knew it wasn't going to take me. I knew that because I had emerged from the deep before, I could do it again.

I squeeze Brooks' hands in mine, feeling tears gathering in my eyes again. "Thank you for encouraging me to swim with you tonight. I needed it. More than you know."

He gathers me into his embrace, and I bury my face in his shoulder again. I remember when my lungs felt like they were carrying an unbearable, thick weight made of shadow. In the depths of my postpartum experience, I could barely draw breath. It was hard to believe that I would ever truly feel soft, dappled sunlight or laugh deeply or love ever again.

But here I am, released from the deep. Released from the heartbreak and shadows of my past, and enveloped in a golden net Brooks and I are slowly weaving from trust, shared happy experiences, and love.

It's there. I know it's there. The love I feel for him is scaling through my ribcage now, threatening to spill over. I hug him even tighter.

"Nora, you are so incredibly strong," Brooks says earnestly into my ear. "Do you believe that? Because if not, I'm going to remind you of it every day."

"How?" I whisper. "By making me do pushups with you?"

"If that's what it takes," Brooks nips at my earlobe. "I promised I'd warm you up after our dip in the ocean, didn't I?" Brooks says, pulling away slightly to brush my damp hair away from my face. The way his eyes rove over me undoes another knot in my stomach. I'm safe with him. I'm realizing that the only way I'm going to learn to trust Brooks...is by trusting him. I have to choose to believe that he is trustworthy, unless he proves otherwise. It's what he deserves.

He makes good on his promise by thoroughly kissing me right there in Booth Six and then again at every single red light we hit on the way home.

TWENTY-FOUR
Brooks

Fourth Friday

"Wassup, Big Dude?" Ollie says, walking with a swagger down the front porch steps of Nora's house.

"Dude...you look awesome."

"Thanks," he says with a little shrug, adjusting his sunglasses on his face. "Where's your gasses?"

"They're in my car. Should I wear them so I can look as cool as you?"

Ollie nods, and his glasses slide down his nose adorably. Nora locks the door to her house behind her and barely has time to amble down the steps before I sweep her into my arms.

"The neighbors!" she wheezes into my ear as if she really cares what they think, but her hand on the back of my neck is telling me otherwise. She likes being held by me. I glance around, and sure enough, there's a man across the road with a rake in his hand, but instead of raking leaves, he's openly staring at us. I swear I see a lady in the house next door peering out the window, but she's gone as quickly as she appeared.

Maybe she's right. I'll save the making out for later, once we're inside and away from prying eyes.

"Who's ready to do some shopping?" I ask once we're all buckled into the car. It's four o'clock and the weak November sun is already setting, but I've got my sunglasses on to please Ollie anyways. He flings his hand into the air and shouts, "Meeee!"

"You've got the list ready?"

"Got it right here," Nora says.

We drive to the only grocery store Kitt's Harbor boasts, which is referred to by locals as The Market since it's tiny and chock full of random bits and bobs along with a limited selection of local produce, dairy products, and overpriced shelf staples. After finding parking on Main, I stow my sunglasses (much to Ollie's dismay), and we head inside. I haven't grocery shopped in a long while, and it feels nostalgic stepping foot somewhere that's been around since I was a kid.

"Welcome in!" Winnie calls out from her perch at the till. She peers owlishly over the gossip magazine in her hands and blinks twice at me from behind her glasses. I raise a hand in greeting and she stares back, eyes wide.

"Hi, Winnie," Nora says. "How's that novel of yours coming along?"

"Oh, just fine," Winnie answers, but her eyes are still fixed on me. "How do I know you, young man?" she asks. "You look familiar."

My eyes dart to one of the sports magazines lining the checkout aisle that has my face on it.

"He's an Alden," Nora answers for me. "The twins' older brother."

"Oh, that's right," Winnie says with a chuckle. "You look just like your sisters. Claire has been helping me with my book, you know. She's got lots of wonderful ideas."

"I'm sure she does," I say. My sister rarely talks about it, but she's an aspiring writer herself.

"We'll let you get back to your reading," Nora says, hustling me along before Winnie can entrap us in a long-winded conversation. From what my sisters tell me, Winnie likes to talk. Winnie waves us off and Nora and I share a smile.

"Okay," Nora says, pulling a cart from the rack and buckling Ollie in the child seat. "First, we need baking soda, dark brown sugar, and some kind of fancy salt."

"Fancy salt?" I ask. "What constitutes fancy salt?"

"You know," Nora makes a sprinkling gesture. "The kind people use to top their baked goods to make them look...enticing."

"So, what you're saying is," I say, bending my head to speak into her ear. "If I sprinkle *myself* with said fancy salt, you'd find me more enticing?"

"Oh, believe me, you're enticing enough as you are."

We locate two different types of sugar and cocoa powder, and then me and Ollie spend five minutes racing up and down the aisle while Nora determines which of the salts available at the market will be up to snuff.

I lurch to a stop and Ollie giggles, his blue eyes shining. If anyone were to see us together, they could easily mistake Ollie as my son. Our eyes are nearly the same color. The thought tugs at my gut as I take off down the aisle again at top speed.

Unfortunately, another patron at the market rounds the corner, and I have to make a lightning-fast swerve to avoid a shopping cart collision. Winnie would for sure kick me out if she saw me pull a hit-and-run.

"I'm sorry..."

My words flicker and die in my throat as the man pushing the shopping cart comes into view. He's dressed in a navy-blue suit, his black hair slicked back in a perfect wave. He eyes me narrowly, though his mouth lifts into something like a smile.

"Brooks," my dad says, his eyes flicking down to Ollie.

"Okay, I think I found the perfect salt," Nora says from behind me, approaching with quick steps before placing the salt in the cart. I don't have time to say anything before she glances up and her gaze collides with the man who played a role in our break up back in high school. She knows the truth now, and that makes me feel even more protective of her. I angle my body so she's slightly behind me, shielding her from my dad.

"Nora," Bill Alden says coolly. "So nice to see you."

His eyes move between me, Nora, and Ollie and I can tell he's taking their measure. He smiles again, tightly.

"When I heard my son was spending more time in town, I was surprised at first, but," he nods to Nora, "now I see he's in good company."

"Go again, Bookie!" Ollie says, squirming in his seat. He's wanting to continue our race down the aisles.

I still haven't said a word to my father. He's intruded on something private and personal, something I want him to have absolutely no part in. He doesn't get to make small talk with Nora and her son. He doesn't get to be involved in my life. He lost that privilege a long time ago.

I'm not putting up with him. Especially not with these two around.

"We were just about to check out," I say, maneuvering my cart around my dad's. Nora glances at me furtively before shadowing me.

"Wait," he says, and his hand latches on my arm to stop me. "I'd like a word."

My jaw clenches, and I draw in a deep breath through my nose. What was it Greta had told me to do should I encounter my father? Oh, yeah. *Do not engage.* No matter what he says, no matter what he does, don't take the bait. *Do not engage.* It's not safe for me to do so.

"I've still got a couple more things left on my shopping list," Nora says, her fingertips grazing my lower back as she sidles past. "We'll meet you at the checkout." I release my death grip on the shopping cart, and she takes it from me. "Goodbye, Mr. Alden."

Dad gives her a flat smile in return, and as soon as she's out of sight, he turns his cold gaze on me, smile gone. It's just me and the man who raised me, facing off in the baking aisle in the middle of the market. I return his glare with a contrasting, easy grin. He'll hate that. It's proof that the casual happiness he always tried to scrub out of my personality is flickering back to life.

"How can I help you, Bill?" I say, addressing him by his first name because that's who he is to me. A distant acquaintance. "Please tell me you're not wasting your time with her...*again*?" he says, his voice laced with condescension. "You would think after the way your season ended, you would be putting your head down and overhauling your game like I suggested instead of giving into...meaningless distractions."

Anger rolls through me at his assumptions, but I try not to let it show. *Do not engage. Don't stoop to his level.*

"Leave Nora out of it," I grit out.

"If I were you, I would be very careful getting involved with someone like Nora Foster. You've been down this road before, remember? She's not built for the life you live, Brooks. She won't be able to keep up."

I scoff, glancing over at the assortment of flours on the shelf across from me before looking back at my dad. "You don't even know her. You *never* knew her."

"And you think you do?" he says. There it is, the bait. The manipulation. He's trying to plant a seed of doubt in my mind again, just like he did senior year. He told me Nora wasn't serious about college and wasn't serious about us. He convinced me that she would only hold me back from reaching my goals. She was a nobody. Going nowhere.

I lift my chin, taking stock of my dad. He's tired. A fancy suit and perfectly styled hair can't conceal the smudges under his eyes and the lines bracketing his mouth. An unexpected wave of pity rises within me. I'm disappointed that he still feels the need to try and control me. Despite the distance I've put between us, he hasn't clued in and grown up and let me make my own choices without adding his two cents.

"Bill," I say firmly, standing tall and staking my feet firmly beneath me. "Nothing you say is going to change my mind. I never ask you for advice because, frankly, I don't need it. I'm doing just fine."

He seems slightly taken aback by my directness, blinking rapidly.

"Hope you enjoy your stay at home," I say.

And with that, I leave Bill Alden standing stock-still in the aisle, my heart pounding in my chest.

As we start assembling our ingredients for our brookies, Nora can tell that my mind is occupied.

"Do you want to talk about it?" she asks softly. Ollie is singing some song about cookies from his perch on her kitchen counter, drawing with his fingertips in a pile of spilled flour.

"How long do I melt the butter for?" I ask, hand hovering near the buttons on the microwave. I'm dodging her question, and she knows it.

"Brooks," she says, taking my outstretched hand in hers. "What did your dad say to you?"

I stiffen. I can't tell her that. It would break her heart to know that the first time Bill and I had crossed paths in years, we'd essentially argued about her. Again.

"He didn't have anything nice to say," I say, which is the truth. "Per usual."

Nora's eyes swell, and she tucks herself against my chest. I sigh, pulling her close and breathing into her hair.

"I'm sorry," she says simply.

"It's okay," I say. "It was bound to happen eventually."

"Yeah, but I'm sure you were hoping for the best."

"Not really. I try not to expect anything when it comes to my dad. He's very consistent."

"I hope one day he'll let go of his pride and see you for who you are," she says, brushing her thumb over my jawline. "He's missing out."

Ollie yelps, and we startle apart.

"Yucky!" he says, pointing to the mixing bowl. "Is yucky."

"Oh, no," Nora says. "Did you eat the cocoa powder?" Ollie nods, wide-eyed. Nora laughs. "Yeah, that's really bitter, buddy. I should have warned you."

We resume our baking, and I try my best to let my interaction with my dad roll off my back, but my mind keeps calling it forward. Replaying his words. It's like every time I interact with him, I revert back to the kid I once was. Desperately trying to grow tall enough to fight him off while simultaneously being squashed beneath his foot.

You would think after the way your season ended, you would be putting your head down and working on improving your game instead of giving into...distractions.

A guilty feeling sinks into my gut. That was exactly how I'd seen Nora when we'd first started talking. A welcome distraction. Have I been using her?

The thought makes me sick.

I didn't think I was *using* Nora, but Bill's comments are making me second-guess myself.

Have I been slipping in my performance on the field? Should I be doing more? Am I endangering Nora and Ollie by being involved with them? Did I rush her when she needed more time?

The questions continue to circulate through my mind, and I find myself growing quiet.

She's not built for the life you live, Brooks. She won't be able to keep up.

I watch Nora laugh with Ollie, joining him in singing his silly cookie song. I watch her drop the cookie dough over the brownie batter, sneaking bites and dancing to music that nobody else can hear. I note the soft smiles she offers me and feel my discomfort multiply.

Maybe I've been doing this all wrong. Maybe I really have been using Nora. Selfishly stringing her along because being with her makes everything in my life feel easier and more manageable. I've loved every minute we've spent together.

But am I what she *needs?*

I've avoided thinking too far into the future, as Greta has advised me to do, but maybe I should start to consider what I'm going to do once spring training starts. Nora's roots are here in Kitt's Harbor. My life, come February, is baseball. All day, every day for the majority of the year. Lots of travel. Weeks and maybe even months apart. How could I ask her to change anything about her life for me? And would she even want to?

"You can do the honors," she says, handing me the container of fancy salt.

"Oh," I say, pulled momentarily out of my mental spiral. "How do I do it?"

"Just grab a pinch," she says, demonstrating for me. "And sprinkle it on top."

"You're putting a dangerous amount of trust in my sprinkling abilities," I say. "What if I over-do it?"

"I trust you," she says simply, giving me a bright smile. "You've got this."

I swallow. I thought I was the trustworthy type, but maybe I've got things all wrong.

I sprinkle the salt, feeling like every flake I drop on the pan is piling up inside me, adding to the mountain of uncertainty.

TWENTY-FIVE
Nora

Fifth Friday

It's a busy week leading up to the holiday market. I spend every evening sorting, pricing, and packing my second run of ceramic goods. Brooks is busy, too, and though I want to be understanding of his schedule, he's been decidedly less chatty ever since our run-in with his dad at the market. I've tried not to read into things too much, but worry niggles the edges of my heart every time he doesn't reply to my texts right away.

I tell myself that it's probably a good thing that he's not distracted during training, meetings, and overall preparation for the coming season. This is what he needs, right? My job is to be understanding of his schedule.

But still. I miss him. Friday can't come soon enough. We haven't talked about what's going to happen after our five Fridays are up, but my hope-filled heart yearns for the best. A continuation of what we've already started. We've come too far to back out now.

> **Nora:** Sorry to throw off our fifth Friday this weekend. To be fair, I signed up for this market well before we had our agreement in place.

> **Brooks:** I've never run a booth at a market before, so this totally counts as trying something new for me. It's you who's breaking the rules.

> **Nora:** Oh, so you're running the booth? Do I get the night off, then?

> **Brooks:** Hey, I can operate a card reader and wrap delicate ceramics with the best of them.

> **Nora:** I'll believe it when I see it, Brookie.

Autumn in Kitt's Harbor is relatively mild, so pending rain, the market is set to be held outdoors at Alice Park. We'll be sheltered beneath our white tent regardless, but I hope the weather holds so visitors can linger and enjoy the holiday magic.

With Thanksgiving around the corner, I expect the market to invite the spirit of the season. In years past, I've been mesmerized by the twinkling lights, the smells of citrus and pine in the air, and the wide variety of baked holiday treats and handmade gifts. We've already added holiday items to our menu at the diner: gingerbread pancakes, candy cane lattes, and cinnamon roll waffles. All Ollie approved, of course.

"Can I bite it?" Ollie asks me, cinnamon stick in hand. He's been "assisting" me for the past thirty minutes in tying sprigs of pine and cinnamon sticks to my mugs with twine.

"You can," I say. "But it might be a little spicy."

Ollie licks the cinnamon stick and shakes his head with his tongue out. "Don't like it."

I press a kiss to his squishy cheek and give him a squeeze.

"Where's Big Dude, Mama?" he asks me later as we're cuddled up on the couch watching his favorite show.

"He's working," I say. A concept well understood by little Ollie.

"I miss him," Ollie says with a heavy sigh, and I press my lips together in a pout. He is precious.

"Yeah, me, too."

I'm arranging the shelves in my booth for the twenty-seventh time, stepping back to ensure it has the "collected" look I'm going for, when someone enters the tent.

"Hi, beautiful," Brooks says into my ear, and I turn into his arms. He holds me tightly for three whole breaths, and though I love the feel of his arms around me, my anxiety rises.

I pull back and study his face, and though he's smiling and handsome as ever and I could cocoon myself in his soft sweater for the rest of the night, something feels...off. He doesn't quite meet my eyes, and his smile is less light-filled and more tired.

This is how it felt before he broke up with me the first time. I sensed it was coming. The same thing happened before I found out about Nate's affair. Maybe I have a sixth sense about this sort of impending doom, or maybe I'm sleep-deprived and paranoid for no reason.

Before I have the chance to ask him what's going on, Ollie comes running over and locks his arms around Brooks' leg in a tight hug.

"What's up, my dude?" Brooks says, reaching down to embrace my son. Ollie then drags Brooks away to show him the booth across from ours which is selling handmade Christmas ornaments. I watch them go, puzzled. Feeling like I'm missing something.

Heavy clouds hover overhead, and I'm certain we'll get a bit of rain, if not a downpour. Sydney joins me at the booth, her blonde curls wild and blue eyes bright.

"How can I help you?" she asks eagerly. I hug her to me, feeling the need to anchor myself before the evening gets underway.

"Thank you for coming," I say. "If you could test the card reader for me and make sure it's working that would be great."

"Where's Ollie?" Sydney asks, peering outside of the tent. She laughs and nods to our right. "Spotted. Looks like he's wheedling a donut out of Brooks."

"Is he really?" I join her, and sure enough, Brooks is handing Ollie a cinnamon donut. Ollie looks up at Brooks with the purest delight and open admiration, and the sight of it makes a knot lodge in my throat. Sydney pulls out her phone and snaps a photo of the two of them.

"You're welcome," she whispers.

Brooks takes Ollie's free hand, and they continue walking through the market. Ollie puttering along happily in his rain boots and puffy jacket, Brooks with his sure strides and confident smiles.

I don't want our Fridays spent together to end. I want this to continue so badly, I feel desperate. Brooks has brought both Ollie and I so much happiness that I can't fathom losing him. Not now. After seeing Bill Alden the other night, I've been wondering what exactly they talked about. Bill was persuasive enough to convince Brooks to dump me the first time; who's to say he couldn't hold the same power over his son now? What if his opinion still holds sway?

Stop it, Nora.

Brooks has done nothing to make me question his intentions. He's been honest with me from the start, and I can't do him the disservice of doubting him now. I've got to trust him. I want him in my life, and I can't let a busy week put distance between us.

I'm just about to chase Brooks down so we can talk things through when someone else enters the tent, causing both Sydney and I to turn.

"Nora," Bill Alden says, looking severely overdressed for a local market in his black pea coat and dress shoes. "May I speak with you for a moment?"

Sydney's brow furrows, and she gives me a look that says, *need me to get rid of this guy?*

But I'm not afraid of Bill Alden anymore. I know what I want, and he's not going to get in the way of me obtaining it. Not again.

"Hi, Bill," I say, mustering up a smile. "Of course."

He gestures out the tent, and I punch my fists into the pockets of my coat as I follow after him.

"Is this a new venture of yours?" he asks, flinging a hand casually back towards my booth.

"Sort of. I've been throwing ceramics for years but have just started selling my work."

"My neighbor showed me a few things she bought from you. A vase. A few plates. They're beautiful. Really something."

"Thank you," I say cautiously. There's no way he sought me out to compliment me on my work.

"Can I buy you a cider?" he asks, gesturing to another tent across the way.

"No, thanks," I say slowly. I plan to get out of this conversation as quickly as possible. I will Brooks to turn around and see me with his dad. *Please come rescue me.*

"Do you enjoy it? Your creative work?"

"I do," I say, shooting an anxious glance back down the tent-lined walkway. There's a decent amount of people milling around, so we're not entirely alone, but there's no sign of Brooks and Ollie. I wish he'd stop beating around the bush and say whatever it is he came here to say.

"I'm not sure if you know this, but outside of my career as a pilot, I dabble a bit in investments," Bill says, his steel-blue eyes cold. They don't glitter the way his son's do. "From a business standpoint, I think you're onto something really great. Have you thought about scaling Noli into something more?"

"I mean, yes?" I say, and it comes out like a question. I cross my arms and glance back toward the mingling crowd arriving at the market. "But I'm not sure now is the right time."

"Why is that?"

What is the point of all these questions?

"Well, I don't exactly have the time between managing Delia's and taking care of my son. Nor do I have the..." I pause, then swallow. I don't want to talk about this with him. I don't trust him.

"The resources?" he supplies, leaning closer.

I say nothing.

"I'd like to have a conversation with you about that," Bill says. "I see an opportunity in Noli, and I'd be willing to invest in your business. Help provide you with some capital to get you on your feet."

I blink up at him, frowning. Why the sudden burst of generosity? There's got to be a catch.

"Of course, that investment would come with certain stipulations. One specifically," Bill narrows his eyes as he smiles.

"And what would that be?" I say, fearing his answer.

"I would be willing to invest a substantial amount of money in your business," Bill says in a low tone. "If you would agree to stop associating with Brooks."

I've felt angry before. A heart-shattering rage when I found out my husband of four years was cheating on me. Countless subsequent rolling waves of bitterness from frustrating interactions I've had to endure with him and others. A hopeless, tear-filled racking of my soul in the depths of postpartum depression. But this? This is different.

It's a direct hit. A cold-blooded attack on the fragile, growing hope that I've protected within me since Brooks entered my life again. The thick, greenhouse glass starts cracking around the tiny seed I've been nurturing.

I glare up at Bill Alden, the anger mounting inside of me, bound to expel from my mouth should I open it.

I can't help myself.

"How dare you?" I hiss. "How dare you try and manipulate our relationship *again*?" Bill's eyes narrow. "Yes, Brooks told me about how you influenced him to break up with me back in high school."

"It was for the best."

"Why are you so threatened by me?" I hate how my voice shakes. I'm not good at confrontation. I hate it. I want to run away from Bill and disappear, but I know things have to be addressed. Pity washes over me as I stare up at the man who desperately wants to pull the strings connected to his child to jerk him around, this way and that. Instead, Bill should be cutting Brooks free and allowing him to grow into the wonderful man that he is capable of becoming all on his own.

"Do you realize that this is why Brooks doesn't want a relationship with you?" I gesture towards him. "You think you're clearing the path to his success by getting me out of the way, but you're not. You're impeding it."

Bill's jaw clenches, and he opens his mouth to speak.

"I'm not finished," I cut in. "If you want to have any sort of bearing over your son's life, you have to have a relationship built on love and trust. Constantly criticizing him and tearing him down only ensures that he is going to run in the opposite direction. And he has."

"Right into your arms again," Bill says through gritted teeth. "It's only because he let you go that he's had the successful career we always dreamed of him having. You were the one thing standing in the way of his success, and once you were removed, he was free to soar. My son is at another crossroads in his life, and if he doesn't stay on the path I set him on years ago, everything is going to fall apart."

"It already has!" I say, my voice rising. "He fell apart at the end of last season because of *you*. Not me. I've been here to help him realize just how great he is after you worked so hard to tear his confidence to shreds. He thinks every time he makes a mistake, every time he falls short or acts like a normal human being, it's the end of the world."

Bill glowers down at me, and a shiver runs under my skin. Is this what Brooks felt as a child when he displeased his father? It's soul-crushing.

"You," Bill says in a cruel kind of calmness, "are nobody to him, Nora Foster. You always have been. You'll soon find that out for yourself, but in the meantime, if you care about him at all, you'll let him go."

Tears are pricking at the edges of my eyes, and I work desperately to keep them at bay.

"Promise me you'll leave him alone."

"No," I say firmly. "I will not."

Bill looks down at me as if I'm the most insignificant person to ever walk the face of this earth.

"Does this mean you reject my offer?" Bill asks. "Think very carefully. I could help you."

"I'll pass," I say tartly.

"Brooks has no plans to continue a relationship with you," Bill says, and his words feel like ice. "Ask him yourself."

I blink, doubt clouding the edges of my vision. Could this be true? Is that why Brooks has been distancing himself from me this week? Is he planning to drop me after tonight, now that our five Fridays are up?

"I will," I say. "But for now, I've got a booth to get back to."

I spin on my heel and march back to my booth as an icy drizzle begins to fall. I'm grateful for the rain. Maybe it will hide the tears burning pathways down my cheeks.

TWENTY-SIX
Brooks

NORA DOESN'T LOOK AT me for the entirety of the holiday market. Not even when a line forms around the corner made up of people who recognize me as they're passing by. Some simply say hello, while others want a photo or an autograph. Normally, I wouldn't mind this sort of thing, but tonight it feels wrong to be taking so much attention away from Nora in her own booth.

She's all welcoming sweetness for those who are interested in her work and make purchases, but I can see the tight smiles she's giving the Stormbreakers fans who have discovered that I'm here. I feel horrible. My intention was to help her run her booth, not draw a crowd for my own personal gain. But I'm trapped. I don't know how to politely turn all of the eager people away, so I smile and make shoutout videos and sign random objects for the duration of the night, too busy to help Nora wrap a single mug or vase. I even catch Sydney giving me an annoyed look as she tends to Ollie, which was supposed to be part of my job. I'd much rather be hanging with him than doing this.

The rain continues to fall, the crowd dwindles, and Ollie starts yawning widely. I finally escape from a lengthy conversation from two very avid local fans and slink to the back of the tent in an effort to hide.

"You tired, buddy?" Nora asks, pulling him in for a hug. He nods pathetically and whimpers. "I've got to get Ollie home," Nora says to Sydney.

"How can I help?" I ask, and Nora's eyes flick in my direction before moving away just as quickly.

"You can help me load these boxes into Trent's truck," Sydney answers instead, seeming to sense the tension between us and attempting to ease it. I'm grateful for the direction and work quickly, feeling a growing anxiety in my chest as I watch Nora in my periphery. I'm afraid that I completely ruined what was supposed to be a special night for her.

Once everything is packed up, and the tent is taken down, Sydney follows us back to the house. I help her unload the truck into the garage while Nora puts Ollie to bed.

"Hey," I say once everything is safely stored away. "I'm sorry about tonight."

Sydney looks up at me with a gentle smile. "I'm sorry for *you*. I'm sure a three-hour meet-and-greet was not in your plans for this evening."

I scrub a hand over my mouth. "I feel terrible."

"It's okay," Sydney says with a shrug. "Nora wasn't herself tonight."

My guilt deepens.

"Just talk to her," Sydney says with a pat on my shoulder. "I'm sure it will all be fine."

She drives away, and I take several steadying breaths in the garage before heading inside. I need to make things right.

I find Nora at her kitchen sink, scrubbing dishes that must have been left from a hasty dinner she'd prepared for Ollie earlier. My pulse races, and my nerves feel frazzled as I approach her in the quiet of her kitchen. I sidle in behind her at the sink, gently placing my hand on the small of her back.

"Hey," I say softly. "Can we talk?"

She continues furiously scrubbing away at a pot and doesn't spare me a glance. "About what?"

"About tonight."

"What about it?" she bites out, tossing a clean pot onto a towel spread onto the counter. I slowly slip the towel out and begin drying the pot. She continues to avoid my gaze.

"Nora," I say, setting the pot and towel down. "Come on. Look at me."

She flings her hair over her shoulder and finally glares over at me, pausing her frantic scrubbing. The look I see flashing in her eyes haunts me. It's the same look she gave me when I broke up with her all those years ago.

"What happened tonight," I say, "was inexcusable." She continues to glare at me, her eyes dancing with emotion. "I'm so sorry that I drew attention away from Noli. I'm sorry that I couldn't help you with Ollie or help you ring up customers. I feel awful about it."

She looks away, letting out a long breath from her nose and staring out the window over her sink into the dark yard beyond.

"Let me make it up to you," I say, reaching for her, but as soon as my fingers brush her arm, she flinches and pulls away.

"I worked for weeks to pull this off," she finally says, her voice trembling. "Every spare second I had, I spent at the wheel. I gave up extra sleep so I could get everything ready. And I still worked shifts every day at the diner like I always have. This was supposed to be special," she says, and when her voice breaks, my heart thuds painfully against my ribs. "Tonight was important to me, Brooks."

"I know. I'm so sorry."

She sniffs, brushing the back of her hand over her nose. Then she sets the dish brush aside and grips the edges of the sink with her head lowered. She looks so defeated. I hate myself for causing her to feel this way.

"Nora," I say, coaxing her into my chest. She buries her face in her hands and starts to cry in my arms.

"I'm not even mad about all the stupid fans who found out you were there," she says, her voice muffled against my shirt.

"You're not?" I ask, confused.

"No," she says. "A good amount ended up buying things, too. Really, I should be thanking you." She lets out a snorty laugh.

"Why are you so sad, then?" I ask, rubbing my hands up the sleeves of her soft sweater. "I thought this was all because of me."

"You're only partially to blame," she says softly, her eyes downcast. "Your dad was there." My grip on her arms tightens as she raises her gaze to mine. "He pulled me aside while you had Ollie."

"What did he say to you?" I ask, furious. How did I not see him there? "Please tell me."

"You first," she says stubbornly, poking me in the stomach. "You've barely spoken to me since last weekend when we ran into him at the market."

I allow my shoulders to drop, my eyes flitting between Nora's. I don't want to tell her. I don't want to hurt her any more. In my session with Greta this week, we'd worked through some of the insecurities our encounter with Bill had stirred up, and she'd counseled me to be upfront with Nora about those feelings and doubts. But now that I'm standing here in front of her, face to face, I don't want to do it.

"You promised," she pleads. "You promised to be honest with me, and I promised that I would be completely honest with you. Please tell me what happened, and then I swear I'll tell you about the conversation I had with your dad."

I sigh, releasing her and rubbing a hand over my forehead. I swallow, not wanting to speak my father's hurtful words into existence again.

"He tried to give me some advice," I say carefully. "Some really terrible advice that I refuse to listen to."

"Let me guess," she says flatly. "Advice about me?"
I nod slowly, feeling a frown pulling at the edges of my mouth.

"He told you to get me out of the picture, didn't he?" she almost whispers, and I see tears pooling at the corners of her wide, brown eyes. I nod again.

"Yeah," I say on a sigh. "He did."

She shakes her head, and I see anger in the tense lines of her face and the set of her jaw.

"He told me the same thing."

My chest aches, and I draw her to me again.

"He offered to invest in my business if I let you go," she says, her voice thick and muffled against my chest. "He said I was a nobody. And after tonight, I think he's kind of right."

"Don't say that," I say angrily. "This is what he wanted. This is how he works, Nora. He tried to make me doubt you and doubt myself, and I'm embarrassed to admit that what he said to me the other day got under my skin."

"I know," she sniffs. "I could tell."

"He's an expert at making me feel inadequate. You would think I would have learned to see through it by now, but I let him get to me, and then I let him get to you..." I trail off, placing my hands on her shoulders so she'll look at me. "I'm so sorry, Nora. This is what he wanted. He wanted us to fight. He wanted to drive a wedge between us. That's what he does."

"Why?" Nora whispers.

"I've been asking myself that question for my entire life," I say with a bitter laugh. "It's a power struggle. That's just the kind of parent he is."

"I'm so sad for you," Nora says, pressing a palm over my heart. "My parents trusted me. I always knew my parents loved me. I don't know what I would have done if I'd had someone always making me feel small like your dad does."

I draw inward, recognizing the feelings of shame and inadequacy that always rise whenever I interact with my dad.

"You were right. I don't think I'll ever please him, and I need to grieve that," I say. "I'll never be perfect. No matter what milestones or achievements I make, it will never be enough. He holds me to a standard that he himself cannot ever achieve."

"That's probably why he hates me so much," Nora replies. "I'm a mess. He thinks I'm going to take you down with me and ruin the perfect image he wants to hold you to."

"You are not a mess," I say firmly. "You are real, Nora. That's what I need. My dad tried to make me feel guilty for going back to you, but I've only been able to move forward and progress these past couple months because I had you by my side. I *need* you, Nora. You keep me grounded. You remind me that it's okay if things aren't perfect. I don't want to lose this momentum that you've helped me create. For the first time, I feel like I'm on the right path for the right reasons, and I want you to walk it with me." I frame her face gently with my hands, and she closes her eyes.

Nora hiccups and claps a hand over her mouth, embarrassed.

"I'm so sorry," she says, laughing. "Sometimes I hiccup when I cry."

We laugh together, breaking the tension of the moment, and I go off in search of a box of tissues. We reconvene a minute later on her couch, our legs and hands tangled together.

"Are you going to take Bill up on his offer?" I ask, teasing. "Cut me loose?"

She blinks over at me, offended. "Absolutely not. I'm not going to allow him to come between us again, Brooks." Her words make my chest swell. "Though what your dad said to me did make me think about what I really want, long term."

"What *do* you want?" I ask, desperate to know. Desperately hopeful that I'm included in her plan.

"I'm okay with being a nobody," she says with a shrug. "If that means I get to live in my own little house and do honest work I'm proud of. And have a family of my own to love and learn from."

"Don't sell yourself short," I insist, but she waves me off.

"No, really," she says. "I don't need a lot to be happy. That's why I've never ventured outside of Kitt's Harbor. I never had big dreams to chase like my sisters did. I just wanted to be somewhere I could feel safe and be loved." She clings to my hands even tighter. "But you, Brooks Alden, you are not a nobody."

Her eyes fill with tears again.

"You have carved out a big place in this world, and I don't want to hold you back from filling it."

"Nora," I plead.

"What are we going to do once baseball season starts up again? You have to go to Florida for spring training. Then you'll be on the road lots for away games, and even when you're in Seattle for home games, your days are filled from top to bottom. Where would Ollie and I even fit?"

I bite my lip and take a deep breath, not wanting to face the facts of what the future is going to look like for me. The disparity between our lives that we've been able to ignore up until this honest conversation.

"I have a son, Brooks. I have to work to provide for him. I have to live close to Nate to abide by our custody agreement. And you have to go back to Seattle. Back to your team."

"All of that is true, but plenty of my teammates are in relationships and have families and they make it work," I say. "Tell me you haven't been happy with me. Lie to my face. Go ahead and try it."

"You know I'm a terrible liar! Of course I've been happy," she cries, half-laughing, half-sobbing. "I've never been more happy!"

"Then let's keep this good thing going," I say. "I've spent these past two months learning what it means to be a man outside of my career. The man I want to be is the man by your side, Nora. The man who takes care of you and Ollie, just like I said I would."

"Brooks, I–"

"We could make it work," I say. "You know we could. I have driven home every weekend to see you, and I don't regret one single mile."

"Won't you have games on the weekends?" she points out.

"Come to my games, Nora. I'd love for you to be there," I counter. "Bring Ollie along. There are always lots of girlfriends there, and the other wives bring their kids to the games, too. Have you ever asked Nate if he'd be willing to adjust your custody agreement?"

"Well...no. I've always been afraid to."

"Why? Nate doesn't seem like he's much of a father to Ollie. I think you could take Ollie full-time if you wanted to. We could approach Nate about it with the help of a lawyer, if that's something you'd want to change."

Nora grows quiet, resting her chin in her palm, her fingers dancing over her lips.

"Nate pays child support. I need that money," she says softly.

"I have money, Nora," I say. "You wouldn't have to worry about that."

Her dark eyes widen, and she blinks rapidly. "I can't take your money."

"What else am I supposed to do with it? My sisters think I'm going to die a bachelor, and I'll have to bequeath it all to them. I can't let that happen."

Nora's determined expression softens, and she smiles at me, but her smile quickly fades.

"My biggest concern and priority is taking care of my son. It has to be."

"Understood," I say. "But who is going to take care of you?" She stares back at me, her expression unreadable. "Let me do it, Nora. Let me take care of you."

"But if I let you do that, if I let you in, there's no guarantee that things will work out between us," she says fearfully. "If anything were to happen, it wouldn't just break my heart, it would break Ollie's, too."

"I would never do that."

"That's what Nate said, too, when he married me."

"Nora," I say gently. "I am not the man I was when we dated in high school, nor am I your ex-husband. Look at my muscles. Unlike Nate, I didn't have to do steroids to build them." I playfully flex my bicep around her shoulders. "You can feel them if you want, just to verify for yourself."

She laughs and snuggles closer to me.

"I'm all in, Nora," I say. "I might not be perfect at being the man you need and the man that Ollie needs, but I will sure as hell try my best."

Nora's eyes flick between mine contemplatively.

"Screw Bill Alden," I say, brushing my fingertips over her ear and into her hair. "I want you, Nora. I've always wanted you. I'm not going to let him or anyone else take you from me again."

She places her hand over mine and leans into it, her gaze filled with a soft affection. "I want you, too," she whispers.

That's all it takes for me to capture her mouth with mine. I kiss her gently, breathing her in and holding her carefully. My heart is pounding against my chest. Words are gathering in my throat. Words I've been wanting to say every time my mouth moves against hers. Every time I pull into her driveway and she's there, waiting for me. Every time she's taken me in and tamed my demons and helped me get out of my head.

"Nora," I mumble against her lips, and our kisses quiet. "Nora..." I rest my forehead against hers, eyes still closed. I wait until she opens her eyes, and our gazes collide.

"I love you, Nora. I think I never stopped loving you," I say. I see the emotion emerge in her expression, drawing her mouth up into an unguarded smile. I kiss her again, and she begins to tremble under my hands. She pulls away, nervously touching my cheek, her eyes darting between mine.

"I love you, too," she whispers. "We can do this. I want to do this."

Her words blanket me, and there's a settling in my soul and in my bones. A tempering of the unknown. I try to convey my dedication to her and to what will hopefully be our family one day with every slow kiss, every brush of my fingertips across her skin.

We're a team now: Nora, Ollie, and me. And if there's one thing I know how to be, it's a team player.

TWENTY-SEVEN
Nora

"Mama!" Ollie says, his mouth dropping into an *O*. "You look pretty." He draws out the last word, and I want to squeeze him to pieces. He's got the sweetness dialed up to eleven today, and I'm not complaining about it.

"Thank you, honey," I say, applying a second layer of red lipstick before inspecting my work in the mirror. "Do you like my lipstick?"

Another nod. He starts reaching for the tube. "I help you?"

"You're so sweet. I'm already done! Let's go get our shoes on."

I finish tying one of Ollie's shoes when a knock sounds at the door. Ollie gasps, and we look at each other in excitement.

"I get it!" he says, scrambling to his feet. I let him attempt to open the door by himself, and he struggles with the knob for a minute before I step in.

Ollie barrels into Brooks as soon as the door swings open. Brooks looks me up and down appreciatively, mouthing the word *wow*.

"How's my little dude?" Brooks asks, shifting Ollie into his arms so he can look at him. He lets out a theatrical gasp. "Wait a second...Nora. We've got a problem."

"What is it?" I ask, playing along as I slip on my boots in the entryway.

"This isn't Ollie," Brooks says teasingly. "This right here is our Thanksgiving turkey."

"No, it's not!" Ollie cries.

"It must have escaped. We've got to get it over to your parents' house or Thanksgiving will be ruined!"

Ollie shrieks as Brooks tickles him, insisting that there's been a mistake, and he is not, in fact, a turkey.

"I'm Ollie!" he giggles.

"I don't know, Brooks," I say. "I think you might be right. Look at the legs he's got on him."

"Those are turkey legs, alright," Brooks agrees. He shifts Ollie to one side and gathers me close, nuzzling me just below my ear. "It's a good thing Ollie is here because, if he wasn't, I would be taking you right back inside your house to order takeout just so I could have you all to myself."

I laugh as he skates his fingertips across my low back. He drops a soft kiss to my cheek.

"You look beautiful."

"So do you," I say, and he does. This deep green crewneck sweater situation he's got going on is working. I grab my sweet potato casserole from the entryway table and move to close and lock the front door. "Let me grab Ollie's car seat out of my car," I say.

"No need," Brooks says, chasing after Ollie as he darts down the porch steps.

I glance at Brooks in confusion. He doesn't offer an explanation, just opens the back door and hoists Ollie inside his Tesla...into a brand-new car seat.

I slowly approach the car and watch as Brooks buckles Ollie into the car seat like he's done it a thousand times before.

"Got you a new seat so you can ride with me even if your mom isn't around," Brooks says, shooting a grin at me over his shoulder. "Do you like it?"

"Yeah!" Ollie says enthusiastically. He looks up at me from inside the car. "You like it, Mama?"

My eyes burn as tears threaten to fall, and I blink quickly, determined not to ruin the makeup I'd spent a little extra time on. "I love it. That is the coolest car seat I've ever seen."

Brooks shuts the car door and turns to face me. I spring myself at him, and he catches me with a *wumph*.

"Thank you," I say, lifting my chin above his shoulder so I don't accidentally get lipstick on his sweater. "I don't even know what to say."

"Just trying to take care of my people," he says, his hands splaying across my back as he draws me in tighter.

"How did you know what kind of car seat to get?"

"I have a couple teammates who have kids Ollie's age. They helped me choose a good one. Hopefully," he says with a nervous laugh.

I pull away and trace his clean-shaven jawline with my fingertips. He brushes his lips over mine, and my eyes flutter closed. He smells so good. I'll take three courses of Brooks Alden over Thanksgiving fare any day.

We arrive at my parents' house about ten minutes later, and I try to prepare Brooks for the events of the evening.

"Everybody's going to want to talk to you," I say. "Well, except for Trent. He's pretty much anti-social. They're going to ask you a lot of questions."

"I'm not worried about it, Nora," he says, flashing me a confident smile.

"Well, I am!" I say. "We should have some kind of signal we can flash to each other if you're feeling overwhelmed or need me to rescue you."

"I'm not sure flashing each other would be appropriate at a family function, but I'm not opposed to it."

"Stop it," I say, smacking his chest with the back of my hand. "How about you give me one of your baseball signals?"

"Baseball...signals."

"Yeah, like something you do with your teammates or the pitcher or whatever."

"I need to educate you. Badly."

"Come on! I'm trying to help you!"

"I'm going to be fine, Nora," he says, giving my hand a reassuring squeeze before reaching for the door handle. "I can handle your family. What you should be worried about is me trapping you in a well-lit corner of your parents' house and kissing you in front of everyone. Your lips look...mmm."

I level him with a look. "Don't even try it."

His dancing blue eyes and confident smirk say he just might.

"I've got something to tell you," I say. Brooks looks over at me expectantly. "Nate texted me this morning."

Brooks' face darkens, and it shouldn't make me happy to see him immediately bristle at the mention of Nate, but it does. I like that he's in my corner now. "What did he say?"

"His wife is pregnant," I say. I'd initially felt angry when I'd learned that Nate was going to be a father for a second time after essentially abandoning me and Ollie. But then I'd read the rest of his text. "He asked if we could meet to discuss our custody agreement. He feels he needs to focus on Heidi and the baby on the way and thought we could adjust things now that you're in the picture."

"Wait," Brooks says with a disbelieving grin. "He's trying to use *me* to get out of playing an active role in Ollie's life?"

"Pretty much."

"What a tool," he says. "But you know what? I say let him use me. Let's keep Ollie all to ourselves."

I snuggle up to him and press a kiss to his cheek, leaving a perfect, red imprint of my lips on his face. I'm not even going to bother to wipe it off.

My prediction proves to be correct. We are smothered from the moment we enter the house, starting with my dad, bless him, who has the undivided attention of his favorite local baseball player. Brooks is gracious and sweet with my dad, sitting next to him on the couch and chatting easily while I help my mom and sisters finish things up in the kitchen. Ollie is climbing all over Trent and Javier, who are putting together a complex puzzle in the living room.

"So," Sydney says, putting the finishing touches on her green bean casserole. "What happened after the holiday market last weekend? Did you guys work things out?"

"I'd say so," Bridget says before I can answer, jutting her chin towards Brooks. "He keeps looking over here every five seconds. He can't get enough of you."

"Shut up," I hiss, but inwardly, my heart is leaping. "Yes, we had some really good conversations. I think we're both on the same page."

"And what page is that?" Mom asks. "Is he going to propose tonight?

My heart stumbles. What if he did? I'm certifiably insane? Because I think if he asked me tonight, I would say *yes*.

Who am I? Gone is the hesitant, fearful version of Nora. Somehow, I'm not scared about a future with Brooks anymore. I've got a cloud of balloons tied to my wrist, pulling me up and onward with him by my side.

"You really like him, don't you?" Mom says, and I nod.

"I do. I want to make things work with him this time around. I'm going to take weekends off so I can be with him in Seattle."

"My neck of the woods!" Bridget says. "With or without Ollie?"

"Well," I say, feeling elated at the news I get to share with my family. "Nate's wife is pregnant, so he wants to grant me full custody of Ollie so he can focus on her and the baby."

"*What*?" Sydney gasps. "Oooh, I'm so happy for you, but at the same time, I want to give that man a swirly in the nearest toilet!"

My mom and sisters gather around me in eager excitement, hugging me in turn. For the first time in forever, I can take a full, deep breath without it getting stuck in my lungs. There's no hitch, no fearful squeezing in my chest. Things are working out, and I'm filled with a deep sense of gratitude and relief.

"So, what about your job?" Mom asks.

I fidget with the edge of the tea towel hanging from the oven. "That's something Brooks and I have been talking about a lot. I don't want him to be my sugar daddy," I say with a laugh. "Though he's very sweet and offered to support me and Ollie financially. As a compromise, I've agreed to let him help me turn Noli into something more."

"I'm so proud of you," Sydney says, growing weepy. "We're here to help you with anything you need."

I look between the women who have anchored me through the ups and downs of the past few years, then over at the men taking care of my son. They are everything to me.

A random timer starts beeping, and the kitchen becomes a flurry as we work together to get the table set for dinner. Sydney made hand-written place settings for each member of the family. There's a lively shuffle as we all locate our assigned seats around the table. I'm squashed between Brooks and Trent, and Mom insists that Ollie be seated in a highchair next to her so I can enjoy my meal. She gives me a wink, and I don't fight her on it.

Brooks takes my hand in his as we bow our heads while Dad prays over our meal, and I lean into his touch. I'm so glad he's here.

"Thank you for having me," Brooks says to my mom over the clang of serving utensils and murmured conversations. "I'm sorry I didn't contribute anything to this beautiful meal."

"You did," I remind him, and a crooked smile tucks his cheek.

"A certain someone found my marshmallow stash in the pantry." I look pointedly at Ollie. "And I didn't discover it until after he was already asleep. Brooks saved the day and had some delivered to my front porch last night." He'd also included a pint of ice cream for me. I've never sprung for grocery delivery because the fees are so ridiculous, but when I'd jokingly told Brooks that the sweet potatoes would have to be served sans mallows, he took matters into his own hands. It warmed me right through when those groceries showed up at my front door.

"Glad to be of service," he says with a smile.

"I would have still eaten them," Trent reassures me, taking a hefty helping for himself when the sweet potatoes make their way around.

I can't remember the last holiday I'd enjoyed as much as this one. My fingertips itch to be constantly clasped in Brooks', and I notice every press of his knee against mine under the table, every glance he spares in my direction. I want him by my side at every family gathering for the rest of my life. He's part of my family now.

He has groceries delivered to my house. He buys a car seat so my son can safely ride in his car, should the need arise. He asks thoughtful and engaging questions to each member of my family, genuinely interested in getting to know them.

For a while, I thought my entire heart would forever belong only to Ollie, but it's expanding like the Grinch's to accommodate Brooks. There's plenty of space for both of them.

The night passes with laughter and warmth, the draining and filling of glasses, and the telling of stories meant to entertain. I feel a deep appreciation for my family and for the love that has always filled our home. Brooks didn't always have that when he was growing up, and I'm desperate for him to taste it now.

The men take care of the dishes before joining the rest of us in the living room. Sydney and Brooks start chatting about photography, and I watch as Brooks' eyes light up with interest.

"I shoot portraits with a 50 millimeter lens, and then if I'm shooting a landscape or a city, I use a wide angle lens," she explains, flipping through some photos she's taken on her phone.

"Can you send me some links?" Brooks asks her. "I think I want to buy a camera."

I knew he'd enjoyed our night spent shooting photos with Sydney, but I didn't realize he'd loved it that much. The thought of him finding an interest he wants to pursue outside of his chosen sport warms my heart.

"Absolutely!" Sydney replies, and I'm grateful for her enthusiasm. I know she'll set him up with everything he might need. "You'll have to let me know if you really do end up buying one. I can give you a crash course anytime."

I sidle up between Javier and Trent who are still hard at work on the puzzle, gazing down at the scene they're slowly piecing together.

"Venice?" I venture.

Javier nods. "Sydney chose it."

"Obviously," I say with a smile. "Trent's favorite place in the world."

Trent snorts, hunched over the table with a frown in place. He's as content as anybody else, but you'd never know it by the somber expression he usually wears. "I'm never going back there."

"What was it that ruined it for you again? The pickpocket or the pasta that gave you raging–"

"Sydney will try to sell you on Venice," Trent interrupts, addressing Brooks. "Don't listen to a word she says."

"Listen," she says defensively. "We had some unfortunate moments in Venice, but it is still one of the most magical cities in the world, in my opinion."

"Do you guys travel a lot?" Brooks asks.

"It's her hobby," Trent says, leaning back in his chair.

"More like passion," Sydney amends.

"So yes," Trent says. "We travel quite a bit."

"Where are you off to next?" Brooks asks.

"You will not believe where I convinced Trent to take me next year."

We all wait for the big reveal. Trent looks less than enthused as Sydney shouts, "Iceland!"

"Iceland," Trent repeats flatly.

"Trust me," Sydney says, planting a kiss on her husband's bearded cheek. "You're going to love it. You guys wanna tag along?" Sydney asks, just like she always has. She's never given up on me even though I've never agreed to accompany her on one of her countless trips abroad.

"Maybe one day," I say. "I should probably fly somewhere domestic first."

"She's never flown before," Sydney says to Brooks. "Can you believe that?"

Brooks looks at me in shock. "What? Never?"

I shake my head. I look like the most boring person on the planet compared to my well-traveled sister. She made a career out of traveling while I got really good at memorizing orders at the diner.

"Well, we might have to change that," Brooks says with a grin.

"Don't you move with the team to Florida soon?" Javier asks.

"Yeah," Brooks says. "In February."

"Spring training?" Trent asks, and Brooks nods.

We'd discussed this the other night. Bless all of the women who date and marry professional baseball players. They never stay in one place too long during the season.

Ollie clambers onto Brooks' lap so he can tell him all about Florida. Brooks keeps glancing my way, and I can tell something's brewing in that mind of his. It's not until he drops me off at home at the end of the night that I find out what it is.

"I like the thought of you being with me in Florida," he says, drawing me to him for a kiss across the console. Ollie fell asleep on the ten minute drive home, zonked out in the back seat.

"You do?" I say, tilting my head to find his mouth again as he threads his fingers into my hair.

"Palm trees...you and me. A little baseball during the day, time together at night," he says with a teasing nip at my lower lip.

"Sign me up," I say. I need no more convincing. I'm terrified of hopping on that flight, but I'll do it if it means we get to be together during those months he'll be living on the opposite coast.

"Do you think you'd be able to take work off?" he asks between kissing stints.

"Send me the dates you'd want me to be there, and I can start looking into it."

"I think Ollie would love it."

He would, and so would I. I couldn't bear to be that far from him, even if it was for a few days. But the thought of paying for flights and a hotel for both of us is already making me queasy, and I haven't even done any research yet.

"I think he would, too. If I do a few more markets I think I could save up enough money to buy our flights."

"Oh, I didn't tell you?" Brooks says. "You're a sweepstakes winner."

"A sweepstakes winner?" I whisper, stifling a giggle so I don't wake Ollie. "I've never been a sweepstakes winner before. What did I win?"

"An all expenses paid trip to Florida during spring training."

I thumb Brooks's jawline affectionately. "That's very sweet of you, but I can't let you do that."

"Just try and stop me," Brooks says, his mouth hitching up in a grin. "But we've still got a couple months together before I leave for spring training. What on earth are we going to do with all that time?"

"We'll have more Fridays," I whisper. "More rollerblading. More brookies–."

"More night swims?" he ventures and then laughs at my scowl.

"I don't know about that," I say. "Maybe more kissing?"

"I can give you that," Brooks says, pressing a soft, warm kiss to the corner of my mouth.

There's a sweet reassurance in his kiss, and I plan to savor every day we have left together before he leaves again. The idea doesn't terrify me like it used to because I know that this time, he'll always come back to me.

TWENTY-EIGHT
Brooks

December

The month leading up to Christmas is a wild whirlwind of preparation for the new year, doubling down on my good habits and training routines, and slow weekends spent with Nora and Ollie in Kitt's Harbor. We fall into a rhythm, a comfortable ease that spreads into every other area of my life. My teammates notice. My therapist notices. My family notices. Claire and Caroline are jokingly (but not?) banking on a spring wedding, and I like the thought of it so much it's embarrassing. In a moment of weakness, I even allowed Claire to show me her inspiration mood board she's made on my behalf. Then, I found a printed version of it hanging in the guest room the following day.

After our initial six therapy sessions conclude, I decide to continue to meet weekly with Greta. The more I implement her ideas, the more balanced and present I feel in my life.

"The way you speak to yourself really matters," Greta reminds me during one of our sessions. "Talk to yourself out loud, if you need to. Speak kindly to yourself."

So, I do.

When I fail to catch a ball, I reassure myself that I'll get it next time. When I work with my trainer in the gym and struggle to perform something he asks me to do perfectly, I say, "All good, man. All good." He thinks I'm talking to him, but really, I'm speaking to myself. When Nora and I have a disagreement or I fall short, I don't allow myself to spiral into negativity and self-doubt. I look her in the eyes and apologize, then say, "I'm still learning. I'll get better at this with time."

Nora assumes the role of my gentle partner. My closest friend. We still seek out new experiences to try together, including a painting class that leaves me certain I was never destined to be an artist.

"Well," I say, hanging my sorry portrait next to Nora's beautiful artwork on her fridge. "I won't be doing that again."

Nora laughs and kisses me on the cheek. "You gave it your best. That's all that matters."

Nate was surprisingly accommodating in the new custody agreement, seeming slightly relieved to pass the baton of responsibility for his biological son to me. I'll never understand him, but at the same time, I'm eager to step into the role he failed to cherish. I may not be Ollie's birth father, but I know I could love him like he's my own. I already do.

The hazy happiness I feel at the idea of us becoming a permanent family nearly swallows me whole. Then, there are moments when I catch myself imagining Nora with a ring on her left hand and a swollen belly, carrying *my* child. I'm willing to move at her pace and respect her timing, but I'm determined to change her last name to mine. I plan to lock her down for good this time.

There's a peace I'm experiencing as Christmas approaches, a rooted contentment I've never felt before. I'm also highly entertained by Nora's endless collection of Christmas sweaters. I never know what sort of tacky, hand-knit creation she's going to emerge in next.

One night, we're seated on her couch, cuddled up after watching a holiday movie. Nora's reindeer sweater jingles every time she moves. She's got her legs over my lap and is lying back on a pillow with her eyes half-open. She's tired. I can tell I'm losing her.

"You still awake?" I say. "I've got something I want to ask you."

"Hmm?" Nora hums lazily. I'd love nothing more than to cocoon her into a blanket and let her sleep, but I need her full attention. "What is it?"

"I want you to come to the team Christmas dinner with me," I say. Nora's eyes flutter open, and she blinks at me. "I want to introduce you to the guys. I want you by my side."

"You do?" she says breathlessly.

"Of course. I want you to bring Ollie, too. If you're comfortable with that."

"He would love it. We both would." Her dark eyes become hooded, and she knots one of her hands into my hair, leaning in close. "How will you introduce me to your teammates?"

"I'll introduce you to everyone as my girlfriend, if that's alright with you. You've already been that...at least, in my head."

She lets out a little giggle.

"Would that be alright?"

"I like the sound of that," Nora says before kissing me softly. She's all I ever wanted, and I'm eager to meld our worlds together for good.

The night of the team Christmas dinner arrives, and we agree that it's best if Nora drives out to Seattle to meet me. She's got Ollie with her, and when they show up at my apartment together, I'm so happy to see them standing there outside my front door I think I might implode.

"Hi, Daddy," Ollie says, and Nora audibly gasps. We look at each other, trying to gauge each other's reactions to his sweet slip.

I snatch Ollie up in a hug and squeeze him tight. He looks adorable, dressed up in a sweater, khaki pants, and the tiniest dress shoes I've ever seen in my life. He rests his little head on my shoulder, and I hold him there, feeling like him accidentally calling me Dad is a sign.

I could do it. I could be his father. I won't be perfect at it, but anything I don't know how to do right away, I know I could learn. I can break the chain and be the kind of father I never had. The kind of dad Ollie deserves.

"Looking fresh, dude," I say, setting him down and offering him knuckles. I turn to Nora and let out a low whistle, looking her over with appreciation.

"Dang," I say as she twirls around. Her black dress is doing good things for her curves. "On second thought, we'll just stay in tonight."

She completes her spin and faces me with a flush on her cheeks and a twinkle in her eyes. "You like it?"

"Love it," I reply, thoroughly smitten. Her dark hair is shiny and smooth, her makeup accenting her beautiful eyes and smile.

"He called you daddy," she says, slinging her arms around my neck. "How do you feel about that?"

"He can call me that, if he wants to," I say. "I like it."

Nora's eyes grow watery, and she blinks up at me. "Thank you. That means the world to me. And him."

I bring her chin up and press a kiss to her mouth. Then, a loud crash sounds from my bedroom.

"Ollie?" Nora calls out, jumping out of my grasp. "I'm warning you now. You're about to find out how kid-proof your house is."

Fortunately, Ollie is unscathed. He was trying to reach a signed baseball I keep on my desk and knocked over a decorative globe.

"You wanna see it?" I ask, handing him the ball. "That ball is signed by Ichiro Suzuki. One of the greatest baseball players of all time."

"Where did you get this?" Nora asks, helping Ollie handle it carefully.

"My dad," I say. "He bid on it in an auction for me. Gave it to me as a gift when I got drafted into the minors."

Nora gives me a small, knowing smile. "This is very special, Ollie. Let's put it back, okay?"

Ollie has no qualms rummaging through my belongings, and soon, we've got a spread of balls, bats, gloves, pictures, awards, and other random memorabilia spread in a growing pile on my bed.

"I try it?" he asks, pointing to one of my hats hanging on a rack. I slap it down onto his head, and he beams up at me from underneath the brim.

"It's a good look on you, buddy."

He pulls the hat off a few minutes later and gasps. "Oh, no!"

"What's wrong?" Nora asks.

"My hair! Mama fix it?"

"Oh," she laughs, combing her fingers through his hair. "Like that?"

"No," Ollie pouts, then runs over to me. "Big Dude fix it."

"You want me to fix your hair? Like mine?" I say, and he nods. "You got it."

I lead him to my bathroom and set him on the counter. He batters his heels against the cabinet drawers while I pull out some pomade and a comb.

"I've never done a kid's hair before," I admit to Nora, who's standing by observing with her hands laced behind her back. "But how hard could it be?"

I take some pomade in my hands and gently apply it to Ollie's soft hair with my fingertips, raking it through. Then, I comb his hair back and style it the way I usually do mine.

"How's that?" I ask him, spinning him around to face the mirror. "Do you like it?"

His face splits into a toothy grin. "So handsome!"

"You both are. Ollie, you look so grown up!" Nora says, helping him down off the counter before sliding her hands around my waist. "Thank you."

"Anytime," I say. And I mean it. "Next time Ollie needs a hair stylist, I'm your guy."

We head to the restaurant, a swanky seafood joint on the water. I let the valet park my car, per the invitation's instructions, and we enter the restaurant together.

"Just so you know," Nora says, sounding nervous as we huddle in the warmth of the entryway, "Ollie might not last very long."

"That's totally fine," I reassure her. "Let me know when you're ready to leave, and we'll bounce."

There's a chorus of greetings as we're led to a table, passing by coaches, trainers, and teammates I haven't seen in a while. Apparently, the Stormbreakers rented out the entire place for tonight. Jonah claps me on the shoulder as we pass and pulls me into a bear hug.

"Tell me you missed me," he says, squeezing all the air out of my lungs. "Say it."

"I saw you like three days ago," I wheeze.

"And who might you be, young man?" he says, crouching down to Ollie's height.

"This is Ollie."

Jonah motions for his daughters to come over. "This is Scarlett. She's seven. And this is Rosie. She's four. How old are you, Ollie?"

He holds up two fingers.

"Two!" Jonah crows. "No way. You look at least twenty-three with that dapper sweater and hairdo."

Ollie turns away, clinging to Nora's dress.

"You must be Nora," Jonah says. "This is my wife, Megan."

"So nice to meet you both," Nora says with a soft smile.

"You're a lucky man, Brookie," Jonah says.

Nora smiles up at me. "I think we're both pretty lucky." Alright. She can't say things like that to me in the presence of others. My teammates might witness an improper amount of PDA if she keeps this up.

Nora starts chatting with Megan, and Jonah pulls me aside.

"So," he prods. "I need the full report. What were all the potential new hobbies you tried out together?"

"We dabbled in roller blading, baking, and cold plunging," I say. "Nora's sister also gave us a lesson in photography, and honestly, I think I could get into it."

"Really?" Jonah asks. "That's awesome. You should take photos of the team. We could make a calendar for charity."

"With you on the cover?"

"Nah," Jonah says, flexing playfully. "That honor would go to Miles. Speak of the devil..."

A big hand closes over my shoulder, and I turn to find Miles and Beau standing behind me.

"Way to show us all up," I say, taking in Miles' bright blue suit. He loves a statement.

"Somebody's gotta be the eye candy here," he says, flashing a smile. "You gonna introduce us to your lady?"

I regain Nora's attention and introduce her.

"You're the one who made those mugs Brooks gave us, right?" Beau asks.

"Yes. That was me," Nora says, looking slightly starstruck. I forget sometimes that her family followed Stormbreakers baseball before I joined the roster. She's probably a big fan of some of these players. But as long as I'm at the top of the list and she's wearing my number on her jersey at my games, I'm cool with it.

We all know she's mine.

"Now, I was never a mug guy, but I am now," Miles says to her. "How can I buy more? I want to get some for my mom and sisters."

Nora glances over at me in disbelief, and I smile with pride. She talks shop with Miles, and they end up exchanging numbers so he can place a larger order. I have a feeling he won't be the last to make this sort of request.

I turn and greet more of the seemingly endless stream of guys lining up to say hello to both me and Nora. I feel the slightest twinge of jealousy at how friendly my teammates are towards her, but then I realize that they're treating her as nicely as they are out of respect for me. They want me to know that if she's important to me, she's important to them, too.

Ollie steals the show during dinner, raving about everything they put in front of him. He devours his food like it's his last meal on earth and cracks us all up with his expressive exclamations.

"My man," Miles says, extending his glass to clink it against Ollie's plastic cup. "You have impeccable taste."

I find Nora's leg and give it a squeeze, the thin satin material of her dress silky under my fingertips. "Are you enjoying yourself?" I ask, leaning close to speak into her ear.

"Of course I am. The food is amazing, the service is top-notch, and the company is pretty good, too," she says, reaching for my hand resting on her leg. I turn my palm upwards, and she slides her fingers between mine.

"Good," I say. We may not have figured out all the logistics yet, but I can't imagine not having Nora and Ollie by my side for every single event like this in the future. They belong here with me.

At the end of the evening, I drive a very sleepy Ollie and a very content Nora back to my apartment so she can get their car. She's staying with her sister Bridget for the night. She'd told me that once Bridget found out they'd be in town she had practically begged them to stay over. We linger in the parking garage, neither of us quite ready to end the night.

"You sure you don't want to stay with me?" I ask again.

Nora looks over at me skeptically. "You know we can't do that."

"Why not?"

"Because," she says. "We have a child with us, and I know you can't be trusted to keep your hands to yourself."

I scoff. "You have so little faith in me. You sure I can't convince you?"

"Hmm..." she hums as I kiss her jawline before coaxing an answer from her mouth. She pulls away and looks up at me shyly. "It would take a higher level of commitment between us for me to stay with you."

"What kind of commitment?" I want her to name it. To say the words out loud. I'm ready.

Nora nudges my nose with hers and smiles. The smell of her perfume on her neck and the line of her collarbones are so tempting. She's probably right. There's no way I'd be able to resist her tonight.

"You'd have to marry me," Nora says, and my pulse pounds in my temples.

I gently skate my thumb over her bottom lip, and she smiles. "Is that all?"

"That's it," she says coyly, her fingers toying with the hair at the base of my neck. "Just a ring on my finger and a promise to love me forever."

"Done," I say, and elation swells in my chest. I can't keep the stupid smile off my face. "When do you want to get married?"

"Next summer?" she suggests, her pretty eyes sparkling.

"How about next spring?"

"Hmm," she hums. "Spring might be nice."

"Tell me when and where you want to get married, and I'll be there," I say, elated. High on the thought of making Nora Foster mine forever. "Where will we live after we're married? Would you move to Seattle with me?"

"Maybe part time," she says with a giddy grin. "But when you're traveling, I'd like to be near my family so I could still have help with Ollie. And I'll still need to work, right? Somebody's gotta pay my mortgage."

"I could do that."

She levels me with a look, and I'm struck once again by her beauty, deep brown eyes and the waves of her dark hair glowing in the dim light inside the parking garage.

"You most certainly will *not* be doing that."

"You're so stubborn," I whisper, laughing. "What would have to happen for you to let me pay your mortgage?"

"After we're married, we'll both pay the mortgage. Together."

"How about after we're engaged?" I say, curling my arms around her across the console and wishing I could pull her onto my lap. "Can I make you my fiancée?"

"Yes," she whispers. "That's exactly what I want."

I smile against her mouth before tipping her chin up to kiss her again. This was the go-ahead I needed. Nora Foster deserves the real thing. And I'm going to be the one to give it to her.

A few days later, we spend Christmas together. We start the day with breakfast at Nora's house before exchanging gifts. Ollie is thrilled about the glove, ball, and bat I give him. Nora gives me a book of photos she and I took on Sydney's camera that night on the beach. She even framed a few prints so I can display them in my apartment. She also buys me an outrageously hideous Christmas sweater that she insists I wear to her family's house later that night.

"It's tradition!" she says.

"So, this is what I'm signing up for?" I sigh in fake frustration. "A lifetime of ugly sweaters?"

Nora beams. "I'll buy you a new one every year."

"Maybe I should take up knitting," I grumble. "I could *make* something better than this."

"Put on the sweater, Brooks," she threatens.

"Oh, you mean right now?" I say, starting to peel off my t-shirt. Her eyes widen, and I grin.

Later in the evening, the Foster family is spread about the living room, their faces washed in soft golden light from the Christmas tree. The house is peaceful and quiet, and I don't think I've ever had a happier Christmas in my life.

"I've got one last gift for you," I say to Nora

318

"What is it?"

I reach into my pocket and draw out a blank envelope.

"A love letter? How romantic."

She slowly pulls a piece of paper from the envelope and scans it, her eyes growing wide.

"Wait, *what*?" She gapes at me. "What is this?"

"I remembered you telling me that you've been using the kiln at the high school to fire your ceramics. I figured you could use one of your own."

I watch tears pool in her eyes as she glances between me and the receipt for the kiln I'd ordered that's on its way.

"Now, here's the catch," I say, pulling her close. "Consider this an investment in Noli. I want you to really pursue that dream of yours this year, if that's something you still want. A few of the guys have already agreed to help share about your products once you're ready to launch."

She nods, still speechless.

"I want you to know that I believe in you. I want to support your dreams, whatever they are."

She hugs me so tightly then that I think she may never let go. Fine by me.

"Nobody's ever done anything like this for me before," she says, pulling away. "Thank you, Brooks. This means so much to me." She stares down at the paper with a stunned smile on her face.

"I may need to enlist some of your nosy neighbors to help me bring it into your backyard when it arrives. The thing is a beast."

"Not the neighbors!" She laughs. "They'll be eager to help if you're the one asking." She carefully tucks the receipt back into the envelope and stands, leaning forward to drop a kiss to my mouth.

"Where are you going?" I say in an undertone. "I'm not finished with you yet."

"Be right back," she says with a mischievous grin. She searches behind the Christmas tree, then returns a moment later with a gift-wrapped box. "Open it."

I carefully tear off the wrapping paper and open the box, my throat growing tight at the sight of what it contains.

"Nora. This is too much."

"It's not just from me; it's from my whole family. We all pitched in to get it for you."

I look around the room, and sure enough, all eyes are on me. I pull out the frame of a DSLR camera, shiny, black, and brand new. Inside the box is a plastic wrapped lens.

"No way," I say, shocked. "You guys really didn't have to do this."

"Sydney helped me pick it out for you." Sydney gives me an air high-five from across the room.

"I saw how much you loved taking photos that day at the beach, and I wanted you to have a creative outlet once the season starts up again," Nora says. "I hope you'll take it with you to practice and spring training and take lots of pictures to show me."

I set the box aside and pull her close. "Thank you. I don't even know what to say."

"I love you, Brooks," she says simply. "Now every city you travel to, you can get out and explore and take photos and hopefully get out of your head and into the world."

Little does she know that she's become my world.

After Ollie goes to bed, we talk late into the night about the future. Our dreams and hopes, our plans together. And for the first time in my life, I see a happy, fulfilling life for myself outside of baseball. Life with Nora will be filled with diapers and dishwashing, wins and losses, highs and lows, mistakes and healing. A tapestry of both remarkable and mundane moments woven together to create something safe, deeply fulfilling and uniquely ours.

TWENTY-NINE
Nora

February

"You ready?" Brooks asks me. I nod, focused on taking deep, steadying breaths as our plane taxis down the runway.

"Can I have a snack?" Ollie asks. He's sitting between us in his car seat, and as much as I wish that Brooks was right next to me so I could bury my face in his shoulder during take-off and landing, I'm glad Ollie's coming to Florida with us. It's going to be a long travel day, but we've been looking forward to experiencing spring training with Brooks for a while now.

"Guess what?" Brooks says to Ollie. "After take-off, those nice flight attendants are going to bring you your very own snacks. Can you believe that?"

"Like what?" Ollie asks.

"They've got cookies. And granola bars. And *chips*!"

Ollie's eyes light up, and I can't help but smile. Brooks keeps both of us distracted as the plane picks up speed down the runway. The rattling and rumbling around me kicks my heart into high gear, but as I hold tight to Ollie's hand and watch the plane rise off the ground below us, I know everything is going to be okay.

After seven hours of flying and one layover in Detroit, we finally make it to Fort Myers, Florida.

I've got crumbs in my hair, stains on my clothes, and have been climbed like a human jungle gym for the majority of the day, but we survived. Tears were shed, movies were watched, and snacks were consumed and spilled. Ollie only knocked over one entire cup of apple juice on our first flight, but our clothes eventually dried. We made it. I want to bend to kiss the ground when we emerge from the Southwest Florida Airport into the thick, humid air.

The sense of relief that fills me as Brooks kisses me while waiting for our rental car is consuming. For the first time in my life, I'm on the other side of the country, but being held in his arms, I still feel grounded. Safe. Home.

Brooks

Spring training feels like the fresh start I've been waiting for. Like I've been holding my breath, and I can finally let it out in one long, slow drag.

I'm surprised by how much I've missed this. Seeing the guys every day. Lacing up my cleats. The smell of wet dirt and fresh-cut grass and sun-warmed leather. The snap of the bat as it connects with the ball. My mind and body are ready to work and jump back into the routines of baseball season. I've put the work in to ensure that I'm able to enjoy playing the game again, and it relieves me when I genuinely do.

We're having fun, enjoying ourselves without the pressure of massive crowds and media attention. There's nothing high stakes about this. It's us getting back into the swing of things, tweaking our lineup, and putting our skills to the test after a few months of training and working hard to refine them.

I bring Nora and Ollie to our morning warm-up the day after we arrive in Fort Myers, and the coaches allow them to come out onto the field to watch me work. Ollie's all about it, chatting with my teammates and coaches, fielding rogue balls, and having a blast touching everything he sees. Nora's chasing after him in my periphery, looking like a fresh-faced, dark-haired bombshell.

She's wearing a jersey with my number on it. And the hat I gave her at the Harvest Market. I can't stop stealing glances at her.

We rotate to the batting cages for hitting practice, and as I step up to the plate I give myself a mental pep talk. *You've got this. No stress. Enjoy it.*

"Yeah, Alden!" I hear Nora yell. I can't help but smile.

"Work that swing, baby!" Miles adds.

I hit a lot and miss a few, but it's all in good fun.

It feels good, being back on the field surrounded by palm trees and warm sunshine after a long, rainy winter. I'm ready for what's to come this season, and I'm grateful to have Nora and Ollie here to support me. It makes all the difference in the world, knowing they're out there in the crowd cheering me on at our game later in the day against the Tennessee Timberwolves.

I'm on cloud nine when I wind up doing two-for-two, a home run and a triple, and 3 RBIs.

"Dang, son," Miles says to me after he belts a solo home run at the top of the fifth. "Where you been?"

The energy is good today, and we feed off each other. We end up winning 6-2.

I'm proud of how I played today, but the thing that gets my heart pumping and my adrenaline racing even more than a great game is the sight of Nora and Ollie waiting for me afterwards.

I pick Ollie up in one arm, then haul Nora close with the other and kiss her fiercely. She seems taken aback by my enthusiasm at first but quickly fits her mouth to mine and knots her fingers into my hair.

"My goodness," she breathes as I smother her cheek with another kiss. "That post-win kiss is something else. Let's hope you keep playing well so I can get a few more of these." She goes in for another kiss and then giggles. "Bubblicious?"

"You know it, girl. Don't lie," I whisper into her ear. "You were checking me out on the field all night."

She gives me a coy smile. "Of course I was."

"It's the baseball pants. They always seem to do it for you."

"Your words, not mine," she laughs.

"Good game, dude," Ollie says, patting my shoulder. I'm so elated to have won and to have them here with me that I can't help myself. I kiss Ollie on his soft little cheek, too. He wriggles and laughs.

He screeches and tries to get away. "You so scratchy!"

I nuzzle my stubble against him and revel in the sound of his giggles and the feel of Nora gathered in close. There's nothing better than this.

During the first week that Nora and Ollie spend with me at spring training, we fall into a routine. I'm bunking up with a bunch of the guys at a hotel near our training facility (with Miles as my roommate), so Nora and Ollie are staying at a different hotel nearby. I bring them an early breakfast to their hotel room, and I can't get enough of the sight of the two of them still in their pajamas with tousled hair. The day is filled with practice and intermittently seeing my two favorite people, who never fail to brighten my day. They come to my games at night, and then I join them back at the hotel later. Most nights when I arrive, Ollie is already asleep, so Nora and I sit out on the back patio and talk.

Nora spent the start of this year training Roman to take over her job at Delia's Diner. She officially stepped down last week and now is free to pursue her dreams of being a full-time mom and part-time artist. Roman has promised us free meals at the diner for as long as he's manager. I plan on leaving him extra-generous tips every time we visit.

On our fifth night in Fort Myers, we play an earlier game, so I'm able to shower and leave with Ollie and Nora immediately afterwards. I tell Nora I want to take them out to get some ice cream before Ollie needs to go to bed.

She has no idea that I'm about to give her what she asked for in December after the team Christmas dinner.

Tonight, I'm going to propose.

◆

"I thought you said we were getting ice cream," Nora says, looking out at the parking lot at Lovers Key State Park.

Ollie gasps from the back seat. "The beach!"

"That's right, Ollie. You've been here for nearly a full week, and you haven't set foot on the beach," I say. "We're going to fix that. Right now."

Nora's eyebrows fold in suspicion, but she gets out of the car and follows me and Ollie down the sandy path towards the beach. I'd scoped out the local beaches in advance and had chosen this spot knowing we could easily find a secluded area all to ourselves. The beach is a two-mile long stretch of powdery sugar-soft sand that tumbles into the warm Gulf Ocean. It's perfect.

"We're just in time to catch the sunset," I say, tossing a smile back over at Nora. She takes Ollie's other hand, connecting the three of us together.

I've played countless baseball games in front of an innumerable number of onlookers, but never in my life have I felt as nervous as I do tonight.

I secretly flew out my mom and the twins yesterday, as well as Nora's entire family, enlisting their help to create a romantic setup on the beach where I'll propose. We trek across the sand to the twinkling fairytale they've created in the distance, and I watch Nora's expression shift in understanding as we draw closer.

328

There's a candlelit walkway that leads to an archway decorated in foliage and flowers. I can see Sydney hiding partially behind the archway, waiting to step out and capture some photos. The rest of our family was instructed to remain out of sight until after I've popped the question.

Our feet sink into the soft sand, and I think I may have actually stepped into heaven. Nora looks absolutely stunning in the warmth of the sunset. We've come a long way in a relatively short amount of time, but I know the time is right for me to ask Nora to marry me. To braid the threads of our lives together into one unbreakable knot.

I'm ready.

I lead Nora up the candlelit walkway and watch her eyes fill with wonder. She takes in the scattered flower petals, the pink-tinged light from the setting sun, and the soft hush of the ocean waves behind us. And then finally, her gaze lands on me.

"Brooks," Nora says, slowly following after me in a daze. "What is this?"

She's sniffling already, and Ollie looks up at her in concern. She pulls him closer as we fall under the archway.

"Hey, Ollie," I say. "Remember this box I showed you earlier?" I pull a small black box from the pocket of my pants, and Nora audibly gasps. I'm smiling so big that my face might actually split.

"What?" Nora says, her voice cracking.

"Do you remember what's inside?"

Ollie nods excitedly. "A wing!"

"Should we show your mom?"

Ollie helps me pop the lid open on the box, revealing a ring with two diamonds, one marquise cut, the other emerald. The stones are angled together and set within a gold band that twists above one stone and below the other.

"Two stones," I explain. "One for each of us."

"This one is mine!" Ollie says, pointing to the emerald cut stone.

Tears are slipping down Nora's cheeks as I get down on one knee. Ollie, totally unprompted, follows suit and kneels down beside me, looking up at his mom with his big, blue eyes.

"Nora Foster," I say, surprised at the emotion swelling within my own chest as I speak her name. "I would be the happiest man on earth if you would let me take care of you and Ollie forever. You're my favorite people, and I want to make you both mine. Will you marry me?"

She hiccups and nods. "Yes! Of course I will. Yes!"

Ollie helps me remove the ring from the box and slide it onto her finger. Then she bends down and tilts her head, her lips finding mine. I taste the salt of her tears and the joy in her smile.

"My *gosh*," she breathes as I stand up. "I can't believe this. The ring is gorgeous. And so thoughtful." She tears up again and gathers both Ollie and me close.

"I talked to Ollie earlier today," I say, and Ollie nods. "And I asked him if it would be okay if I married his mom. What did you say, Ollie?"

"Yes!" he says, pumping his fist in the air. Nora laughs and gives him a squeeze.

"Tell you what," I say, bringing Nora flush against me. "Once we're married, I'll put on those baseball pants you like every night, if you want me to."

"I'd expect nothing less," she says. Then she frames my face with her hands and presses a slow kiss to my mouth.

EPILOGUE

Nora

Two years later...

I stare down at the pregnancy test on the bathroom counter in disbelief. I try closing my eyes and peeking at the test again to see if I'm imagining things, but that only seems to make the lines deepen.

"Brooks?" I call out. When he doesn't immediately answer, I assume he's still out in the front yard, loading boxes of my ceramics onto the shelves we've set up outside. We're having a tent sale this afternoon to clear out my inventory.

I take the pregnancy test with me and wander with slow, dazed steps into my studio. Our house is half-packed already, and I have to sidle past boxes of our things set to be loaded onto a moving truck and taken to a storage unit in a few days.

After five great years of playing for the Stormbreakers, Brooks' agent negotiated a killer contract with the Utah Archers. We talked about it for weeks, weighing the pros and cons of moving our family to a new state and all that would entail. It was a moment of bravery for both of us when we said yes to a new adventure. A fresh start for all of us. It feels like leaping into the frigid ocean all over again: a little bit crazy, but oddly refreshing at the same time.

I've got the window in my studio open so the brisk breeze can draft into the space while we pack things. The soft morning light is filtering through the curtains as they flutter, dappling across the prints of photos Brooks has taken since we've been married. There are candid captures of me and Ollie, cityscapes and landscapes, and even a few shots of our garden and the trees lining our backyard that I found to be too beautiful not to display.

I love this room. It's where we had our (second) first kiss and where I started my now-thriving business. After we got married, I was glad that Brooks agreed that we should keep my home in Kitt's Harbor. We bought a second small home in Seattle so we could be nearby when he plays at Boeing Park. Both homes are stamped with proof that we live and love well, and knowing that our family is growing makes me sit in wistful nostalgia of the happy life we're living right now.

But things are about to change for us. Big time.

"Did you need something?" Brooks sweeps into the room, his steel blue eyes making my already nervous stomach flip. He's got his hat turned backwards on his head and a week's work of stubble growing on his cheeks. We'll be married for two years in April, and I still never tire of calling him my husband.

"Yes," I say slowly, hiding the pregnancy test behind my back. "I've got something to tell you."

His eyes pinch, and he frowns with concern. "What's going on? Are you still feeling sick? You can go lay down and I'll get the rest of the stuff set up."

"You're very sweet," I say, beckoning for him to come closer. "I need to show you something."

He takes three strides to close the gap between us, looking worried. "Did Ollie break something again? I'll have a talk with him when he gets back from–"

"Brooks," I say softly, slipping the pregnancy test around so he can see it. "Honey...I'm pregnant."

"*What?*"

He takes the pregnancy test from me and stares down at it, open-mouthed.

"Are you sure?" he asks in awed disbelief.

"Those lines are clear as day," I laugh. "We're having a baby, honey."

He kisses me, and I melt into him, his mouth fusing with mine. Brooks pulls away, his eyes softening as he grins. Then he kneels down, right there on the studio floor, tugs me towards him by my hips and presses a soft kiss to my belly.

"I can't believe this," he says, rising to his feet and kissing me again. "We're having a baby."

I can already picture Brooks cradling a tiny baby in his arms. My heart swells at the knowledge that this time, I won't be carrying, delivering, and caring for my child all by myself. I'll have Brooks beside me every step of the way. I cling to him even tighter.

We both stare down at the pregnancy test again. Proof that I'm carrying new life. Proof that Brooks and I are as crazy about each other now as we were when we were seventeen.

Proof that with a little time, a lot of patience, and a lot of mistakes, even the most fragile hearts can heal.

"Good thing our new house has a third bedroom," he says into my ear, sounding shocked. "I never would have thought I'd be playing for the team that caused me so much grief, let alone having a child in Utah."

"I never thought I'd be married to the sexiest baseball player in the sport and carrying his baby, but here we are," I say, linking my hands behind his neck and kissing him again.

A knock sounds at the door. It must be Ollie, back from playing with some of the kids in the neighborhood.

"Let me help you finish packing up your studio, and then, I'll take Ollie to grab some lunch so you can rest," he says. "Roman owes me a free meal at the diner, anyway."

Roman runs a tight ship, but he always makes sure Booth Six is available for us when we come in to visit.

"I won't say no to that," I sigh, letting him hold me.

"Hey, you," he says, tipping my chin up so I meet his gaze. He's practically quivering with happiness. "I've never been more excited in my life."

"I'm going to remind you of that when you're holding my hair back while I'm puking during this first trimester."

"Bring it on, girl," he grins. "I'm ready."

Brooks answers the door and brings Ollie into the studio to see me.

"I've got something to show you, Ollie," I say, kneeling down in front of him. Brooks goes down on one knee, too, propping Ollie up on his leg. Both boys look at me in expectation, their blue eyes and dark hair giving them an uncanny resemblance, despite their lack of shared blood. My throat knots as I look between them.

"So...you know how I've been feeling sick the past little bit?" Ollie nods. "Well, I thought it was some kind of stomach bug, but just to be sure, I took a pregnancy test this morning."

"A what test?" Ollie asks.

"I'll show you," I say, lifting the pregnancy test up to his line of sight. "See these two pink lines right here?" he nods. "Those lines mean that I'm pregnant."

"Pregnant?" he asks, looking confused.

"I have a baby in my belly," I explain, feeling a flutter in my gut at the realization that another tiny human is already growing inside me. It's the most profound kind of miracle.

"It means you're going to be a big brother," Brooks adds.

Ollie gasps, his mouth dropping open and eyes glimmering with excitement.

"You're gonna have a baby?" Ollie asks, pressing his palms to his cheeks.

"That's right," I say. "You'll be the best big brother ever!"

And he will. I know it.

Ollie stands and flings his arms around my neck. Brooks wraps his arms around the both of us, and we stay there, kneeling on the floor in a family hug that makes tears streak down my cheeks.

"I love you, boys," I say, kissing them each in turn.

Ollie starts chattering about whether or not the baby will be a girl or a boy, and how he'll be a big helper when the baby comes. I have no doubt that he will.

Brooks enlists Ollie's help to carry the rest of the boxes out to the front yard for the tent sale with a pep in his step and a light-filled smile on his face. I'll give him ten more babies if it means I get to see him happy like this again.

The afternoon passes in a silvery haze. I greet our friends and neighbors who come by to stock up their favorite Noli goods in person for the last time. I carefully wrap plates, mugs, cups, paint palettes, and vases, knowing my hand-crafted treasures are going to be well taken care of. Every time Brooks catches my eye, we share a secret smile. Elated at the private knowledge that our family is growing.

Knowing that we would soon be saying goodbye to Seattle, living in Florida for spring training, and then moving to Utah for the start of baseball season was already filling me with a mixture of emotions. Adding pregnancy on top of all of these changes fits the bill for my life since I met Brooks. He continually eases me out of my comfort zone and helps me embrace change. It all somehow feels manageable with him by my side.

After the sale is over, I pause in the doorway at the front of the house, watching my two boys working together to take everything down. I place a hand over my belly and rub my thumb absently back and forth.

This is it. All I ever wanted is right here within my reach. I've got my own little house (well, two technically, but soon it will be one again). I've turned my passion into a successful business so I could do honest work I'm proud of. And above all else, I've got a beautiful family of my own to love and learn from.

And a secret shelf in our bedroom closet stocked with Fruit by the Foot and Bubblicious bubblegum.

THE END

Enjoyed Brooks & Nora's story? I'd love for you to leave a review on Amazon or Goodreads!

BONUS SCENE!

Enjoy a bonus scene written from Brooks' POV when you sign up for my newsletter on my website: haileygardiner.com.

ALSO BY HAILEY GARDINER

Kitt's Harbor:
Girl Meets Grump

Falling For Franklin Series:
The Holiduel
The Retreat
The Make Up
The Duet

ACKNOWLEDGMENTS

I'd first like to thank my angel Grandpa Bagby for taking me and my sisters to Dodgers games and for playing catch with me as a kid. I know you'd be proud of this book. For me, baseball is associated with happy times spent together, and I will always love the Dodgers because of you!

I'd also like to give a shoutout to my boy Mookie Betts, the all-star shortstop I studied while writing Brooks' character. What a stud! His YouTube videos and stellar performance highlights made writing my first sports romance so fun!

To my Bookstagram friends–I wish I could hang out with all of you in real life! You make every release something I look forward to. Thank you for being supportive, encouraging, and understanding as I worked my tail off on this book. I hope it brings a little light to your life!

To Lenae, Amanda, Jenessa, and Sara, your ideas are sprinkled throughout this book and it now feels cohesive and especially tender thanks to your input. You each inspire me as writers and humans and I'm grateful to call you my friends.

To my editor, Heather: we did it! Again! Thank you for being not only a top-tier editor, but also a wonderful friend.

So grateful to know you! Whenever you decide to bake Carol's croissants, I'll be your taste tester.

Thank you to MaryAnn for knocking out that final proofread and for loving this story.

And last but not least, to my husband Cayden. Who knew your athleticism and baseball knowledge would one day come in clutch for your author wife? You can now say that you helped co-author a romantic comedy. How does that FEEL? I'm incredibly grateful for all of your help with this story and with our boys so I could have time to write it. This book wouldn't exist without you.

ABOUT THE AUTHOR

Hailey Gardiner writes cheeky, sweet romantic comedies in an effort to finally put her wildly active imagination to good use. Hailey is a master at quoting movies, will eat any dessert that's salted, and loves raising two book-loving boys with her husband.

Official Website: www.haileygardiner.com
Instagram : @authorhaileygardiner
TikTok: @authorhaileygardiner
Join **Hailey's Happily Ever After Reader Group** on
Facebook
Sign up for Hailey's newsletter for monthly updates and
exclusive content.

Made in United States
Orlando, FL
09 July 2025

62799614R00204